D·E·A·T·H
OF A TALL MAN

Books by Frances and Richard Lockridge

Dead as a Dinosaur

Death Takes a Bow

Death of a Tall Man

The Dishonest Murderer

Hanged for a Sheep

Killing the Goose

Murder Is Served

Murder Out of Turn

Murder Within Murder

The Norths Meet Murder

Payoff for the Banker

A Pinch of Poison

D·E·A·T·H
OF A TALL MAN

FRANCES & RICHARD
LOCKRIDGE

HarperPerennial
A Division of HarperCollinsPublishers

Originally published in hardcover in 1946 by J. B. Lippincott Company.

DEATH OF A TALL MAN. Copyright 1946 by Frances & Richard Lockridge. All rights reserved. Printed in the United States of America. No part of this book may be used or reproduced in any manner whatsoever without written permission except in the case of brief quotations embodied in critical articles and reviews. For information address HarperCollins Publishers, Inc., 10 East 53rd Street, New York, NY 10022.

HarperCollins books may be purchased for educational, business, or sales promotional use. For information, please write: Special Markets Department, HarperCollins Publishers, Inc., 10 East 53rd Street, New York, NY 10022.

First HarperPerennial edition published 1994.

Designed by R. Caitlin Daniels

Library of Congress Cataloging-in-Publication Data

Lockridge, Frances Louise Davis.
    Death of a tall man / by Frances & Richard Lockridge. — 1st HarperPerennial ed.
      p. cm.
    ISBN 0-06-092513-2
    1. North, Jerry (Fictitious character)—Fiction. 2. North, Pam (Fictitious character)—Fiction. 3. Private investigators—New York (N.Y.)—Fiction. 4. Women detectives—New York (N.Y.)—Fiction.
I. Lockridge, Richard, 1898– . II. Title.
PS3523.O243D434 1994
813'.54—dc20   93-45826

---

94 95 96 97 98 ❖/CW 10 9 8 7 6 5 4 3 2 1

D·E·A·T·H
OF A TALL MAN

• 1 •

Monday, April 16, 8:58 a.m. to 3:03 p.m.

Deborah Brooks watched her step getting out, in accordance with instructions, and the elevator door banged heavily behind her. She turned right, walked half a dozen steps and let herself into the office through what all of them called the "back door." This door closed behind her soundlessly and she flicked up a tumbler switch without looking. Her fingers slipped off it; then her mind overtook her reflexes and she noticed that the lights in the corridor were already on. She looked at her watch and it said eight fifty-eight. Grace was early then, which was unlike Grace who came as exactly on the hour as if she wound herself each morning. It was more probable, Deborah thought, that her watch was slow. Machinery was fallible.

Deborah went down the short corridor and past the first closet. She opened the second and took off her light coat—and noticed that Grace's coat was not, after all, neatly on its customary hanger. Deborah noticed this with a fraction of her mind. She peered into the mirror on the inside of the closet door. She closed the door, pulling it toward her, and then went the rest of the way down the short corridor and opened the door which led from it into the bathroom. The light was not on there and she flicked it on. She looked at herself carefully in the mirror over the washbasin. She looked a moment and then stuck out a pink tongue, suddenly, and looked at it with care. That was something she had done since she was a little girl; there was something magical and reassuring about it. Even now, when she knew that the magic and the reassurance came, somehow, from a past which she could never regain—and knew that the gesture was meaningless—she still stuck out her tongue at herself when she faced a mirror. Sometimes she did not even look at her tongue after she had stuck it out. But when she stuck it out, even when she did not look at it, she was a child again and her father was saying, "Stick out your tongue, Debbie," and he was looking at it and nodding gravely in approval. That meant she was well; that she was not confronted by those strange discomforts which meant that she could not play and go to parties. Her father could tell when those discomforts were coming, merely by looking at her tongue. That had been the magic, when she was very little. Even when she understood that her father was a doctor, and so could tell things by looking at you that others could not tell, the magic still, in some not very clear fashion, remained. If you stuck out your tongue and looked at it, you warded off evil.

Deborah withdrew her tongue, which looked much as it always did—pink and rather strange. Tongues were strange when you looked at them, and curiously meaningless. Except the tongues of cats and dogs, particularly cats. Cats and dogs had tongues that could go places. Humans merely had what amounted to carpets in their mouths.

Deborah looked at her face. It should, she thought, reflect anxiety; it should show worry. But it was a very young face, and did not, really, show either. It was smooth and lines had not yet set in it; there were no shadows that should not be around young eyes. It was also, in an impertinent fashion, rather beautiful. Deborah Brooks nodded at herself. She thought: "I do look sort of pretty." She examined her forehead, which was a little reddened. Even an April sun could get its effects, if you sat in it long enough—or ran in it, playing the first tennis of the new season. There was also a small reddened place on the bridge of her nose.

She powdered forehead and nose and the redness abated. She washed her hands and dried them on a paper towel. She went out through the door on the opposite side of the bathroom, passed through the small, neat storage room beyond without thinking about it and, through a door in the left wall of the storage room, into the long waiting room. The lights were on there, too. But she saw no one, and heard no one, as she walked the length of the room—her dark brown hair swaying with her movement—to her desk at the other end. She sat at it a moment, reaching in for the dustcloth in the lower right-hand drawer. She was crouched over the desk, dusting it, when she heard a sound to her right and turned, the hand which held the dustrag still resting on the desk. She looked across her shoulder and up. Then she smiled at the tall man who was smiling at her.

"Dan!" she said. "How nice." Then she stopped for a moment and when she spoke again her voice was faintly puzzled. "Only—" she said, and stopped again.

Dan Gordon was tall and slender; perhaps, as Deborah told herself, he was really thin. Certainly he was thinner than he had been before. His face, particularly, was thinner than it had been before, and there were lines in it that had not been there before. The lines went away when he smiled, in that oddly lopsided fashion. He smiled more with the left side of his face than with the right, so that his smile was never on quite straight. It was just, he had told her, that one side of his face was more flexible than the other. It was just the way he was made.

Dan Gordon smiled now, and for that moment his smile was as it had always been; as Deborah remembered it for most of the years about which she remembered anything. He looked almost as he had looked when he was sixteen and she was twelve; as he looked when he was twenty and she was sixteen and, more or less suddenly, she had been no longer merely a female nuisance who lived next door, as next doors went around North Salem, which was an expansive area. She could not remember when he had not been a part of the bright magic of the future. But girls, she supposed, noticed such things earlier than boys did.

"Hello, Debbie," he said now. He spoke in a quick, hurried way, as if there were insufficient time for speech. He smiled again, but this time his smile, too, was quick and hurried—as if there were not enough time for smiles. "I told you I was going to talk to him."

Still without moving from her domestic crouch over the desk, she shook her head. The soft brown hair swayed excitedly.

"No Dan," she said. "Not here. Not now. There couldn't be a worse time. Please, darling."

He was ten feet from her, standing in the doorway which led to the inner corridor—to the office and the examining rooms. But she could see, even at that distance, that his forehead was damp with sweat. She could see, as he reached for his cigarette case, took a cigarette from it, that his hand trembled. Neither of these things was obvious. The tremor, particularly, was hardly perceptible. Even in two months it had lessened markedly. But she had always seen everything about Dan with unusual clearness, ever since she could remember.

"Don't watch me, Debbie," he said, suddenly, harshly. "Damn it all, don't watch me!" His voice was angry. Then, almost at once, the anger left him and he smiled again. He looked, in an odd fashion, hurt and rather baffled. "Darling," he said. "Debbie, I'm sorry."

"You don't have to be sorry," she told him. But she sat down rather quickly in the chair behind the desk and for a moment made a business of putting the dustrag back in the bottom drawer on the right. Only when she had tucked it in, with more care than was needed, did she look up at him again. Then she smiled. "You know you don't have to be sorry," she said.

"Listen," he said. "You don't have to be sorry for me, either." Again his voice had a harsh surface.

She did not look away this time. She kept on smiling at him.

"I'm not sorry for you," she said, "you give me a pain in—"

He crossed the ten feet quickly and leaned over her. His lips pressed hard on hers, and he did not hurry the kiss. There was sufficient time for kisses, apparently. When he did end it, he still bent near her; his fingers were warm against the nape of her neck, under the brown hair.

"The hell I do," he said.

"The hell you do," Debbie Brooks agreed. "The hell you do, darling." Her right hand went up and her fingers touched his wrist for a moment. "And," she said, "I'll watch you when I want to. Who else would I watch?"

"That's right," he said. "You watch me."

He stood up and moved around the desk. He sat on it for a moment and looked down at her and then he moved again. It seemed difficult for him to remain in one place. She watched him. He moved behind her and stood in front of the window behind her desk. She could feel him there, even when he was motionless. She spoke without turning around.

"You can't talk to him this morning," she said. "It isn't the time. And he'll only have a moment. He's operating."

He was always operating, Dan told her. He came from behind her and sat on the edge of her desk.

"I'm going to talk to him," he said. "I know damned well it isn't your plan."

"It isn't what I want," the girl said. "But—"

"But you listen to God," Dan said, and now his voice was angry again. "You're a trusting baby, and you listen to God Almighty. Only he isn't."

The girl merely shook her head.

"What does he know about it?" he asked. "What does anybody know about it?"

The girl smiled faintly. She said it was his business, after all.

"Being God?" the man wanted to know. He was very irascible. He stood up and walked almost the length of the long room and then came back and stood in front of her desk. He looked down at her, and again he smiled, the smile running lopsidedly across his face. "I'm sorry," he said. "I'm always sorry, Debbie. Only—"

"I know," Deborah Brooks said. She paused for a moment. "I'm not sure he's right," she said. "Maybe he's not right. But he doesn't ask a great deal, Dan." He started to speak, but she shook her head. "He doesn't ask a great deal. And—he's done a great deal, Danny. You know that. You know why I—why I listen."

"To hell with gratitude," Dan said. "What makes you think we've got so much time, anyway?"

She smiled suddenly.

"Because I'm twenty," she said. "There seems like a lot of time."

She watched his face. His forehead was damp again. "I don't mean there could ever be enough," she said. "You know I don't mean that, Dan. That I don't—" She broke off. "I'm telling you things you know," she said. "Things we've been all over. And you know it isn't gratitude. That that isn't the word. It's a little word."

He looked at her unhappily. Then, nervously, he shrugged his shoulders.

"All right," he said. "So it isn't gratitude." He looked at her. "Of course," he said, "it could be a fixation."

Her half-smile went away.

"Sometimes," she said, "you're impossible, Dan. Sometimes I feel as if you're a different person. You know perfectly well you can't talk to him this morning. Or any morning. You know how—how concentrated he has to be."

He looked down at her, his eyes enquiring. She stretched out her left hand to him. There was a diamond on the third finger of her left hand. It had been there for three years, and as she held out her hand she looked at it. He looked at it, too. Then he took her hand and leaned across the desk and kissed the finger on which the ring was. Then, with a quick movement, he sat down in the chair by her desk. He put his elbows on the desk and took his chin in his two hands and looked at her. Suddenly she laughed.

"You look—" she said.

"Like a dog worshipping a bone," he said.

"Danny!" she said. "What a way to say it!" She reached out and took his wrists in her two hands. "Now, soldier," she said. "I want you to listen—"

Miss Grace Spencer, R.N., let herself into the "back door" at nine five, thinking harshly of the New York subway system, which undermined punctuality. She hung her coat and hat in the closet beside Deborah's, took a clean uniform off a hanger, and went into the bathroom. She changed quickly and went back to hang her blue suit and white blouse in the same closet. Then she went through the bathroom to the storeroom beyond and at the lab sink, washed her apparently immaculate hands in antiseptic soap. It was an unforgiving soap; her hands were roughened from many washings in it. Grace Spencer regarded this fact, as she did each morning, with half her mind; she lamented it perfunctorily and went about her business. She checked supplies on the glass-protected shelves; she made notes of three items which, within five days, would need reordering. Then she went back through the bathroom and began her check of the examining rooms. It was, she thought—and this, too, she thought each morning with half her mind—rather a nuisance to have to pass through the bathroom to get to the examining room area. But it was, generally, an efficiently planned office. It would be worse if the bathroom were accessible only through the storage room. You couldn't have everything.

A number of people were, later, to find the planning of the office interesting. If they had followed Grace Spencer through it that morning as she ran her professional eye over the rooms which lay in her special country, they would have satisfied that interest—except that at nine fifteen that morning nothing had yet happened to arouse their interest.

When Grace Spencer entered the office, she came into a short, fairly thick, corridor which began with the "back door" and ended with the door to the bathroom. She went into the bathroom and out of it by a door in the opposite wall to the storeroom and laboratory. In the wall on her left as she entered the storeroom there was a door at the far end which, if she had opened it, would have let her into the waiting room at the end opposite to that in which Deborah Brooks's desk stood. But Grace Spencer did not use that door. After she had washed her hands, and checked the supplies, she went back the way she had come. When she closed the door as she left the bathroom, she stood at the intersection of two corridors—that through which she had entered and another which now, as she faced the "back door," stretched toward her right. This was a much longer corridor. Six doors opened into it along the wall which, as she turned down it, was on her left. At her right, built into the wall, was a cabinet with a leaf which, when dropped, made a kind of desk. That was the center of Grace Spencer's activities; that was where, in the event she had nothing else to do, she sat. There was a telephone there.

The six doors along the wall of the corridor opened into small cubicles which were examining rooms. These rooms also opened directly into one another, in series. The room nearest the "back door"—six in the numbering which began at the far end of the corridor—opened into what they called the "back-door hall" as well as into the transverse corridor.

Grace Spencer went into Room 6, which was identical with the other five rooms. It had a window and beneath the window a counter; it had a low chair with a neck rest and a higher stool; it had a powerful, hooded light. The counter was covered with a white cloth. Grace whisked the white cloth off and spread a fresh one. She switched the light on and switched it off again; the big bulbs burned out quickly. She went on, satisfied, to Room 5, entering it without reentering the corridor outside. She repeated her operations there, and in the next four rooms. Room 1, like the others, had two doors—one into the corridor, and the other leading directly into a large private office. Grace did not enter the office from Room 1. She went instead into the corridor and back along it to her desk. She let down the leaf and moved a memo pad, a file of patients' cards and two pencils onto it. She had surveyed her country and all was well. It was nine twenty-five and she had five minutes. She went back down the transverse hall, which also ended in a door. That door was a second way into the private office. At the right there was a doorway with no door in it. She turned through that and stood in it, and now she was standing where Daniel Gordon had stood twenty minutes earlier. She looked at Deborah Brooks and smiled. People usually smiled when they looked at Deborah; in a world so filled with unsatisfying objects, and unsatisfying human objects in particular, she provided encouragement.

"Hello, baby," Grace said. "How's the business girl?"

The business girl was sorting mail into two piles. She looked up. When she spoke her voice was unanimated. She said, "Hello, Grace."

"You got a little burn," Grace told her. "Too much weekend, baby?"

Deborah shook her head.

"Grace," she said, "did you see Dan?"

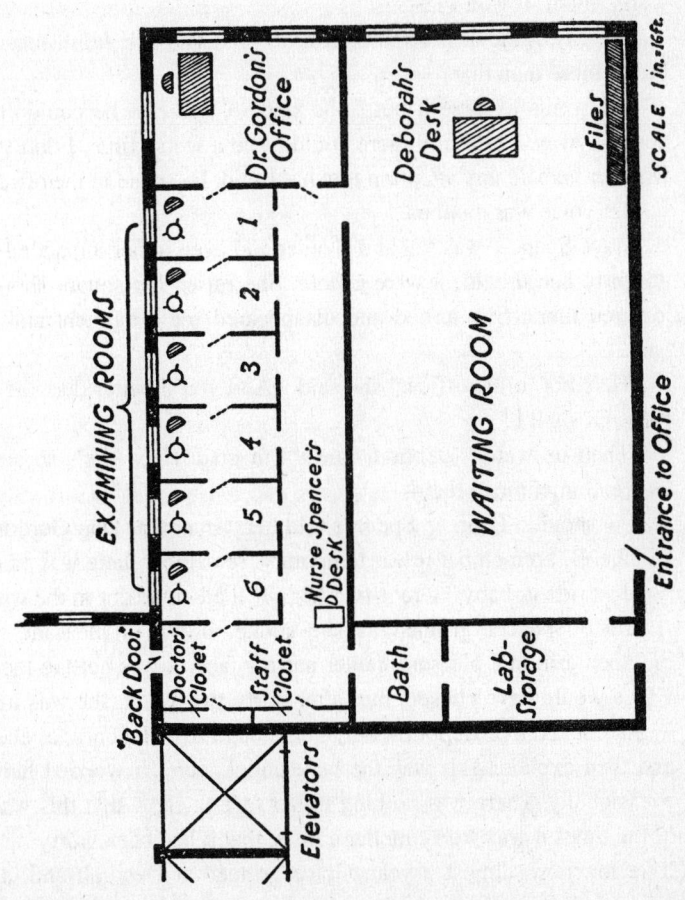

Floor Plan of Dr. Andrew Gordon's Office

"No," Grace said. "I didn't see Dan."

"He was just here," Deborah told her. "He wanted to—to talk to his father. About us. He's—he's upset."

"Look, baby," Grace said. "Of course he's upset. It's nothing to worry about. It won't last."

The girl at the desk shook her head. She said she didn't mean that. It was more than that.

"He wants to have it out," she said. "I told him he couldn't—not now, anyway. I told him there couldn't be a worse time. I don't know whether he paid any attention to what I said. Is—is he in the office?"

Her voice was anxious.

Grace Spencer was tall and slender and even in her unpadded white uniform, her shoulders were square. She raised her square shoulders, lowered them. She turned and disappeared for a moment and came back.

"He's not in the office," she said. "And you'd better dust the desk, baby. Or shall I?"

"Then he went," Deborah said. "I'm glad. He's—he's so strange, Grace. Sometimes I feel—"

She shouldn't, Grace Spencer told her. Grant that Dan Gordon was strange. But remember it was temporary; remember there was cause.

"Just ride it, baby," Grace told her. "It'll all come out in the wash."

Grace Spencer grinned as she spoke; it was a pleasant, wide-mouthed grin in a pleasant, rather narrow face. It was not the face that Grace would have chosen, but, after thirty-two years, she was used to it. She looked like Hepburn, only not enough like Hepburn, as she now and then explained. It was the way things were; it worried her only occasionally. There was nothing in her face to show that this was one of the times it was worrying her a little; that it had been worrying her a little for, now, almost a year. Grace grinned at Deborah and, as she grinned, pushed at her short, curling, sandy hair, changing its appearance not at all. Deb smiled at her.

"I know," Deb said. "But—"

She did not finish because a door at the far end of the long waiting room opened and Dr. Andrew Gordon came in. He came in through the "front door," which was unusual. Almost never did any of them use the front door; that was for patients.

Dr. Andrew Gordon was in tweeds. He was of medium height and rather heavy, but he moved quickly, with a kind of crispness. His hair was graying; his eyes were sharp and comprehending behind rimless glasses. His mouth formed a straight line, but now the line broke. He smiled. He came, smiling, down the room toward Deborah and Grace and said, "Morning, ladies," as he came.

Deb Brooks stood up and came around the desk, holding out half a dozen letters.

"And," she said, "some very nice checks, Doctor."

"Good," Dr. Gordon said, and took the letters. "You got sunburned, Debbie. See it, Grace?"

"Grace saw it," Deborah told him. "Apparently it's the first thing you see—anybody sees."

"Oh no," Dr. Gordon said. "I shouldn't think that, Debbie. Not the first thing."

The smile held but the voice now was casual; it was running out a conversation after the mind had gone on to something else. He went past Grace in the doorway, shuffling the letters in his hands as he went. Grace followed him. The telephone on Deborah's desk rang and she said, "Dr. Gordon's office," into it. Then she said, "Oh, yes, Mrs. Overall, I'm sure he can." Then she listened.

"Not this morning," she said. "The doctor is tied up all morning. It will have to be after lunch—the regular time."

She listened again.

"Any time between three and five," she said. "Of course, the earlier the better. I don't think you'll have to wait too long." She listened again. "I'm glad," she said. "I'll tell the doctor. Goodbye." She put the telephone back in its cradle and it rang again. She lifted it. She said, "Dan!" and her voice had a different texture. She listened momentarily.

"Of course I will," she said. "It'll have to be a drugstore, you know. I've only got half an hour."

She listened again. She said, "You don't need to." She said, "All right, maybe it would be better." She listened again and said, "You know I do, darling." Her voice was very soft when she said that.

She put the telephone back in its cradle and sat for a moment looking across the room, seeing nothing—nothing except a kind of brightness which was the way things were going to be.

During the next ten minutes—from nine thirty-five to about nine forty-five—five men came in. They were compensation cases, referred by insurance company physicians; such men came on two days a week, mornings and afternoons, usually five at a time, more rarely in groups of six. Today's first group was typically varied in appearance and attitude. They were tall and short, thick and thin. Some of them were aggressive; some were uncertain, hesitant. Compensation cases were usually like that, Deborah had discovered; their varying attitudes were intended to disguise an uneasiness which was common to all of them. Deborah greeted them and recorded their referral cards; she returned the cards to the men. When they were all in, Grace Spencer took the cards and guided the men to the examining cubicles, one man to each, from Room 1 to Room 5. She left each man's identifying card handy beside him. And, from Room 1 to Room 5, the doctor examined them. He was quick that morning; he had finished by a quarter after ten.

Nurse Spencer collected the cards, which the men left behind in the cubicles. She slipped the cards into the file on her desk in the corridor and went to the doctor's private office. The doctor was sitting at his desk and looked up at her.

"Ralph Tober may call," Dr. Gordon told his nurse. "Tell him to keep on with the drops and see me tomorrow." He shook his head. "I wish we could tell him something better."

"It isn't going to work?" Grace said, only half as a question. Dr. Gordon shook his head.

"I'm not God," he said. He was looking at a card on his desk as he spoke, not at Grace Spencer. If he had looked at her, her face might have told him she found his last remark unconvincing. But probably it would have told him nothing of the kind; it was a pleasant face he was used to, with good, clear brown eyes. Normal vision, no evidence of undue strain. The undue strain which was sometimes elsewhere in Grace Spencer when she looked at Dr. Gordon was not apparent, even to an outstanding specialist. It occurred to Grace Spencer, sometimes, that Andrew Gordon was excessively interested in what people could see out of their eyes, and insufficiently concerned with what other people could see by looking into them. Not that, as things stood, it would make any difference to her; it was fortunate, indeed, that he never saw anything in her eyes except their physical efficiency.

"If Mrs. Fleming calls, as she undoubtedly will," Dr. Gordon said, "tell her yes, she's got to keep on wearing dark glasses, and I'm very sorry if she thinks they are unbecoming. Tell her a white cane would be even less becoming."

"All right," Grace said. "Actually, it would be fun to tell her just that."

Dr. Gordon smiled fleetingly. He agreed it would be fun.

"However," he said, and let it go at that.

He looked at more cards and stood up.

"In short," he said, "continue treatment as before. If the roof falls in, I'll be at the hospital." He smiled at her. "And," he said, "unavailable." He stood for a moment, looking abstractedly out of the window. Abstractedly, he took a full package of cigarettes from a pocket and his precise fingers found the opener tab of the cellophane wrapping. He flicked it off and his fingers, which seemed so much more deft than most fingers, felt for the package opening.

"You're operating, Doctor," Grace said. It was something she said three times a week; something she said on Mondays, Thursdays and Fridays at, approximately, ten twenty-two A.M.

"Damn," Dr. Gordon said, as he said at approximately five seconds after ten twenty-two A.M. on Mondays, Thursdays and Fridays. He put the unopened package of cigarettes back in his pocket. He said, "Thank you, Nurse," with the calculated bitterness which was part of the formula. Then he smiled.

"Compensation cases again at noon," Grace Spencer said. "It's Monday."

Dr. Gordon nodded; this was a formula recurrent only twice a week, on Mondays and Fridays. He said he remembered. He said he would probably be a little late.

"Probably," Grace Spencer agreed.

Dr. Gordon already had his light topcoat back across his arm and was moving toward the door. He still held most of the letters, open now. At Deborah's desk he paused and dropped them in front of her.

"Appointments, Debbie," he said. "Nothing Friday afternoon." He started away. He turned back. "Unless it seems to be really urgent," he said.

Deborah said she knew. Dr. Gordon went on across the waiting room, but at the front door he paused again.

"Give the boy my love when you see him," he said, and went out. It was between ten twenty-five and ten thirty.

For the next two hours, both Grace Spencer and Deborah Brooks afterward agreed, nothing out of the ordinary happened. There was the usual number of telephone calls—some for appointments, which Deborah handled; some for advice and counsel, which went to Grace. Mrs. Fleming did call. Grace Spencer assured her that it was essential to continue to wear the dark glasses, even if they did make her look like an owl. Deborah made half a dozen appointments for the next two days and refused one for Friday afternoon. She answered letters and typed up the office records of the compensation cases.

At eleven thirty a small elderly man in a neat blue suit and an immaculate white shirt, slightly frayed at the collar, came into the office. He came hesitantly and stood just inside the door, peering down the room at Deborah. Deborah smiled at him and, encouraged, he came to her desk. He peered at her through red, swollen eyes. He spoke doubtfully, hesitantly.

"I was sent here," he said. "The insurance people, they—"

Deborah's smile and nodding head made him welcome.

"Of course," she said. "You're a little early, Mr.—"

"Weber," he said. "Fritz Weber. I didn't want to keep anybody waiting, miss."

Deborah smiled at him again and he smiled back. He was an unusually nice little man, Deborah thought. He held a card out to her; she took it, recorded it, and returned it, telling him it was to go with him into the examining room. He was, she told him, to go to room No. 1, and the nurse would show him where it was. But for the time being, he was to find a comfortable chair somewhere and—Deborah checked herself. From the looks of his eyes, she had better not tell him to find himself something to read.

"Just rest for a while," she said.

Between eleven thirty-five when Mr. Weber was attended to, and eleven fifty-five, five more men came—men varying in size and manner, three of whom were wearing dark glasses and one other of whom, judging by the lesion in his right lower lid, should have been; all looking like men who worked for a living with their hands. They identified themselves as Robert Oakes, John Dunnigan, George Cooper, Henry Flint and Jose Garcia; they appeared in that order and were assigned examining rooms in the order of their arrival, Weber going to the first room, Oakes to the second and so on. At noon, Grace Spencer came to the door and said, "If you gentlemen—" and they stood up, with varying alacrity, differing degrees of confidence. Grace took their cards, which Deborah had numbered in pencil in accordance with the room assigned. Grace took them into the corridor and, moving down it, dropped them off at the appropriate cubicles. Then, beginning in Room 6, she worked back, leaving in each room the card of the man occupying it. She then retraced her steps, working back from Room 1, dimming the lights in the rooms of the men wearing the dark glasses and gently lifting away the glasses; putting drops which stung and caused tears in the eyes of Henry Flint, No. 5, and John Dunnigan, No. 3.

She finished at twelve fifteen. When she emerged from Room 6, she found Dr. Gordon coming in by the back door. She watched him leave his hat and coat in the front closet. She thought he looked unusually well and pleased; she deduced that the operation had gone well. As he went down the longer corridor to his office he lighted a cigarette. He stopped at the door leading to the reception room long enough to raise his eyebrows enquiringly at Deborah and to hear her say, "Nothing important, Doctor." Then he went on into his office and closed the door behind him. It was assumed afterward that, during the next three or four minutes, he washed up in his private lavatory and put on the fresh white coat left ready for him by Nurse Spencer. It was about twelve twenty, a minute one way or the other, when he opened the door from his office into Room 1 and began his examinations.

Whatever preoccupations Dr. Andrew Gordon had when he opened the door leading from his office to the first of the examining rooms vanished as he closed the door behind him and looked down at the first waiting patient—little Fritz Weber, blinking his red and swollen eyes. He must, it was realized afterward, have had at least as many personal problems, sharp-edged worries, churning in his mind as most men have. He must have been thinking about Dan, and of the girl of twenty—their Debbie—who loved Dan. He must have been thinking, at some time that morning, about the fact that Dan Gordon would be twenty-five in a few months' time, and about what that birthday would mean. And as he thought of that, he may have had memories—with what emotions no one could more than guess—of a woman dead for almost a decade, and of that woman's brother, who was anything but dead. Dr. Gordon must have thought about Evelyn Gordon, eighteen years his junior and his wife, and of their Eileen, who was only six and had hair as soft and bright as her mother's. One of these thoughts would have led to another and all of these would have led to others still—to thoughts of Lawrence Westcott and, perhaps, of Grace Spencer. A man's mind can become a clutter of thoughts and worries, like a storeroom long unordered.

But when Dr. Gordon stepped into the first of the six examining rooms and looked with entirely professional interest at Mr. Weber, and, of Mr. Weber, only at Mr. Weber's eyes, he was able to sweep all this clutter out. It was that ability to concentrate—the unjealous among his confreres had long ago decided—which made him so very, so exceptionally, good at his job. At a given moment, Andrew Gordon could eliminate everything else and become a doctor—a man in a white coat. Possibly, Grace Spencer had sometimes thought, the wearing of the white coat helped; perhaps it was in some degree a symbol. A good many oculists, working in their own offices, worked in tweeds and blue cheviots. Andrew Gordon never did. The act of putting on the crisp white over his suit coat may have been his way of dramatizing, for himself, a step across some invisible line, on one side of which he was a man of fifty with the ordinary worries of his kind, and on the other only a doctor, with eyes only to observe and a mind only to diagnose. And there was also the fact, of course, that the white coat had a desirable effect on many of his patients, lending them assurance that all was as it should be. Like other people, although usually with more difficulty, Dr. Gordon's patients read the better magazines and knew that oculists wear white coats as inevitably as they wear reflectors strapped to their foreheads.

Now, as science in a white coat, he examined Fritz Weber's card, noting the provisional diagnosis of the insurance physician who had referred Weber to a specialist, no doubt in the hope that the specialist would find Weber's eyes in ideal condition and that hence the insurance company would have no liability in behalf of the firm for which Weber worked and in whose shop Weber had incurred an eye injury which had left him, so far, half blind. Science in a white coat looked at the card and then at Weber, who said, uneasily, "Good morning, Doctor." Science, impartial as between Weber and an insurance company, examined Weber's eyes; it made notes on Weber's card. It told Weber, with impersonal friendliness, that he should leave his card, that Dr. Mergrim of the insurance company would be communicated with, and that Weber should go home and avoid using his eyes. "Wear dark glasses for a few days," science advised Mr. Weber, who blinked and nodded. Science in the white coat moved on.

"Good morning, Doctor," the patient in Room 2 said, also uneasily, and the man in the white coat—the man who represented science—looked into his eyes. "Hello, Doctor," the man in Room 3 said. The man in Room 5 said "Hello, Doc," and there was a kind of asperity—of challenge—in his voice. The man in Room 6, who spoke with an accent, said "Good morning, sir." In each of the six rooms the representative of abstract science examined eyes and made notes on a card and undertook to communicate findings to the physician representing the insurance company. And each patient, following instructions, left his card behind, to be picked up later by Nurse Spencer, to find its way eventually to Dr. Gordon's desk and to serve as a memorandum of diagnosis.

* * *

Grace Spencer, after she had checked the patients in advance of the doctor, relieved Deborah Brooks at the reception desk in the waiting room. That was a minute or two, as nearly as she could afterward decide, after Dr. Gordon had returned from the hospital—she guessed it as about seventeen or eighteen minutes after twelve. Deborah Brooks went through the storeroom and bathroom—pausing to powder her nose and to worry briefly about the sunburn on it—and then out the back door. It took her, she thought, two or three minutes. At a guess—the guess of Lieutenant William Weigand of the Homicide Squad—she went out the back door about the time Dr. Gordon entered the first examining room. She had met no one as she left.

Debbie returned from lunch at twelve fifty by Grace's watch. Grace thought she looked a little worried, but she could guess why the girl might be worried and had not mentioned it. She had turned the reception desk over to Debbie and had gone through storeroom and bathroom, pausing to wash her hands, and then to her desk in the examining corridor. She had reached it, she thought, at about five minutes before one.

Her statement covering the next quarter of an hour, made partly in answer to questions by Lieutenant Weigand, read as follows:

Miss Spencer: I sat at my desk so that I would be available if the doctor needed me. He sometimes did. I never went to lunch on compensation days until he had finished his examinations. I—

Q. Compensation days?

A. The days he examines patients sent to him by insurance doctors. They come in two groups, morning and afternoon. He always started the second group a little after noon and then went directly to lunch.

Q. Thank you, Miss Spencer. And he was still examining when you were relieved by Miss—Brooks, is that right?

A. Yes. He had finished examining four of the patients and they had gone. He was examining the fifth.

Q. Let's see. Did you go into the rooms?

A. Oh, no. I wouldn't do that. Not unless he called me. Of course, we never bothered him when he was examining.

Q. Then how did you know—?

A. Oh, I see what you mean. Why, the patients were told to leave as soon as the doctor had finished with them. I checked the rooms, and the doors of four of them were open. The doors to the corridor, I mean. And the rooms were empty. So I knew he had finished with those patients and they had gone.

Q. I see. But the door—the corridor door—of the fifth room was still closed. I take it, incidentally, that when you speak of the rooms by number, you begin numbering from the doctor's office?

A. Yes. And the door of the fifth room was closed. Then I sat at my desk. And in a few minutes the door of the fifth room opened and the patient came out. I directed him to go out the back door.

Q. Thank you, Miss Spencer. Then?

A. I just sat there, keeping one eye on the door into the corridor—what we call the "back-door hall"—from Room 6. The doctor didn't call me. There is a call button in each examining room, so that he can get me, if he needs me. He didn't. Then at one seven—

Q. You noticed the time exactly?

A. I was in—I wanted to do an errand on my lunch hour. And I had to be back by two. It depended on him whether I had time.

Q. Right.

A. He came out at one seven. The door opens out toward me, so I only got a glimpse of him. He got his hat and coat and—

Q. Please, Miss Spencer. I'd like to get all the details just here.

A. Details? Well—he just came out into the hall from Room 6, went across the hall to the closet and—well, just took off his hospital coat, got his hat and went out. Through the back door. That's all I can think of—all the details, I mean.

Q. Right. How long did this take, would you say?

A. Not long. Two minutes perhaps.

Q. That long? Two minutes is really a rather long time, under certain circumstances.

A. Oh—perhaps a minute, then.

Q. So you would think that he went out—out of the office entirely, I mean—at about eight minutes after one. Nine minutes at the most. Right?

A. I'd think so.

Q. I hope your watch is accurate, Miss Spencer.

A. Oh, it is. I'm sure it is. I haven't changed it and—what time is it now?

Q. Four thirty-three.

A. Then mine's right if yours is.

Q. Right. Then? After the doctor went out?

A. I decided I would have time to do my errand—easily.

Q. (By Sergeant Aloysius Mullins) What was your errand, Miss?

A. I wanted to buy a pair of stockings.

Q. (By Sergeant Mullins) Oh.

Q. (By Lieutenant Weigand) And then?

A. I went to the other closet. The one nearer the bathroom door. You know? I got my own hat and coat—I just put my coat on over my uniform—and went out. I suppose it took me another two minutes. Or one minute.

Q. Then you left at—say—one ten or one eleven? Didn't you meet the doctor outside? Waiting for the elevator?

A. It must have been about then. No, I didn't. I'd just missed a down elevator; I could tell by the indicator. I had to wait, oh—you've unsettled me about times. I'd think two or three minutes. The elevators are crowded just after one, of course.

Q. While you waited, you didn't see Dr. Gordon?

A. No.

Q. (By Sergeant Mullins) Or anyone else?

A. Oh—other people, of course.

Q. (By Sergeant Mullins) I mean—you didn't see anybody going in what you call the "back door." Into the office, I mean. Dr. Gordon going back, say? Or anybody else? You were where you could see the door?

A. The door is right next to the elevators, Sergeant. I'd have noticed if anybody went in. Nobody did.

Q. (By Sergeant Mullins) Oh.

Q. (By Lieutenant Weigand) Why, Mullins?

A. (By Sergeant Mullins) I sort of thought it would be interesting, Loot.

Q. (By Lieutenant Weigand) And then you went to lunch—and did your errand—and returned, Miss Spencer. Getting back at about two o'clock?

A. Yes. About then.

Q. Thank you, Miss Spencer. You've been very clear. The rest of it—we'll let that go for now. Right?

A. Please, Lieutenant. I can't—

The scene is belied by the coherence of Mullins' notes. There is nothing in the transcript to show how often Grace Spencer's voice broke; how she hesitated; how her hands moved and twisted as she talked; how, after she said, "I can't," her head dropped on Debbie Brooks's desk and rested on her folded arms and how her broad, slender shoulders shook.

Grace Spencer came back from lunch at about two o'clock that afternoon. She let herself in through the back door, hung her coat in the closet she shared with Deborah Brooks, took her time about washing up in the bathroom and then went on through the storeroom into the waiting room. Deborah had her typewriter swung out—and was making an erasure. She was too preoccupied to notice Grace for a moment and Grace stood just inside the waiting room, looking down it with a faint smile on her face. Then Deborah looked up and saw her and smiled in turn. Her smile was rueful.

"I ought to be better," Deborah said, and Grace walked down the room toward her. "Only, I don't seem to get any better."

She was all right, Grace told her. Anyway, she would be all right.

"After all," Grace said.

"After all," Deborah agreed, "I'm new at it. I seem to be new at everything, Grace."

She was, the nurse pointed out, only twenty. Few people were not new at things at twenty.

"Most girls have had training by that time," Debbie said. "Years of training. And I can't even type a letter saying all right, come Tuesday at three o'clock and the doctor will work you in, without having to erase three times. Andy's very patient. And he just has me here because he's nice."

"And," Grace said, "because he's known you since you were a—a kitten—and knew your father and mother for years—and, anyway, there's more to the job than typing. You coo very nicely, Debbie."

"Grace!" Debbie Brooks said, with some indignation.

"On the telephone," Grace said. "When appropriate. To dear little old ladies who can't understand why they can't see as well as they could when they were dear little girls. To men who are so important they can only come when the doctor is at the hospital operating. To—"

"You make me sound like an—like a drip," Debbie said. "I mean literally a drip. Dripping."

"All right," Grace said. "You're a sweet child."

"Yes, Mama," Debbie said. "Yes, Grandmother. All right, Miss Methuselah."

"You looked worried when you came back from lunch," Grace said. "Tell mama. Danny?"

The younger girl nodded.

"The same?" Grace wanted to know.

Debbie nodded again.

"He insists on our going ahead, whatever Andy says," Deborah told her. "He won't wait; he says he's tired of waiting. He says things are snafu. He says—oh, he says everything, Grace. I've told you. And he's right. And Andy's right, too, and—it's a mess."

Grace smiled faintly. Things were so easily a mess at twenty. You had so little time at twenty; even when you were only thirty-two you had more time. It was a most ingenious paradox.

"The doctor thinks six months will do it," Grace said. "Surely you two can wait six months."

"Did you ever—" Debbie began and stopped suddenly.

"Yes, my sweet, I ever did," Grace told her. "Longer than that. Much longer."

"I don't know why," Debbie said. She said it honestly, and with a kind of surprise.

"Maybe men are afraid of nurses," Grace said. She was light about it. "Maybe it's the starch, baby. Anyone want me?"

"Mrs. Fleming again," Debbie said. "She says if she could take them off for just a couple of hours. Or even just when she arrived. And will you call her?"

Nurse Spencer would call Mrs. Fleming. She did, there on the desk telephone. She was gently final with Mrs. Fleming; she was sorry; she had checked with the doctor; the doctor was firm. Not even for a couple of hours. But of course, Mrs. Fleming's eyes were Mrs. Fleming's eyes. Then she listened, her own expression one of resignation. Debbie laughed a tiny, low-pitched laugh, watching Grace's face. "I—" Grace said and had to stop again. She waited. "I wouldn't," she said quickly. "The doctor definitely does not approve, Mrs. Fleming. Goodbye." She put the telephone back in its cradle, looked at Debbie and said, mildly enough, "Damn fool."

"That was all?" she said then.

That was all, Deborah told her.

"One of the compensations is going blind, poor guy," Grace said. The man in No. 1. "I don't have to be a doctor to tell that."

"Oh," Debbie said. "Can't Andy—?"

"Not even your Andy," Grace said. "It would take God."

Debbie Brooks closed her own eyes for a moment and then opened them. Grace Spencer nodded at her.

"I do that too," she said. She straightened. "However," she said, and went from the desk and through the door into the examining-room area. The door to the doctor's office from the corridor was closed. She went into the first room. The door leading from it to the doctor's office was also closed. The doctor was back, then, and did not want to be disturbed until office hours began at three. She checked the first examining room, and went on to the next room. Patients left things sometimes; a kind of light debris. She found none until she reached Room 5, which smelled of a pipe. And Room 5—Mr. Henry Flint—had knocked out his pipe on the floor. Grace looked at this debris with resentment. Room 6—Mr. Jose Garcia, with an address in Harlem—had left no debris. Grace went to the storeroom and got fresh cloths to cover the six little tables in the six rooms. She got a dustpan and whiskbroom; she changed the cloths in the rooms and removed Mr. Flint's debris. She rubbed the wax linoleum lightly with one of the used cloths. She opened the windows slightly to air the rooms and switched off the lights. She disposed of the used cloths in the storeroom hamper, emptied the dustpan and looked at her watch. It was two thirty. She returned to the rooms and picked up the referral cards and carried them to her desk. She entered the names and addresses neatly in a kind of ledger. This took her about five minutes. She went back to the reception room and sat down in the chair at the left of Deborah Brooks's desk, stretched out her long legs and looked at them and said she had seen a hat that would knock your eye out—would knock your mind out, for that matter—on her way to buy stockings.

"In that little place on Madison between Fifty-first and Fifty-second? West side of the street?" Debbie said. "If it was, I saw it. The one that went up like this?" She demonstrated.

"Other side of the street," Grace told her. "It went down like this." She demonstrated. "Between Fifty-second and Fifty-third."

"Tell me," Debbie said, and licked an envelope closed.

"Why don't you use the sponge?" Grace said.

"Gets my fingers gummy," Debbie told her. "Go on. Feathers?"

At ten minutes of three, an elderly woman dressed in black came in to the waiting room with a younger woman. They went to a sofa against the wall and the younger woman helped the older to sit down. Then the younger woman came to Deborah and Grace—who had got to her feet, unhurriedly, when the two entered. Grace went behind Deborah's desk into the examining-room corridor and Deborah said, "Good afternoon, Miss Newsome."

"We're the first?" Miss Newsome said. "I hoped we would be."

"The very first," Deborah assured her. "It will only be a minute, I'm sure. The nurse will see if the doctor is ready for your aunt."

* * *

Grace went to her own desk and sat at it a moment, doing nothing. Then she took a compact from a drawer in the desk cabinet, looked at herself in its mirror and touched her nose with powder. Then, ready, she stood up and walked down the corridor to the door leading to Dr. Gordon's office. She knocked lightly on the door and, without waiting for an answer, opened it. Dr. Gordon was sitting at his desk across the room, near the windows. As he sat there, he should have faced away from the windows, toward the door in which Grace Spencer stood a moment—stood and instinctively, meaninglessly, raised her right hand toward her lips.

Because Dr. Andrew Gordon was not facing her. His face lay on the smooth glass of the desk top, the head twisted, so that the right cheek rested on the glass and the eyes could not be seen.

"Doctor!" Grace said, but already the knowledge that he could not hear her was in her mind. It had come as blackness comes in the narrowing world of one who is about to faint. But Grace Spencer was not about to faint. She crossed the room to the doctor. She had to go around him to reach his left hand, dangling by his side. His body pressed the right arm against the desk.

Before her fingers touched his wrist she knew. She did not need to feel for the pulse. But her fingers, trained until they seemed to work without direction from her mind, did feel for the pulse on the wrist which, although it was not cold, was too cold for life. The fingers did not fumble. They did not find a pulse.

Grace did not scream. But when she stood up, her face was colorless and her wide mouth was set in a contorted line. She did not touch Andrew Gordon again; she looked at him with eyes which were wide and blank. Her lips were stiff; so stiff she could hardly move them. But she spoke as she stood, looking down at Andrew Gordon's body.

"Andy," she said. "Oh—darling. Darling."

Her voice was low in the emptiness of the room.

Slowly her eyes focused again. They did not have far to look. In the back of Andrew Gordon's head, visible even through the hair, there was a deep depression. It was not a horrifying wound; it had not bled; it was probable, she realized, that the skin was not broken. It was merely that the posterior portion of a human skull had been pushed into the brain under it.

She turned away and started toward the door and seemed to stagger a moment and then caught herself and went on, quite steadily. She went out of the private office and into the doorway leading to the waiting room. Deborah Brooks looked up at her, and then half rose with a little cry. Grace's head moved to summon her. Deborah came to the nurse and was drawn back, beyond the vision of those in the waiting room, into the corridor. Grace spoke in a low voice; a voice which did not tremble.

"The doctor's dead, Deborah," she said. "He's been—somebody killed him."

The nurse saw the color leaving the girl's face, saw the lips begin to move before they went slack, and caught the light, slender body as it began to sag. She lowered Deborah to the floor and stood for an instant looking at her. Then she made up her mind and, leaving the girl lying flat, her head pillowed only by the long brown hair, went to Deborah's desk in the waiting room. She stood behind it and the people in the room—there were five of them now—looked up at her, their differing faces alike in curiosity and expectancy.

"I'm very sorry," Grace Spencer said, and her voice was steady, even professional. "Dr. Gordon has been taken suddenly ill. It will be impossible for him to see anyone today. Miss Brooks will—will communicate with you about future appointments."

The waiting patients were no fools. They looked at Grace's white, set face and they did not argue. Grace waited for them to go and then, still rigid—still standing—she pulled the telephone closer and dialed. When she had finished there was a moment's pause. Then, quite slowly and distinctly, Grace Spencer spoke.

"I am reporting a murder," she said.

The murder of Andy, her mind said. *The murder of Andy. Oh darling—darling.*

• 2 •

MONDAY, 1:05 P.M. TO 4:55 P.M.

Grace Spencer's report reached the police telegraph bureau at 3:03 P.M. It went out immediately to the East Fifty-first Street station, headquarters of the Seventeenth Precinct. It went also to the office of Lieutenant (Acting Captain) William Weigand, commanding officer of the main office Homicide Squad. But Weigand was not in his office; he was explaining things to Deputy Chief Inspector Artemus O'Malley, in command of the Detective Bureau.

"So there we stand," Bill Weigand said, not for the first time. "We know he did it. The D.A. says sure he did it. And the D.A. says if we want a false arrest suit, go right ahead and pick him up. The D.A. says juries want evidence."

"That," O'Malley said, "is what you always get from these damn lawyers." He regarded the younger policeman reproachfully. "Especially nowadays," he said. "Like I've told you."

"Well," said Bill Weigand, "sufficient unto the day."

"What?" said Inspector O'Malley.

"Nothing," Bill told him. "A quotation. Misapplied. However, Inspector, that's the way things are. You'll find it all in D.D. 14."

Inspector O'Malley was morose. He said he had. He said it was a hell of a note.

"It looks to me, Bill, like you slipped," he said. "I don't say you slipped. I say it looks to me like you slipped."

"Possibly," Bill said. "I'm sorry, sir."

"What's sorry?" Inspector O'Malley wanted to know. Bill merely nodded, agreeing by implication it wasn't much.

"If you have any suggestions, Inspector," he said, politely.

O'Malley shook his head firmly. He said Bill knew he didn't interfere with responsible officers, which was untrue; he said that he couldn't do everything, could he? He said, "You young cops!" with a falling inflection and an air of great weariness. Bill Weigand, who was used to this, merely waited, with politeness.

"All right," O'Malley said. "O.K., Lieutenant. Put it on the back of the stove. Maybe it will boil."

"Right," Bill said. "I can't think of anything else. It isn't as if—"

A buzzer sounded on Inspector O'Malley's desk. O'Malley looked resentfully at a box with a grid on the front of it. He reached out, hesitated, pushed firmly down on a lever on the box. The box gave a harsh wail and O'Malley jumped.

"Damn' gadget," O'Malley said, with compressed fury. He pushed the lever up again. He yelled at the box.

"Well!" he yelled.

The box cleared its throat, a little nervously. Bill Weigand recognized the throat.

"Sergeant Mullins, sir," the box said. "Report of homicide in the Medical Chambers, East Fifty-third Street. Looks important, sir."

"Why?" said O'Malley, without compromise in his voice.

"It's a doctor, sir," Mullins said, and cleared his throat again.

"What's important about a doctor?" O'Malley said.

"Yes, sir," Mullins said. "I see what you mean, sir."

"The hell you do," O'Malley said.

"Yes, sir," Mullins said. "I thought the papers, Inspector. Medical Chambers and everything." Mullins, in the box, cleared his throat again. "I thought the Loot—I mean, I thought you'd want to know, Inspector."

Bill Weigand watched O'Malley subside. O'Malley began to subside, he noticed, when Mullins said "papers." It was a word to conjure with, and Mullins had conjured. It was a word like "commissioner," like the two words "district leader." Bill Weigand did not smile, but there was a smile in his mind.

"Yeah," O'Malley said. "The papers. Why didn't you say it was in the Medical Chambers?"

Mullins, without stopping to clear his throat, said he was sorry.

"Is it a name?" O'Malley wanted to know. This time Mullins hesitated.

"Seems like I've heard it," he said. "Dr. Andrew Gordon. He's an optician."

O'Malley looked at Weigand, and Weigand nodded.

"Oculist," Weigand said. "Eye doctor. Well known, I think."

"He's an oculist, Mullins," O'Malley said. "Sure he's well known. Don't you read the papers?"

"Yes, sir," Mullins said.

"Well," O'Malley said. "Stand by, Sergeant. Weigand will pick you up if he wants you."

He flicked the lever on the box down. The box wailed. He flicked it back up again.

"Damn gadget," O'Malley said.

Bill Weigand was standing up. O'Malley nodded.

"Ought to take it myself," O'Malley said. "You young cops. But naturally, I've got a hundred things."

"Naturally," Weigand agreed.

"Well," O'Malley said, "what you waiting for, Bill?"

Bill wasn't waiting. He was moving toward the door. Deputy Chief Inspector O'Malley watched him go. Deputy Chief Inspector O'Malley leaned back in his chair, bit the end off a cigar and then laid the cigar in a brass ashtray. He leaned his head back against the high, upholstered rest on his chair. He closed his eyes, so that he could think better.

Pamela North, bent over so that her body above the hips was parallel with the floor, backed out of her apartment door. She held her hands down, palms out, and made small pushing motions with them, meanwhile saying, "No, no." A small cat, made of India rubber, with a cafe au lait body and upstanding, deep brown ears, looked at her out of blue eyes and made a low, surprised sound. Pam North continued to push the air with her right hand and reached for the door with her left, planning to pull the door closed. The small cat crouched and waved a suddenly bushy tail. Pam got the door with her fingertips and began to pull it toward her. The cat waved the bushy tail. The door was only six inches ajar when the cat moved. It was a movement so fluid, so lithe and, above all, so rapid, that the eyes could hardly follow it. Now you saw her; now you didn't. It was like a flame of a candle going out.

It was Martini North going out. She went over Pam's grasping right hand. She landed running; she frolicked down the apartment-house corridor.

"Teeney," Pam North said, in deep reproach. "You're a bad girl."

Martini stopped when she heard what was, for her, the operative portion of her name. She stopped, it seemed, midway in a leap. She sat down, all in one motion, and looked around at Pam. The little cat's eyes were round and surprised and innocent. It was clear that she was seeing Pam for the first time.

Pam left the door part-way open and advanced.

"Bad cat," Pam said, in low, sad tones. "Bad cat."

Martini watched Pam's approach with pleased interest. When Pam was two steps away she crouched and smiled. Pam said, "Nice Teeney," in tones of caress. She reached out a hand. Teeney threw herself over her own shoulders, landed trotting and went down the corridor. Her trot was ridiculously purposeful. It was also, apparently, downhill. Although she was not pleased, Pam laughed.

"Teeney," she said, "you have the silliest hind legs. Here, Teeney."

Martini stopped and sat down facing Pam. She raised her right rear foot, looked at it with wonder, and used it to scratch her right ear. Pam sat on her heels.

"Teeney," she said, in a voice of great interest. "Look, Teeney!"

Pam herself looked. She looked at her own fingers, briskly patting the carpeted floor. She used her nails to scratch the carpet, producing a small scraping sound.

Martini unwound herself, wrapped her tail around her bottom neatly, looked at Pam North's face and then bent her head slightly forward and looked at Pam's finger. Pam continued to scratch the carpet. Martini's interest grew; she subsided to the floor, with her legs under her. Then she began to swish her tail again. It had become a normal tail; now, for the second time, it bushed. Flattened on the floor, moving with infinite secrecy, Martini began an advance. Each leg moved with its own poised caution. Each foot came down like a petal falling, touched the surface in exploration, by infinitesimal degrees took the weight of cat. Martini was creeping over a jungle floor, wary of the faintest sound of crumbled leaf. Muscles rippled along her little, compact body. She advanced by inches. She stopped, waited, advanced again. Her eyes were fixed on Pam's finger. She was four feet away, three—she was almost within reach of Pam's hands.

Then she leaped for the kill. She leaped sideways, so that she passed the hand. As she passed it, half in the air, half on her feet, she flicked it with her right forepaw. And she touched Pam's hand with all claws sheathed, with infinite lightness. Landing, she continued. She continued at a lope, rocking like a hobbyhorse. She reached the partly open door, made a sharp right turn, and went through the aperture. Pam moved, with only human celerity and grace, after her. Martini was sitting inside the door. She was washing her back. She paid no attention whatever to Pamela North, so Pamela North closed the door gently—so as not to pinch Martini if she changed her mind—and went on about her business.

Cats, Pam thought to herself, are certainly something. It must be very funny to be a cat, she told herself, as she waited for the elevator. Because you don't know what you're going to do next and I don't think you recognize your hind feet when you see them. The elevator stopped and Pam got in. "And certainly not your tail," Pam continued. It was only when the elevator man turned and looked at her that Pam realized she had, as she unpredictably did, spoken aloud. He was an elevator man she knew quite well. Still.

"I said, have you seen the mail?" Pam told him.

"Oh," the elevator man said, and looked relieved. "It doesn't come until about one thirty usually, Mrs. North. The second delivery, that is."

Pam looked at her watch. It was one fifteen. It *is* always later than you think, Pam thought. She reflected. And hungrier, usually, she added. If she walked briskly, she could get to Charles, which was only around the corner, in two or three minutes. The trouble with not having anybody to lunch with was that you forgot to go when you planned to, and then you got hungrier and ate more and if you weren't careful you spoiled your dinner. Things would be simplified if Jerry didn't have to go to his office or, since he obviously did, if he didn't have to have so many lunches with agents and people.

She walked across the lobby and through the door. And she was confronted by a miracle. In front of the door—not across the street or down at the end of the block, although either would have been itself miraculous, but actually in front of the door—there was a taxicab with its flag up! It was almost impossible to believe. Even as—with that wild surge of exultation which, that spring, so few New Yorkers ever had the opportunity to enjoy—Pam North leaped across the sidewalk, skepticism fought for the upper hand.

It would be waiting for someone. It would be a taxicab which would go only in one direction, and would shake its head glumly—longsufferingly—if urged to go in another. It would be time for it to go over to the upper West Side, where all taxicabs seemed to live, and pull in. It would have a broken clutch. It would be out of gas. Or it would be merely whimsical.

As she leaped, Pam's face took on that look of entreaty which, that spring, was the fixed expression of all New Yorkers who sought to become passengers in taxicabs. She looked anxiously at the driver, who regarded her with detached speculation. He was middle aged and jaundiced. He knew his power. Above good and evil, above—oh, infinitely above—the tiny needs of small scurrying folk, he waited her coming. It was not for him, *deus ex machina*—and what a *machina,* to be sure!—to indicate in advance his final, august decision. He pretended he did not know what Pam North was about. Not until she was opening the door, perhaps not until she was in and seated, would he look at her with slow surprise—surprise and effrontery—and say, "No, lady," and give whatever whimsical reason he used between one fifteen and one twenty on Mondays.

There were several ways of meeting this, if you were unwillingly a pedestrian that spring and sought to improve your lot. The simplest was the take-it-for-granted technic. Utilizing that, you merely assumed taxicabs were what they had once been, available, and entered and spoke firmly. Then the driver spoke more firmly and, usually, you got out. The next—Pam's own favorite—was the please-it's-just-a-short-run method. That involved a bright, but suitably submissive, smile, to be turned on just as you reached for the handle of the door. A slight wistfulness helped, sometimes. Frequently this method got you refused before you were entirely in the cab—a concession, this.

There were other methods. There was the stern, I'll-tell-a-cop-on-you method. There was the desperate situation, or I've-got-to-get-to-the-hospital method—seldom efficacious, particularly when used by women. There was the promising or Boy-what-a-tip-I'm-going-to-give-you method. And there were variants of all these. They were alike only, at last, in their common inadequacy. And all involved, first, the miracle of the cab-with-its-flag-up. That was where you began.

Pam was beginning there. Her first startled leap—which was a little, somehow, like one of Martini's leaps—carried her halfway across the sidewalk. It was involuntary, almost a reflex. The rest of the way, Pam moved more slowly. She only trotted. The taxicab did not move. Sometimes they merely went away while you were reaching for them, remote in their contempt. This, at worst, was one of the coquettish ones. It might be wooed. Pam reached it, and still it did not move. She reached out a hand and touched its door handle. The touch was almost a caress. She looked quickly, with her prettiest smile, at the driver. He looked at her with no comment in his face. But his face did not reject her; did not utterly reject her. It reserved decision. Gently, so as not to frighten the taxicab, Pamela North turned the door handle. (There had been a time, dim now in memory, when taxicab drivers reached back and opened the door for passengers. It was strange to remember that time, even mistily—even fleetingly.) Pam turned the door handle. It was probable, of course, that the door would not open. Many taxicabs, in those months, opened only on one side. Some did not, it appeared, open at all. They were merely decoys. This one opened.

The door did not fall off, which was always, also, slightly to be expected. It was secured inside by a heavy rope, but the rope allowed a medium-sized opening. It was quite sufficient for Pam North, who was barely medium sized herself. She slipped in, still cautiously—there was a chance, naturally, that the cab might be half filled with original settlers—and, when she found herself alone, sat down gingerly on the edge of the seat.

Now, slowly, with majesty, the driver turned toward her. Now was the moment. He was about to speak. Tensely, perched more tentatively than any bird, Pam North waited. He spoke.

"Where to, lady?" he said.

His voice was almost like anyone's voice. It was not harsh or condemning; it was not even notably contemptuous. Its tone accepted Pam as, at the least, a candidate for the human race—an entry, not yet scratched.

A delicious feeling of warmth spread through Pam North. She had a taxicab! *She had a taxicab!*

It was only then, suddenly, that she realized she did not in the least want a taxicab. She was not going anywhere, except down the street and around the corner to Charles. It was a bright, warm day. She had never felt better in her life. She had been overtaken, and overcome, by conditioned reflexes—the reflexes built up among New Yorkers through many, many months of almost hopeless longing, interrupted by short, mad dashes. Few, in those days, could watch an empty taxicab go by, or pause momentarily, without some reflex response—a slight watering of the mouth, a momentary twitch of the taxicab-waving arm, a tensing of the leg muscles in anticipation of a spring. Pam North merely carried these responses farther than more phlegmatic people did. But she had carried them quite a distance, this time.

For a moment, but only for a moment, she felt a strange hollowness, an inadequacy. But it lasted only for a moment; when she spoke there was no hesitancy.

"Saks Fifth Avenue," she said. There was nothing to indicate that it was merely what had come first into her mind.

This was another turning point, of course. It might be that this was a taxicab which would only go downtown. But Pam doubted it; acceptance, although long delayed, seemed to have been complete—complete, at any rate, within reason. Not Brooklyn, of course. Not the Bronx. Certainly not Long Island City. But almost certainly Saks. Perhaps even the upper East Side, if she wanted to go to the upper East Side.

The taxicab driver did not respond, but he made a sound. It was hardly contemptuous at all, that sound. He reached across and pushed down the flag. He started up. (There was something, rather dreadful, wrong with the transmission, Pam's ears told her. But the taxicab moved.) Pam sat back in her seat.

Now, she thought to herself, whatever am I going to buy at Saks? When all I want is lunch? She considered a moment. Oh well, she thought, probably that will take care of itself.

It took care of itself reasonably well, as it turned out. Pam found several things she needed without going off the main floor. She had no particular feeling of guilt, having long needed a new purse, anyway. What feeling of guilt she did have, vanished when she bought Jerry a dozen handkerchiefs which she was sure he needed and then, after some speculation, a new tie. He needed a new tie, and she always bought his ties. Neither of the Norths thought this at all comic, nor did Pam at any time buy Jerry a new tie of which he did not highly approve.

Since she was there, she decided, there could be no harm in looking at new dresses, because there might be something entirely too good to pass up. She took the elevator and looked at dresses for some time, and found one that might be too good to pass up and tried it on, and looked at herself in all the mirrors. Then she decided that Jerry had better see it before she bought it, on account of the line, and arranged to have it put aside for twenty-four hours, on the chance. She reclothed herself in the lightweight wool dress which was not far from the color of Martini—a very useful, and not coincidental, similarity; Martini was shedding—but which had red pockets, which Martini did not have. She tossed her light spring coat over her arm and tapped briskly toward the elevator, stopping only long enough to make an appointment at Antoine's desk for the next afternoon. (She did not keep the appointment; she did not return with Jerry to consider the reserved dress. The next day was not to be, in any detail, as she planned it.) In the elevator, she looked at her watch and was startled to see that it was now two thirty. Two thirty-five, really, making the necessary corrections for deviation.

She was really hungry now, she thought, going out the Fiftieth Street door and turning toward Madison. She wanted something reasonably substantial, like hamburgers. She turned up Madison, walking briskly, thinking of hamburgers. She found them in Hamburger Heaven, sitting at the counter. She had two and a cup of coffee and then, after a momentary pause of doubt, a large piece of cake. She had another cup of coffee and a cigarette with it and was pleased because if she had gone to Charles she would almost surely have had a cocktail and this way she hadn't. The taxicab had really been a godsend, Pam North decided.

She pressed her cigarette out in the ashtray—and was faintly repelled when the man next to her, finishing, simultaneously, dropped his, still afire, into his almost empty coffee cup—slipped from the stool, paid her check at the counter and went out into Madison. Now what? she thought, turning downtown. Now a bus—miracles never struck twice in one day—home and then it would be almost time for Jerry. It was three ten now. She walked down Madison and looked in several windows, and then, because she was enjoying her walk, went through Fifty-fourth to Park. It was three twenty when she reached Fifty-third. As she waited on the curb to cross Fifty-third there was a siren wail and a police car came very fast up Park, swung into Fifty-third and went west, lurching around the front of a car which had not stopped quickly enough. Halfway down the next block, it turned in toward the right-hand curb and slowed to a sudden stop. There were two cruise cars already parked there. And a crowd was gathering. As she watched, several people standing near her turned into Fifty-third and began to run toward the police cars.

The police car which had come up Park was not a cruise car. It was a car she knew; it was the Homicide Squad car from Centre Street. She knew it very well. She had ridden in it—perhaps, she sometimes thought, illegally—with Bill Weigand. Where it went, there was trouble—a certain kind of trouble.

It was another reflex, longer conditioned—and harder to explain—which led Pam North now to turn into Fifty-third Street, walking toward the police cars and the crowd gathering there. She did not run. She did not go eagerly. But she went.

When Bill Weigand, Mullins, Detective-Sergeant Stein and Detective Barney Jones went into the offices of Dr. Andrew Gordon on the eighth floor of the Medical Chambers, there were already a good many people in the offices. There had been, for some reason not immediately apparent, a uniformed patrolman standing near a door which opened beside the elevators. Weigand and the others went around the elevators, following directions given them by the elevator operator, turned left into a broad corridor and went to another door outside which a second uniformed patrolman stood. He opened the door for them. Inside there was a waiting room and the first of a good many people. They looked up as Weigand and the others came in; they looked up with a kind of worried, half-frightened, expectation. They looked up with strained, puzzled faces. Bill Weigand had seen many faces like those. He did not seem to look at the people in the waiting room. But he saw them.

One of them did not look up. She was blonde and slim, and she was lying on her back on a sofa against the wall. She was not looking at anything and her face was white; it was evident that she had fainted. Standing near her was a nurse. Tall, slender, broad-shouldered, the nurse was. Bill felt that, before she turned slightly to look at him, she had been looking at nothing. There was remoteness in the lines of her face; it was as if she had only partly returned from nowhere. At a desk, down the room from the entrance door, near another doorway guarded by another uniformed patrolman, a very young girl with long brown hair was sitting. She had been crying. A tall man, not much older than she, stood by the desk. He might have been looking down at her. Now, he was looking at Weigand, and with the other emotions—the emotions he shared with the nurse, and the girl at the desk—there was something else in his face. Antagonism? They'd see. There was still another man—a man in his middle fifties, at a guess—and he was standing in front of one of the upholstered chairs along the wall. He was standing as if he had just got out of the chair. He was a solid man of medium height, and he had short gray hair. There was strain and puzzlement on his face. No antagonism.

Bill Weigand did not appear to look at any of these people and Mullins, Stein and Jones, following him, did not seem to look at them either. The four, in file, went toward the policeman standing in the doorway near the desk, and he saluted as Bill came up. There was sharp light momentarily on the wall behind him; in a moment there was another flash of light. The photographers from the precinct were at it. It was quick work.

The lieutenant of the precinct squad was watching the photographer who, standing on a chair, was shooting down at something which was shielded from Weigand by the photographer's body. The flash went off, the photographer got down. He went around to the other side. The body was that of a man, rather heavy, of middle height. It was slumped forward, head and shoulders resting on the desk. The precinct lieutenant walked a few steps toward Weigand.

"Well," he said, "there it is, Bill."

Bill said he saw it.

"Gordon," the precinct lieutenant said. "Andrew. An eye doctor. Somebody bashed the back of his head in."

"Well," Weigand said. "Well, well."

"Yeah," the precinct lieutenant said.

"The M.E.?" Bill said.

"Coming."

"Right," Bill said. He jerked his head toward the waiting room. He said they seemed to have picked up quite a few people. The precinct lieutenant shook his head at that. He said they hadn't picked them up.

"Found them," he said. "Here when we came. The babe passed out on the sofa is the guy's wife. The young fellow is his son. I don't know exactly who the gray-haired guy is. The other two work here."

"Right," Bill said. There was movement at the door and he looked around. A small, round man with a black bag came in. He had a pink face and a pink bald head. He waved his free hand at everybody and said, "What've we got, boys? What've we got?" He did not wait to be answered; it was greeting, not enquiry. He crossed briskly to the desk and looked at the body. He regarded it; bent over it. He straightened up.

"Somebody bashed in his head," he told them. "Blunt instrument, boys."

Bill Weigand smiled at him.

"Thanks a lot, Doctor," he said. "We needed you to tell us."

"Sure you did," the doctor agreed cheerfully. "Obscure to the lay mind, naturally. You hit somebody with something heavy—hit him on the head—and the skull caves. Always assuming he's not a policeman. Messes the brain up."

"Always assuming he's not a policeman," Bill Weigand said.

"Smart boy," the doctor told him. "Then he dies. Like this one." He turned and faced Bill Weigand. His face was not as cheerful as his words. There was a hurt expression on his face, like the hurt expression on a child's face.

Bill smiled, faintly.

"Funny, aren't we?" the doctor said. "All right. Who was he?"

"Didn't you notice when you came in?" Weigand asked. "His name's on his door. Gordon. Dr. Andrew Gordon."

"All right," the doctor said. "I hoped he wasn't. Never met Gordon. He was a good man, you know. Very good man."

Bill nodded.

"One of the two or three best," the assistant medical examiner said. "A damned good eye man. The boss called him in once or twice. Very interesting malignancy, one case was. Question: Contributing cause? Gordon said no." He turned and looked at Gordon's body. "Now he's dead," he said. "Pity."

"Right," Bill said. "How—"

"Long," the assistant medical examiner finished. "When was he found?"

"About three. Thereabouts."

The doctor looked at his watch. He turned back to the body; he touched the forehead; he lifted the head and looked at the eyes. He went behind the body, picked up the dangling hand and held it by the wrist. Then he lifted the body back in the chair, moving quickly, expertly. He opened the unbuttoned suit coat, placed a clinical thermometer under the arm and pressed the arm down against it. Leaving the thermometer there, he went across the room and looked at a thermostat on the wall; he returned, removed the thermometer and looked at it.

"Warm in here," he said. "Makes a difference, of course. You want a guess?"

"Yes," Bill said.

"Not later than two," the doctor said. "Not earlier than—oh, say twelve thirty to be safe. Few minutes one way or the other."

Bill Weigand only nodded.

The doctor lowered the body again so that it lay in its original position on the desk. He bent over it and examined the wound. He pressed it lightly with his fingers. He sniffed his fingers. "Used something to keep his hair down," he said, casually. He stood looking at the head.

"No skin broken," he said. "Something round and smooth. About as big as your fist. Something like—oh, a big knob on a cane. Hell of a big knob for a cane, of course. Almost as big as a baseball, only smoother. Fit anything you can think of?"

"Oh yes," Bill said. "A big knob on an ornamental poker. A knob off an old brass bed. A heavy paperweight, rounded on one side. A round stone, thrown by somebody. I can think of plenty of things."

"Good," the doctor said. He looked down at the body again. "Damn shame," he said quickly. He picked up his bag. "Well," he said, "you know what to do with it, Bill. You'll get your report copy."

He went, quick and pink—and with the puzzled expression of a hurt child. Weigand looked after him, smiling faintly.

"Hates murder," Bill said, more or less to the precinct lieutenant. "Can't understand anybody so—unkind. Won't be able to eat dinner tonight, poor guy. We get ourselves into funny jobs."

"Yeah," the precinct lieutenant said. "You boys taking over?"

Bill nodded, abstractedly. Except for the men on the doors, he said, they would take over.

"The nurse found him," the precinct lieutenant said. "That's about as far as we'd got. O.K.?"

"Right," Bill Weigand said. He crossed the room and stood looking at the body. He looked around the room. He crossed it and opened the door leading into the first of the examining rooms and looked at the room without going in. He went to the other door beside it and out into the corridor and looked down it.

"Funny setup," he said. "We may need a sketch of it, Barney. O.K.?"

"Sure, Loot," Detective Barney Jones said.

"A rough, for now," Weigand told him.

"O.K.," Barney said.

The precinct lieutenant, two other detectives from the precinct squad and the two photographers went out, in a long file. Weigand waited until they had gone through the waiting room. Then he went to the door. He stood looking into the room, and the people in it looked back at him, worried again, waiting uneasily. He stood for a moment and was about to speak when the door at the end of the room, which had just closed on a police photographer, opened again. Bill Weigand looked down the room at Pam North.

"Is this—" she began, and then she saw Bill.

"This is the place," Bill Weigand told her, his voice grave and businesslike. "We've been waiting for you, Mrs. North."

Pam looked, momentarily, very much surprised. She looked hurriedly at Bill's face.

"I—" she began.

"Yes, Mrs. North," Bill Weigand said, his voice very official. "You're late. However, now that you are here." His official voice had resignation in it. "Now that you are here, we'll go ahead. In here, Mrs. North."

Pam, still looking puzzled, came down the room. All the people in the room looked at her. Bill took her arm as she passed him, in a gesture which seemed one of direction.

"Ouch!" Pam said, in a low voice. "Bill!"

Bill herded Pam North in front of him into the private office of the late Dr. Gordon. He closed the door behind them.

"Now!" he said.

"Hello, Mr. Mullins," Pam said. "Mr. Stein." She looked at Barney Jones, who looked at her with round, appreciative eyes.

"Jones, miss," Barney told her. He looked at Bill Weigand.

"The sketch, Barney," Bill said. "The sketch."

"Yeah," Barney Jones said. He went to the door leading to the first examining room, opened it and went through.

"Now, Pam," Bill said. "How did you do it this time?" His voice was no longer official. It was merely very interested.

Pam told him. She left out the part about the captured taxicab.

"And how did you get in?" Bill said.

"Well," Pam said, "I'm afraid I used your name. And they seemed to think you'd sent for me, Bill—one of them seemed to think I was a relative or something—of the victim, I mean, not of you—and—"

"Right," Bill said. "Jerry won't like it."

"O'Malley won't like it," Mullins said. He said it gloomily. He closed his eyes and opened them again. "At all," Mullins said.

Pam had seen the body. Her face was grave, suddenly. She turned to Bill and her face was still grave.

"It was a—an impulse, Bill," she said. "A sudden thing I do like—like the taxicab. I didn't tell you about that. But coming here was like that. I'm—I'm sorry."

Bill smiled at her.

"Officially," he said, "I regard your actions, my dear, with—" He decided not to keep it up. "Actually," he said, "I'm glad to see you, Pam."

Mullins shuddered; he made his shudder audible. Somehow he had got directly behind Pam, who jumped.

"Mr. Mullins!" she said. "Don't do that!"

Mullins was embarrassed.

"Look, Mrs. North," he said, "it wasn't to make you jump. It was just—I was thinking of the inspector." He paused, considering. "Maybe

I shouldn't," he said. "Only he's sort of a hard guy not to think of, Mrs. North. You know that."

"She's here, Mullins," Weigand told him. "I let them think out there that she was—official. A policewoman or something. So she's here. I'll think about the inspector."

"You won't like it," Mullins told him. "But it's O.K. with me, Loot."

Pam looked at Bill and her eyes asked a question.

"They are uneasy," Bill told her. "Off balance. At least, I hope they are. Because they're the people we have to work on to begin with. The police have taken over—something impersonal has taken over. Not me—not Mullins or Stein—the police. You, Pam—you, unexplained—might have broken it. So I let them think you were police, too."

"Oh," Pam said. "Then what do I do?"

"Sit tight," Bill told her. "Try not to say anything and if you do—" He considered that, rejected it as hopeless. "Try not to say anything," he repeated. "Listen. And—use that mind of yours all you want to, Pam." He smiled at her, and this time it was Bill Weigand to Pam North. "Very nice little mind," he assured her.

His smile went away. He opened the door of the private office, went to the doorway of the waiting room and looked at the men and women in it. The blonde who was, apparently, Mrs. Gordon was sitting up. There was a dazed look on her face. Weigand's eyes went over her. They stopped on Grace Spencer. He made a motion with his head when he saw she was looking at him.

"Will you come this way, please?" he said.

He watched her as she crossed the room toward him. She was tall for a woman and thin, but it was an attractive, straight thinness. She moved well on long, slim legs; her shoulders were broad and square and they were held well back. Her face was faintly brown, as if tan from an earlier, hotter sun still lingered on it. When she reached him, he stood aside to let her pass. In the inner office, she did not look at the body, still sprawled across the desk. She looked beyond the body, out of the window behind the desk. But it was not as if she saw anything through the window.

It was shock, Bill Weigand thought. Rather severe shock. Natural enough, but after all she was a nurse. He looked quickly at Pam. Her eyes were thoughtful as she looked at Grace Spencer.

"I'm sorry about—" Bill said, and his head barely indicated the body. "It sometimes takes a little time for the ambulance—"

Grace Spencer spoke then. Her voice was light, clear, and without expression.

"I understand," she said. "I quite understand."

Then, when Bill Weigand indicated a chair, she moved toward it, still moving well but moving with a kind of abstraction. It was almost as if she did not realize she was moving. She sat in the chair with her body straight and her knees together and her hands in her lap. Bill's eyes, not seeming to, watched her hands. Sometimes it is hard to keep hands from moving. Her hands were not moving. But you could guess that only determination kept them quiet. She did not look at Mullins or at Stein; she did not look at Pamela North. She looked at Weigand, and waited. When he spoke, his voice was quiet, without emphasis.

"I'm told you found Dr. Gordon," he said.

"His body," she said. "Yes. I found it."

He waited.

"It was about three o'clock," she said. "A few minutes before three. The patients had begun to arrive. I—"

She told him of finding the body, of dismissing the patients, of summoning the police. Then she paused and looked at the man from Headquarters and waited. There was an expectant stillness about her. But her concentration had faltered a little as she talked. Her hands were twisting together.

"You acted very properly," Bill told her. "Now we want to find out everything we can about what happened here today. You understand that, Miss Spencer? You realize why?"

"Dr. Gordon was murdered," she said. "I do understand." She let her voice hang an instant at the end of the sentence. Bill Weigand interrupted.

"I'm Lieutenant Weigand," he said. "From Headquarters. These other men are Detective Sergeant Mullins and Detective Sergeant Stein. This is Mrs. North. She works with us." He paused. His voice did not alter; it was detached, official. "Frequently," he said. Pam looked at him and looked away again.

"Thank you," Grace Spencer said. "You have my name. I am—I was—Dr. Gordon's nurse. I have been with him for three years. I am thirty-two years old and unmarried. I live—" She gave him an address in the Murray Hill district.

Weigand nodded at Mullins, but Mullins had his notebook out. He nodded back.

Grace Spencer began to tell what she knew of the events of Dr. Gordon's day. But almost as soon as she began, they were interrupted. Two men in white came to the door of the office, looked in and then waited. Weigand said, "Just a moment, Miss Spencer," and conferred with them. He turned back, hesitating a moment. Then he turned to Grace Spencer.

"They're going to remove the body," he said. "It—it wouldn't be pleasant to watch. I think we might move somewhere else, Miss Spencer. Would you suggest—?"

She suggested one of the examining rooms, but Bill shook his head. They were very small rooms. The waiting room would be better, except for the others there. He preferred— Then he thought of the solution, and smiled faintly. It would be appropriate. He spoke to Sergeant Stein and Stein went into the waiting room. There was the sound of movement there, and in the examining-room corridor. Stein came back, and nodded. The others were now in the examining rooms.

"The younger man and the girl wanted to be together," he said. "I let them. All right?"

Weigand nodded. After all, if they wanted to plan their evidence, they had already had opportunity. And it was sometimes helpful if witnesses tried to plan their evidence. It so often involved them in contradictions. The human mind was seldom as logical as it tried to make itself.

The questioning of Grace Spencer moved to the waiting room. She sat at Deborah Brooks's desk and Pam sat on one of the sofas near by. Mullins put his notebook on a corner of the desk. Grace Spencer went on with her story. She told of checking on the compensation cases, of relieving Miss Brooks—Deborah Brooks, the receptionist—while the doctor proceeded with his examinations.

"There was nothing unusual about the doctor when he returned from the hospital?" Weigand asked her. "He was much as always when you told him the patients were ready?"

"Yes," she said.

He told her to go on. She told of Deborah Brooks's return, of her own resumption of her desk in the corridor.

"I sat at my desk so that I would be available if the doctor needed me," she said, and Mullins took it down.

• 3 •

MONDAY, 4:55 P.M. TO 6:05 P.M.

They gave Grace Spencer time, not hurrying her, not speaking. It would be better for her now that the tension had broken into tears. And it might be better for them. Waiting, Bill Weigand looked across at Pam North, and she tried to tell him something with her eyes, with her lips soundlessly forming the words. He could only guess at what she was trying to tell him, but he took a chance on the guess. He nodded. Then he looked back at the slender nurse and watched her shoulders shake under the white uniform. Then, suddenly, she lifted her head and looked at him. Her eyes were wet and her face contorted. He could see the effort which drew her face back into its accustomed lines.

"I'm sorry," he said. "This is always difficult. I realize that."

She tried to smile. She made a bad job of it.

"Have you any ideas about it, Miss Spencer?" he said. "About who might have wanted the doctor dead?"

She shook her head. He watched her. He did not think she hesitated before she shook her head, but it was a possibility.

"The back door," he said. "What you call the 'back door.' Is it locked?"

She nodded. Then she spoke, trying to keep her voice steady.

"It has—whatever you call them," she said. "A snap lock. It is locked from outside after you close it. Unless you set it before you go out."

Weigand nodded.

"And so far as you know," he said next, "no one had tripped the lock—set the catch so the door could be opened from outside without a key—at any time today?"

She shook her head. Then she looked doubtful.

"Anyone could have," she said. "The doctor when he went out to lunch. Anyone. There's no way of telling unless you look. The key works just the same."

"Yes," Weigand said. "I realize that, Miss Spencer." He paused a moment. "Do you know of anything around the office that is like a knob—a smooth knob? Or a small, heavy ball? Of metal, perhaps?"

She looked puzzled. Then, as she understood, she said, "oh," in a voice which was only a breath. He watched her eyes. He thought they reflected a thought; rejected it—or kept it hidden.

"No," she said, "I don't know of anything like that. Unless—no, I don't know of anything."

"Unless what?" he said.

"Nothing," she said. "How large would it be?"

Bill Weigand told her it would fit in a hand. Comfortably. So that the fingers could curl most of the way around it. That, he said, was what he thought.

"No," she said. "I don't know anything like that."

He thanked her again and asked her to stay. In one of the examining rooms, he suggested.

"Will the lab be all right?" she said. "There—there are some things to do. I may as well do them."

The lab would be all right, he told her. In an hour or so, he hoped, she could go home.

They watched her cross the reception room and go through the door at its end. Then Pam looked at Bill and waited, and after a moment—during which he looked at the closed door—he looked at her. He asked her what it was.

"She was in love with him," Pam said. "With the doctor. Wasn't she?"

Bill Weigand nodded slowly. He said he thought she was.

"And now," he said, "do we quote Oscar Wilde, in unison?"

"About each man, only it would be a woman, and the thing he loves?" Pam said. "And all that? I wouldn't, even if I thought so. Because I don't think it's particularly true. I think it's just something somebody says in a poem. Don't you?"

As a general rule, Bill said, he thought it was something somebody said in a poem. In this instance—

"Oh, in this instance," Pam said, as if it were another thing entirely, "I don't know, Bill. I don't even think I know. But she does know about a knob, I think. Or a ball you could hold in your hand, with your fingers curled—" She stopped. She didn't like the idea. It was an ugly picture. "Could it have been that, Bill? Would that have done it?"

Bill Weigand raised his shoulders and let them drop. They wanted something heavy and spherical. Or half a sphere. They wanted something smooth. A ball on the end of a stick, by preference. Otherwise a ball held in the hand. In which case, it would need to be fairly heavy, or the hand which held it—the hand and the arm—uncommonly strong.

"Or the skull thin," Pam said.

Bill Weigand agreed. It could be that way, of course. But thin skulls left murder to chance; they were something murder could not count on. There was no way, he thought, to tell the relative thickness of a skull by looking at a head. Only if it had been broken before, and mended, and so been examined by men competent to tell— He broke off and nodded, more or less to himself. And while a physician finding a skull thinner and more brittle than the ordinary, might not tell an ordinary patient—or would he?—he would be rather more likely to tell another doctor. Who, in turn, might mention it, as an interesting medical idiosyncrasy, to someone else. Weigand shrugged again. This was speculation with no basis. His head gestured to Stein, who came from the doorway to the examining corridor.

"The other girl," Weigand told him. "The kid."

Stein brought her out. It took him longer than they had expected, and, standing behind her, Stein raised his eyebrows to Weigand. It meant he had something to tell, but that it would keep.

The girl was about five feet four, Weigand guessed. She would weigh a hundred and ten, or a little more. She was very young; her hair hung to her shoulders in soft waves. When she walked, she neither swayed nor moved in that forced staccato which sometimes denied, by suppressing, undulation. Her forehead and the bridge of her nose—a straight nose, not too small, giving character to her face—were slightly sunburned. And she had been crying.

She was Deborah Brooks, twenty years old; she lived with another girl in an apartment on Madison Avenue. A one-room apartment, Bill Weigand guessed. When he asked her where she lived, she began to cry a little. Sobs did not tear at her, as they had at Grace Spencer; her eyes filled and overflowed and filled again, quietly.

"Really," she said, "I live—I lived—with Andy. In North Salem. Since father died. That's almost three years. And it was more home than anything else."

"Dr. Gordon?" Bill said. He spoke gently. His tone enquired.

It took a while, but she explained. Her father had been a very old friend of Dr. Andrew Gordon; years ago, her father and mother had been friends of the Gordons. Years ago. Bill Weigand looked puzzled and the girl saw it. Her mind worked under the smoothly flowing hair, behind the long-lashed brown eyes. "Not Eve," she said. "His first wife—Sally. Years ago." And years ago her mother had died. Her father had died a little over three years ago and the Andrew Gordons—the present Andrew Gordons—had, in a fashion, adopted her. The families had always been close; they lived neighbors at North Salem—"next door," Deborah said. She had been left alone at seventeen; entirely alone. And Andy had asked her to come and live with them. She had. And then, when she had begun to talk about doing something, Andrew Gordon had said that, if she liked, she could be his receptionist. Until—

She stopped.

"Until what?" Bill said.

"Oh," she said, "until I decided I wanted to do something else. There wasn't anything decided on."

But that was not, Bill Weigand thought, what she had intended to say. He waited a second.

"Of course," she said, "I'm engaged to Dan. But there isn't anything definite. Not really."

It occurred to Bill that, for some reason, she had not meant to tell him that—and had then decided that she had better tell him. He repeated the name. "Dan?"

"Dan Gordon," she said. "The boy—I mean the man—who was by my desk when you came in."

"The doctor's son?" Weigand asked.

Her eyes were dry, now, but they were still shining. Perhaps they did when she thought of Dan Gordon, Weigand thought. She nodded an answer to his question. Then, suddenly, her eyes clouded.

"He isn't really—" she began, and stopped. Bill waited. He thought she was worried about something.

"Yes?" he said, when she did not go on.

"I was going to say, he isn't really as—as bad-tempered as he sounds," she said. "It's because—" Then she stopped again. After a moment, Bill said, rather idly, that he didn't know how Dan Gordon sounded. He looked at Stein, and Stein nodded quickly. So that was it.

"I assume," Bill said, "that he said something in front of Sergeant Stein when he asked you to come here. Right? And that you're—laying a backfire?"

She looked puzzled for a moment. Backfire meant something a motor did, evidently. She decided not to bother with it. She looked up at him, her eyes wide open.

"People misunderstand Dan," she said. "That's all. The sergeant may have—"

Weigand cut through it, this time. He spoke to Sergeant Stein. "What did he say, Sergeant?" Weigand wanted to know. His voice was crisp.

"He said: 'Damn it all, Debbie, I told you I wouldn't stand for it!'" Stein told Weigand. "He was angry. At least, he sounded angry."

Weigand turned to the girl. He did not need to put his question into words.

"It wasn't anything," she said. "He's—he's worried and unhappy. He didn't know the sergeant was there. It didn't mean anything." Weigand waited. "It was just about—about my getting another job," she said. "He said he wouldn't stand for it. He wasn't angry; just emphatic. Dad left me some money and so that's all right, and Dan doesn't want me to work. That's all."

She spoke more quickly than she had before. She spoke as if there were a hurry to get it said. And she was unconvincing. There could be no doubt that she was unconvincing.

But Bill Weigand did not meet the issue. He merely nodded, as if it were now all quite clear, and took her through her day. The times she gave coincided with those given by Grace Spencer. She had had a quick lunch at a drugstore counter between about twelve twenty and ten minutes of one.

"Alone?" Weigand said.

She shook her head, hesitated a moment, said Dan was with her. He had met her in the building lobby and had gone to lunch with her. He had not returned to the office. She had left him in the lobby two or three minutes before she got back to the office. Before she left, she had seen Dr. Gordon only momentarily. She had gone to the bathroom to "freshen up" before she went to lunch, but she had not gone into the examining-room area at any time that day—except that she had come through it when she arrived in the morning. When she returned from lunch, she had come in through the waiting-room door, as she usually did when the doctor was working.

Weigand shifted his questions. When had Mrs. Gordon—the young, blonde Mrs. Gordon—come to the office?

"Eve," Deborah Brooks said. "Evelyn. She used to be Evelyn Carr." She said this as if it might mean something, hesitating after it. It meant nothing. "She came a few minutes after Grace telephoned," Deborah said. "For the police. And—we had to tell her. And she made a little sound and fainted. She came to once, in about ten minutes, and then the other policemen came and she fainted again."

It had hit her very hard, Weigand suggested, with no comment in his voice.

"I guess so," the girl said. She strengthened it. "Of course," she said.

"And the other man," Weigand said. "The older man. Who is he?"

He was Nickerson Smith. He was Dan Gordon's uncle. Grace Spencer had telephoned for him after she had called the police.

"Actually," Deborah Brooks said, "I hardly know him. He was never at North Salem. I don't think he was. The others didn't see much of him."

"You hadn't met him before?" Weigand suggested. She hesitated; she didn't think she had. She might have, but if so he had made no particular impression. He had arrived a few moments before the first of the police; he had said—"oh, what people usually say—how shocking it was." Since Evelyn Gordon was unconscious, he had said these things generally, to all of them; perhaps most to Dan.

Bill Weigand got this much, hesitated a moment, told the girl there was nothing more for the moment.

"As a matter of fact," he said, "you can go, if you like."

She shook her head. She said that, if it would be all right, she'd like to wait for Dan. He nodded to that and watched her get up from the desk and go toward the doorway leading to the examining-room corridor. Then his head summoned Stein. Stein was to get this uncle, this Nickerson Smith. Stein went for Smith.

"And she's in love with the son," Pam North said. "And—is afraid about him."

"Or for him," Bill said. "You saw that. It wasn't her getting a job he was angry about. It was something else."

"Yes," Pam said. "Oh, yes."

Then the door at the far end of the long room opened and Grace Spencer came back. She came back quickly. Weigand turned to her. She was no longer shaken; her face was unsmiling and the eyes were dark and, somehow, dulled. But she was in control again. She was only halfway down the room when she spoke, quickly.

"Lieutenant," she said. "Where were his glasses?"

Bill raised eyebrows at her, as she came on toward them.

"The doctor," she said. "He always wore glasses. But they weren't on—on the body. Had they fallen off and been broken?"

Weigand remembered the scene; he built it back into his mind. It did not include glasses, or any obvious fragments of glasses. He made a picture in his mind of the lifted head, when the assistant medical examiner had raised it. There had been no glasses. He turned to Mullins, but Mullins was already on his way. It took him only a minute. He came back shaking his head.

"Nope," Mullins said. "No glasses. On the floor—on the desk. No pieces of glasses."

"In the desk?" Weigand suggested. Grace Spencer shook her head at that. And Mullins said, "Huh-uh, Loot." Grace said, "He wouldn't have taken them off; he never did."

So now they wanted a murderer and a pair of glasses. Nickerson Smith came through the door, with Sergeant Stein behind him. Weigand nodded abstractedly, and indicated the chair at the desk. Grace Spencer stood looking at Nickerson Smith, who looked sad. Smith said, slowly, heavily, "Well, Nurse?"—but it was neither question nor statement. The words merely filled a silence.

"In just a moment, Mr. Smith," Bill said. Then he turned to Grace Spencer. He thanked her.

"There was something else," she said. "Something I forgot. It was nothing, I suppose. I forgot to tell you one of the patients came out after the doctor did, and while I was getting my coat."

"Yes?" Weigand said.

"Out of the sixth room," the nurse said. "He came out into the corridor by my desk, hesitated a moment, and then went out the back door."

Bill thought a moment.

"Was that the way the others went?" he asked. "After the doctor had finished with them."

"Yes," Grace said. "It wasn't important, I knew. But it was in that period you wanted me to be exact about and it was something I forgot."

Weigand said he understood. He said he was glad she had remembered it, even if it wasn't important. He said they wanted to get everything, no matter how small. His tone let her go. She had half turned, when Pam North spoke.

"When you saw Dr. Gordon leaving," Pam said. "Coming out of the sixth room and getting his hat to go to lunch. Was he just as he always was?"

Grace Spencer looked at her.

"I mean," Pam said, "did he seem nervous? Or frightened? Or anything—as a man would who was going to be murdered?"

Grace looked at her again. She looked at Bill.

"Well," Bill said, "did he? Was there anything out of the ordinary? Even any very little thing?"

"Why—no," Grace said. "I don't remember anything. I see what you mean." She looked at Pam. "I guess I do," she said.

"Strained," Pam said. "As if something were wrong. Did his face show anything? Or did he—oh, move differently. As if he were nervous or—or worried?" She looked at Grace. "*I* don't know," she said. "I don't know whether there was anything. Or what it would be. But was he different? As if—oh, say, he'd got a telephone call in his office just before he started the examinations. A call that worried him. Say—oh, say somebody called him up and said 'I just saw your wife having lunch with that other man.' I don't mean she was, of course. I mean, just something like that. Or 'They've found out. What are you going to do now?' Or anything."

She stopped and waited. Grace looked at her. There was a faint line between her eyes.

"By the way," Bill said, "could he have got such a call? Without its going through Miss Brooks's desk?"

"Oh, yes," Grace said. She spoke abstractedly, as if she were answering the easier question first. "He had a direct wire, of course. With an unlisted number. He could have got a call."

"Without your hearing it?" Bill asked.

She said yes, again, still in the abstracted tone. She said the whole office had been built to suppress sound. Particularly if the private telephone rang once, and was quickly answered, she would not have heard it. Or it would not have registered.

"About the other," she said. "I do see what you mean." This was to Pam North. "I—I think he looked just about as always. Unless—" She broke off and looked over Pam's head at nothing. Pam waited. After a moment she spoke.

"There was something?" she said.

There was a little pause. Then, very slowly—and not quite certainly—Grace shook her head.

"I thought—" she began, and then she stopped. "But I really can't remember anything. It's just—" She stopped again. Pam started to speak, but stopped when Bill shook his head at her, very gently. Then she nodded at him.

He means if we go on we'll—set up something, Pam thought. Build up something. Whether it's there or not. Because she's upset and she might begin to think something up without knowing it. Like thinking you've forgotten to lock a door when you haven't or like Jerry's turning off the oil stove in the country that time, and then thinking he hadn't, and driving back miles. And Bill's right, probably. Only—

"There may be nothing," Bill said. "There's no reason—no necessary reason—why there should be anything, Miss Spencer. Don't try to force it. But it might help if you—if you let your mind make a picture of Dr. Gordon as you saw him that last time. It might help."

"I know," Grace Spencer said. She still spoke slowly. "I—I don't think of anything now, Lieutenant. But—I do feel a little—uneasy." She smiled faintly. "As if there might be something. But perhaps you've created that feeling."

Bill nodded. He said they didn't want to. Only if there was something, they wanted that. If he were hurried, for example— He broke off, because there was something in Grace Spencer's eyes. She spoke quickly enough when his words stopped.

"Oh," she said. "I think he was hurried. He—he moved as if he were in a hurry. I do remember that. As if he were late to an appointment." Then she stopped and her eyes grew wide. Because, it was clear, the thought that he had had an appointment came into her mind. An appointment with death.

Bill Weigand brought her back.

"Does that—that memory he was hurrying—satisfy you?" he said. "I mean, is that what made you feel, as you called it, 'uneasy'?"

She hesitated a moment. She did not look, Pam thought, entirely satisfied.

"It must have been," she said.

Weigand thanked her again. He hesitated; said she could go home now, if she cared to. She nodded acceptance of the permission and walked, straight, held-in, back toward the lab. Weigand turned to Nickerson Smith.

It took only a few minutes to get the essentials. He was Dan Gordon's uncle; he was the brother of Dr. Gordon's first wife. He had an office three floors up in the same building; he was an agent for a physicians' supply company. He had been in his office when Grace Spencer had called him, a few minutes after three, and he had come down at once, on the chance there might be something he could do.

"Not that there was," he said. "But I was the nearest relative." He smiled faintly. "I mean I was the closest," he qualified. "In a physical sense."

He waited. It occurred to Weigand that he was, for practical purposes, disposed of. The next question was routine; Weigand prefaced it with an explanation that it was routine. It was something they asked everyone.

"From the medical evidence," he said, "your brother-in-law appears to have been killed between around twelve thirty—a few minutes earlier or later—and two o'clock. But since he was seen leaving the office at about ten minutes after one, we can narrow that a little. Naturally, we want to know where all the people who were—well, associated with him—were during that period. Make it from about one ten to two thirty, to be on the safe side."

Nickerson Smith nodded as Weigand spoke. He replied as soon as Weigand had finished. He was matter-of-fact about it.

"I was in my office from one o'clock until Nurse—" He paused for the name. Weigand gave it to him. "Nurse Spencer called me," he said. "For about fifteen minutes of that time—from one until say one fifteen, I was alone. Then my secretary came in. I don't know whether she noticed what time it was, of course. And I didn't. I'm guessing. But I'd say she came in about ten or fifteen minutes after one. She can assure you I was there the rest of the time."

He considered his own statement.

"That seems to leave some five minutes unaccounted for," he said. "Assuming the doctor went out at one ten and my girl came in at one fifteen. But—"

Weigand nodded. The rest of the sentence could be taken as implied. If the doctor left at one ten; if Nickerson Smith was in his office three floors or so above at one fifteen, Nickerson Smith was out. Because he would have had to come down three floors, meet the doctor, persuade—or force—him to return to the office, walk back with him to the private office, kill him—and make sure he was dead—and retrace his steps. All of which, Weigand agreed with himself, couldn't be done in five minutes. Fifteen would be more like it, and quick work at that. If his secretary agreed, Nickerson Smith was out of it.

Weigand thanked him and thought that would be all. Smith got up, started across the reception room, hesitated and came back. When he came to speak, he hesitated again and then asked whether he could ask a question. Weigand nodded.

"About the boy," he said. "About Dan. I hope you don't—I hope he isn't—"

"Under suspicion?" Bill said. "Of killing his own father? Why should he be, Mr. Smith?"

"I'm glad," Smith said. "He shouldn't be, of course." He looked at Bill Weigand then as if he had just heard something Weigand had said. "His own father?" Smith said. "But he wasn't, of course. I supposed you knew."

"No," Weigand said. "Obviously I didn't."

"Stepfather," Smith said. "My sister had been married before and he was her son. Not Andrew's. He took Andrew's name when he was old enough to decide." He nodded, keeping it straight. "My sister was Andrew's first wife, you know."

Weigand said he knew that.

"And," Smith said, "there's no doubt the boy's manner is—unfortunate. He can appear to be very violent. Not that he is, you understand. His own worst enemy, really. But meeting him for the first time—"

His tone seemed rather anxious. "I can see how you might get an unfortunate impression, Lieutenant."

"Had he quarreled with his stepfather?" Weigand said. "Is that what you're getting at?"

"Oh, no," Smith said. "Not actually. Dan was devoted to his father—really. It's just that—"

He stopped, and smiled. He spoke again in a tone of great frankness.

"Put my foot in it, haven't I?" he said. "Fond of the boy, you know. Hope I haven't given you ideas."

Weigand shook his head. He assured Smith, inaccurately, that he had been given no ideas. He watched Smith go.

"Ingenious," Pam said. "Or is he?"

Bill told her he could stand to know that one himself. He watched Smith close the office door behind him. Then Bill's head summoned Stein. Stein was to get him Dan Gordon.

"He's with the girl," Weigand said. It occurred to him that it would have been better, after all, to keep people separated.

Stein went. He returned. He looked a little red. And he brought Deborah Brooks, not Dan Gordon.

"He wasn't with the girl," Stein said. "She was by herself. She says he's—gone."

There was action then, quick and, on Weigand's part, angry. As she watched it begin, Deborah Brooks began to cry again.

The action got nowhere. Dan Gordon was not in the office. And the patrolman who should have been outside the back door was in the men's toilet. It was one of those things. Dan Gordon had, not knowing whether there was a guard outside the door, taken a chance. The patrolman had taken a chance. Dan's luck was in; the patrolman's was out. He would go to some dismal beat on Staten Island, or in distant Queens. And where Dan Gordon had gone was anybody's guess. And why he had gone—

Bill Weigand turned on the girl, then. He was not gentle or suave, any longer. His questions were crisp; his attitude was obvious. And

Debbie Brooks put her head down on her desk and her answers were muffled in her arms, and by her sobs. He had just gone. She had tried to persuade him not to. She had told him it was dangerous, that it wouldn't work. But he had gone, anyway.

"How long ago?" Weigand said.

Fifteen minutes. Twenty.

"And you didn't think of letting us know?" Weigand asked her, his voice unrelenting.

The girl looked up then. She did not try to stop the flow of tears. She let tears run down her cheeks. She merely looked at Bill Weigand, and she did not need to answer him. Nor did he need an answer.

"Of course you thought of it," he said. "And you decided it would be better to cover up for him." He gave her a chance to answer, and she did not take it. "You were a fool," he said, flatly. "He couldn't have done a worse thing. You couldn't have done a worse thing than help him."

She put her head down on her arms again. Weigand looked at her a moment and spoke to Stein.

"Have Barney take her home," he said. "If he's finished the sketch?" Stein nodded. "Right," Weigand said. "See she gets home." He turned to the girl. "And stay there," he directed. "If Gordon shows up, get in touch with us. Do you understand?"

Her head moved on her arms. She understood.

And she was as unlikely to get in touch with anybody if her Dan came back, as she was to shave off that softly waving brown hair, Bill told himself. Less likely. So that that would have to be taken care of. Humanity was frequently exasperating; particularly humanity in love.

· 4 ·

MONDAY, 6:05 P.M. TO 8:35 P.M.

Bill Weigand used the telephone on Deborah Brooks's desk. She stood and listened to him, and now her eyes were dry and wide. Curtly, Weigand directed that an alarm be sent out for Dan Gordon, twenty-four years old, six feet or a little over, wearing a gray tweed suit with a discharge button in the left lapel, weighing about 160, thin face, brown hair and eyes. It was amazing, Pam North thought, listening to him, how much he had seen of Dan Gordon at what must have been little more than a glance.

"Oh, yes," Weigand added. "Face slightly asymmetrical. Noticeable particularly when he smiles. Smile goes up one side of his face a little. Right side I think—wait a minute."

He turned and looked at Deborah Brooks. His look demanded. Her voice was faint and frightened. But she said, "Yes."

"Right side," Weigand confirmed. He listened then. "Probably not," he agreed. "He won't have anything to smile about. However—" He listened again. "Suspicion of homicide," he said. He said it curtly. Deborah Brooks made a sound which was half a cry, half a spoken protest. "Right," Weigand said, into the telephone, and put the telephone back in its cradle. He looked at Debbie.

"What did you expect?" he said. He seemed really to wonder what she had expected. "He's near the scene of a murder—at any rate, by your own story, he was in the building lobby downstairs at about a quarter to one. He could have waited until his—stepfather, is it?—came down. And he runs away while we're getting ready to question him."

The girl was shaking her head and her eyes were frightened. She tried to speak, or seemed to try to speak, but again she made only a small sound which was not a word, but a little cry. She was very small, standing there, and very lonely, and Pam started to move toward her. But Bill shook his head at Pam and there was no mistaking what he meant. Pam stopped in her motion, and looked a little puzzled. It was not like Bill to be this way, she thought.

"And," Weigand said, still in the dispassionate voice of a policeman, still without inflection, "and we'll pick him up, Miss Brooks. Don't think we won't. Don't think for a moment we won't." He stopped and looked at her. "Every policeman he meets will be after him, Miss Brooks," he said. "Men he doesn't know to be policemen will be after him. Wherever he goes—wherever he runs."

"He didn't—" the girl began. Her voice choked. The effort she was making was clear; there was a kind of gallantry in the effort. "He didn't run," she said.

Weigand caught her up.

"He ran," Weigand told her. "What would you call it?"

It seemed easier for her to speak, now. She was pulling herself together under pressure.

"You don't understand," she said. "It's the way he is. He—he can't just stay in one place and wait. It's—it's as if something was pushing him. Making him go. He can't just stay and wait." She looked at Bill Weigand anxiously, watching his face. "That's all it is," she said. "He just can't." She looked at Weigand again. "Please see," she said.

Weigand shook his head. He laughed shortly.

"He ran," he told her. "He ran from a murder investigation. People have one reason for doing that—one obvious reason." He did not give her time to answer. "Barney!" he said, and he raised his voice. "Where the hell are you?"

Barney Jones came to the door. Weigand barely looked at him.

"I want this young woman taken—" he began. Then he did look at Detective Barney Jones. "Well?" Weigand said.

"This," Jones told him. "I was roughing out the plan at the desk in there and wanted a ruler. I opened the top drawer and—this. It looks to me, Loot, like—"

Weigand interrupted him by holding out a hand. Carefully, Jones transferred the object he was holding, gingerly in a protective handkerchief, to the lieutenant's waiting fingers. Bill looked at it. It was heavier than it looked, more substantial. It was a very solid chunk of glass, shaped into half a sphere. Obviously, it was a paperweight. It fitted neatly into the hand, curved side up. Bill Weigand balanced it in his hand, and then Pam, who was now very close, pointed.

"It's dirty," she said. "I mean—it's dulled, isn't it? Greasy?"

Bill Weigand looked at the curved surface. It was dulled. He raised it toward his nose and sniffed a moment and lowered it. He nodded slowly.

"Perfume," he said. "Sweetish."

Mullins spoke then. His voice was hurried.

"Listen, Loot," Mullins said, "the M.E. said there was something on the guy's hair. The doctor's."

"Yes, Mullins," Weigand said. "Yes—he said that. He smelled it on his fingers." He hesitated a moment. "The body's gone?" he said. Mullins looked unhappy. He said the body was gone—out the back door.

"Look," Pam said, "let me." She leaned close to the half-sphere in Weigand's hand. She sniffed. She stood up and closed her eyes and remembered. "It is," she said. "It's the same. And you know I—"

She stopped because Weigand's smile finished the sentence. She resumed. "Well, I *do*," she said. "Better than most people, anyway." She challenged contradiction.

"Right, Pam," Bill said. "I know you do."

"Then this," Pam said, and indicated the glass weight, "this is what he—somebody—used?"

Weigand nodded slowly. But he did not seem entirely satisfied. He said he supposed it was.

"Only," he said, "why put it back in the drawer? Which drawer, Barney?" Barney told him the left-hand upper drawer. "Why?" Weigand said. "To hide it? But it wasn't really hidden. Why?"

Nobody had an answer for a moment, and then Pam had.

"Maybe he was just neat," she said. "A neat murderer." Nobody replied to that. "Look," Pam said, "while you think about it, Bill, I want to call Jerry. All right?"

"In a minute," Bill told her. He turned back to Barney Jones and held out the weight. "Wrap it up and take it along," he said. "Technical lab. See if it is hair oil. And so forth. And take this young woman home on your way. See she gets home." He looked at Debbie Brooks. Her eyes were wet again. "See that you stay there, Miss Brooks," Bill told her, in a voice without sympathy.

Barney Jones wrapped part of the *Daily News* around the glass paperweight, loosely. He got his hat from one of the chairs. He said, "All right, Miss Brooks," and they went to the door together. Jones moved beside and a little behind her; he opened the door for her. His manner was protective. The door closed.

"Bill!" Pam North said. Her voice was indignant. "You deliberately—you went out of your way to be tough. You wanted to scare her!"

"Obviously," Bill said. "Of course, my dear."

"But—" Pam began.

"Because I want her to run," Bill explained. "I want her to get scared and run. To her boy—to young Gordon. To warn him."

Pam looked at him and said, "Oh!"

"And you'll follow her," she said. "You think she knows where he is?"

"We'll follow her," Bill agreed. "I think there's a good chance she can at least guess where he is. Better than we can."

"Oh," Pam said again. She considered it. She shook her head.

"I suppose it may work," she said, "but I don't think it's very fair. Can I call Jerry, now?"

She dialed. She said, "Hello, darling." She listened. She said, "I know." She listened again. She said she was sorry. She hesitated.

"Well," she said, "actually it's a murder. I just sort of—well, I was just walking past and—" She stopped, and she had the expression of somebody who has been interrupted. Bill listened, amused, to the sound of Jerry's voice coming from the telephone. The words were not distinguishable; the tone was unmistakable.

"I didn't," Pam said. "It isn't fair to say I look for them. But I found I could get a taxi and so of course—"

She was interrupted again.

"No," she said, "not exactly. It would be silly to tell a taxicab man to drive straight to the nearest murder. At least, I think it would."

The interruption was shorter this time.

"Listen, dear," Pam said, and her voice was firm. "It's too long for the telephone. Bill will want to use it. It's just as I said—I was passing by and there it was. So of course—" She was not interrupted. She let it die away. "And, Jerry," she said, "I got you a new tie." She listened. "Of course it isn't," she said, with some indignation. "There isn't any blood on *anything*. Not even the body. It's—it's a very neat murder."

She listened again. Then she told him where she was. Then she listened. Then she said, "But, Jerry—" and then she hung up.

"He's coming," she told Bill Weigand. "Jerry's coming up to get me." She smiled faintly, gently. "He says to take me home," she added. There was the faintest possible emphasis on the word "says."

The telephone rang then. Bill picked it up. He said yes, this was Weigand. He listened.

"Right," he said. "We're still here. Will be for some time yet." He listened again. "Now's as good a time as any," he said. "Come along, Mr. Smith."

He cradled the telephone and looked at his watch.

"Mr. Smith has decided there's something we ought to know," he said. "He's been thinking things over. He's coming down to tell us."

"What?" Pam said.

Bill Weigand looked at Mullins, and Mullins looked back at him. They both seemed interested.

"What?" Pam repeated.

Bill Weigand shook his head. He said he didn't know. He said it was always interesting when people began to volunteer things.

"Helpful," Mullins said. "Helpful guys. Where would we be without 'em, Loot?"

"Right," Weigand said. "Where indeed, Mullins?"

"Maybe he does just want to help," Pam said.

Bill Weigand said there was no doubt of it. He wanted to help—somebody. The question was, who?

They waited, then. It was not a long wait. The door opened and Nickerson Smith came in. As he came in, Bill looked at his watch again.

"Quick work, Mr. Smith," he said. "Four minutes, on the nose."

"Really?" Mr. Smith said. He seemed pleased. "I was lucky with the elevator," he said.

He came across the room to them and, when Bill Weigand motioned, he sat down beside the desk. Bill sat in Debbie Brooks's chair. He said, "Well, Mr. Smith?"

It took Nickerson Smith a time to get started. He said that he felt himself to be in an unfortunate situation; he said he had hesitated. But what he had to tell would come out sooner or later, whatever he said. He thought it would be better all around to have all the facts available from the outset.

"Know where you are, that way," he explained to Bill Weigand.

He realized that what he said might be misunderstood, that his saying it might be misunderstood. "Look as if I'm trying to direct suspicion," he said. It wasn't that.

"Actually," he said, "Dan's the last man in the world to do anything like this. Even now. I know him, and any suspicion of him would be absurd."

Weigand was patient. He did not follow any of the alleys Smith opened for him. He agreed in general; he agreed in detail; he praised Smith's attitude, and mentioned how much better it would be if all people were as reasonable and straightforward. But he did all this in few words. Gently, he nudged Nickerson Smith from generality toward particulars. He got him there.

Dan's mother—"my sister, that is"—had been a wealthy woman.

"From our father, you know." She had left her estate to her son, Dan. Her estate amounted to about two million—"then," Smith added. The income was to be used for his education, and other needs; the principal to go to him when he was twenty-five. "In six months—no, nearer five, now." She had made her husband, Dr. Andrew Gordon, and her brother executors.

"Now," Nickerson Smith said, "I'm the sole executor, of course. That's the pinch."

Weigand nodded and waited.

"Because," Smith said, "it isn't anything like two million now. That's the catch. It's not more than half a million, if that. Gone with the wind."

Weigand made regretful sounds.

"What wind?" he said.

That, Smith told him, was really the rub. "It's embarrassing," he said. "I feel guilty as hell. The fact is—I left things to Andrew. Too much to him, I realize now." Smith diverted himself; explained. It would be easy to explain if Weigand had known Andrew Gordon, alive. He was—"forceful." He was a man who got his own way. And, of course, Dan was living with him as his son. It was natural that he should have the greater share in controlling the estate; it was simpler for him, for example, to pay school bills, and college bills; to fix Dan's allowance as a boy. "But," Nickerson Smith said, "I realize that these are merely excuses. I was negligent. I can't deny that. Easygoing. And Andrew was not the businessman he thought he was."

Under the terms of the will, Smith explained, the executors were allowed considerable latitude. Gordon had taken it—unwisely. He had invested the money—"with the best intentions, understand" and, to be brief, he had lost three quarters of it. At least three quarters.

"Actually," Smith said, and he sounded morose, "actually, I'm equally liable, of course. Subject to censure. Perhaps to legal censure. But there it is—spilt milk. Anyway, that's the setup."

"And—?" Weigand said.

Smith looked at him.

"That's all," he said. He looked relieved. "Maybe I've been worrying myself too much," he said. "Not about the money itself. I don't mean that. There I worried too little, obviously. But about any possible connection of all this and—what happened to Andrew."

"You thought there might be a connection?" Weigand said. He was polite, interested.

"No," Smith said. "Not really. I'm glad there isn't."

"You thought the son might have heard of this—this shrinkage?" Weigand said. "Possibly from Dr. Gordon himself? And that the boy wasn't—shall we say, as understanding as you are, Mr. Smith? That he might, indeed, have been very annoyed? Furious, even? Having a notoriously bad temper?"

Smith was shaking his head.

"The boy isn't really the way he seems," he said. He spoke earnestly. "I realize how he seems to those who first meet him. He's—so quick and—well, angry. About little things. But underneath he is really—oh, not like that. That's all surface." He paused. "I'm certain it is," he said.

Weigand said he saw. He said it slowly, somewhat doubtfully.

"Then you don't think, knowing young Gordon, that he might have had—well, say, a sudden attack of rage when he heard about what had happened to his money? And—well, acted accordingly?" Weigand spoke slowly still.

"No." Smith was emphatic. "That's what I want to make clear. I don't think that at all. I don't think it's possible. That's partly why I decided to tell you this myself. So I could explain how I, knowing him very well, feel about the boy."

Bill Weigand said he appreciated that. He said he appreciated having been told about the estate; that he appreciated the cooperative attitude Mr. Smith had shown. And he was interested in hearing the opinion of Dan Gordon held by a man who knew him well. Smith grew contented under praise; his relief that it was over, and that he had done wisely, was apparent. He went, promising further cooperation up to the limit of his ability.

Bill Weigand and Pam North looked after him. It was Pam who spoke.

"Was he afraid you'd suspect Dan," she said, "or—" She raised shaped eyebrows.

"Precisely," Bill said. "Or that I wouldn't. I wondered, too. I wondered very much."

"And, of course," Pam said, "there's this—the doctor is dead, isn't he?"

There was no doubt of that, Bill agreed.

"Dead men," Pam said reflectively, "have so little to say for themselves, don't they?"

Evelyn Carr Gordon was last, and at that time she seemed also to be least. She was entirely recovered from her faint when they sent for her; she was very calm, sufficiently polite, immeasurably withdrawn. The withdrawal might have half a dozen explanations; it was a waste of time to try to choose among them. It might represent only her manner. It might represent shock. Or it might indicate carefulness—a defensive carefulness.

She was Evelyn Carr Gordon, 32. She was blonde, her hair done high. She was attractive, in a not unexpected fashion—the fashion of straight nose, rounded chin, blue eyes framed in long lashes. She had been crying, they thought; her eyes had the look of crying. But she was not now; her voice was steady and she was composed. And she had little to tell.

She had come to town on the ten thirty-three, driving to Brewster for the train. She had got in a few minutes after noon, had done one or two errands and had gone to the Longchamps at Fifty-ninth Street where her husband had said he would meet her if he could. He had not come; after she had waited for perhaps ten minutes, she had got a table not far from the Madison Avenue entrance and had ordered a cocktail and then lunch, keeping her eyes on the door. He had not come. It was matter of fact in her statement, and Bill Weigand probed into that. Hadn't she been surprised? Or worried?

She looked, then, a little surprised.

"No," she said. "Oh, no, Lieutenant. It was only a tentative engagement."

"Still," Bill said.

She shook her head. She said that he did not understand. She said it often happened.

"He met me when he could," she said. "It was our understanding. He could never tell. An unexpected patient. An unexpected turn in some case at the hospital. I understand—and he knew I would understand. Today was like—oh, like many days. I said I was coming in. He said—or perhaps I said—we might meet at lunch. At about one. He didn't even need to say, 'if I can make it.' That was understood. I would wait a few minutes, then I would get a table, then if he didn't come I would go on with my lunch. If he didn't come, I'd know he couldn't come. It was merely—sensible."

Weigand nodded. Probably it was; any way of acting that people agreed upon could be sensible. This sounded sensible. Pam North's eyes narrowed for an instant and then opened again. Of course it was sensible. She often wished that she and Jerry would be sensible, like that. No, Pam thought, I don't really. But it is a sensible, quiet way to live.

Mrs. Gordon had finished lunch, she thought, at about a quarter of two. She had gone to a little shop down Madison to do the shopping which had brought her to town. She had got some play dresses for Eileen.

"Eileen being?" Bill said.

"My little girl," Mrs. Gordon said. "She's six." The shaped lips smiled a little. "Going on seven," she said.

The dresses were what had brought her to New York. But because Dr. Gordon had not joined her, she had eaten more quickly than she expected, and so had had more time. It was about two fifteen when she finished buying the dresses. She went to another shop and looked at hats.

It should be easy to follow her, if they decided to follow her, Bill thought. As, naturally, they would. Longchamps, a shop, another shop. Somebody would remember.

She had found a hat. She had worn it and had the hat she had been wearing mailed to North Salem. This—her slim fingers went up to her head. Then for a moment she looked puzzled.

"Where is it?" she said. "I wore it here. I—" She remembered, then. "I fainted, didn't I?" she said. "Somebody must have—" She looked around the room. "There," she said, and pointed. There was a hat on one of the chairs. It was impertinent and bright, even when abandoned on the chair. Pam North, distracted, walked to the chair and picked up the hat. She held it up and looked at it; she turned it upside down and looked into it. She nodded at it and then, as an afterthought, at Mrs. Gordon. She took the hat to Mrs. Gordon, who put it on the desk and looked at it again. Then she looked at Bill Weigand.

"And?" Weigand said.

"I came here," she said. "To—to show Andy my new hat. And then—" Her voice broke for the first time. She waited a moment, and swallowed. "To show my husband my new hat," she said, clearly. "Then they told me. Grace told me." Her voice was steady, now.

That, for the moment, was all of it. Weigand expressed sympathy. He told her she could go.

"Home?" she said. "Back to the country?"

"Yes," Bill told her.

"And the—" she said, and balked at the word.

They would be in touch with her, Bill said. In a day or two. "There are certain tests," he said, phrasing it gently. She grew a little white at that, but she nodded. She picked up the hat and went to a mirror over the false mantel to put it on. When she was satisfied, she looked at Bill again as if to say something, and then said only, "I'll go then, Lieutenant." She went down the room to the door. She moved well. Dr. Gordon must have been proud of her.

"And now?" Pam said, as the door closed. Before Bill could answer she spoke again. Her voice sounded worried. "Where's Jerry, do you suppose?" she said. She was trying to keep worry out of her voice. Bill smiled at her, and said Jerry would be all right. He'd be along.

"Now," he said, "a hundred things, more or less. Background on everybody. But they're already on that. A checkup on everybody's movements. By the way, did the hat come from the shop she said?"

"That's what the label says," Pam told him. "Naturally."

Bill agreed with that.

"Of course," Pam said, "labels can go in and out. On fur coats and things. But I don't think this one did, do you? Because the hat is new, certainly."

Bill shook his head. He said he didn't think this one did. He thought it belonged in the hat, and that the hat was new that day.

"We'll check, of course," he said. "Detectives must be suspicious, like it says in the book. Suspicious of shopping trips, suspicious of afternoons spent at desks, suspicious of young men on the loose in building lobbies at appropriate times—young men who run away."

"And of girls of twenty, in love with—flighty men?" Pam said.

By all means of girls of twenty, Bill told her. Particularly when in love.

"And," he said, "of six compensation patients. Of a nurse with opportunity—and in love with her doctor. At the moment—of anyone who could have met Dr. Gordon after he left here, persuaded him to return on some pretext, killed him while the nurse was out at lunch and the other girl was sitting at her desk answering the telephone, and gone away again through the back door."

"Where's Jerry?" Pam said. "I thought he was coming for me."

"I don't—" Bill began, and was interrupted. A patrolman—a very weathered patrolman—opened the reception-room door and looked in. He came part way in, looked behind him, and remained where he could look in both directions.

"Lieutenant," he said, "there's a guy here. Been here about ten minutes, this guy has. Says you know him."

The patrolman's voice scorned this ridiculous claim. Weigand raised eyebrows.

"Want I should send him over to the station?" the patrolman said. "Or you want to see him? Been here about ten minutes, but you was busy."

A voice came around the patrolman from the hall. It was indignant.

"Shut up, you!" the patrolman said, facing toward the hall.

"—your staff of half-wits," the voice said. "Tell this damned cop—"

"Jerry!" Pam said, and started toward the door. "Darling! Where have you been?"

The patrolman dissolved at Bill Weigand's gesture. Jerry North took his place. Jerry was running a hand through his hair.

"Listen, Pam," Jerry said. "For half an hour—"

"You're late," Pam told him. "We were worried about you."

"This cop—" Jerry began. Pam smiled at him and said, "Darling!" in a tone of sympathy. Then she considered and looked at him again.

"Of course," she said, "he didn't stop *me,* come to think of it."

There was no triumph in her tone. Or, at most, very little. Jerry grinned at her and came down the room and she went to him and told him that his hair was mussed. Jerry merely smiled at her. She took both his hands, then, and looked at him more carefully, as if to see that he was really, all of him, in front of her.

"Look," she said. "If we had a date for lunch you'd call me up if you couldn't, wouldn't you? Whatever I'd said?"

"What?" Jerry said. Then he looked at her eyes. "Of course, Pam," he told her. "Always."

"Because the other's so sensible," Pam said, with conviction.

Bill was on the telephone. He was telling people to do things, now. He hung up and looked at them.

"You," Pam said, "call Dorian and tell her there's a murder. Or—why don't we have dinner together? The four of us." Mullins came back through the door from the examining area. "And Sergeant Mullins, of course," Pam said.

"Hullo, Mr. North," Mullins said. He seemed to consider a moment. "Well," he said, "here we are again."

They sat at the bar in Longchamps at Fifty-ninth and Madison.

"Before anything else," Pam said to Jerry, who was next to her, "did you feed Martini?"

Jerry nodded, and sipped a martini.

"How was she?" Pam said. "I hated to leave her but—"

"You had to attend a murder," Jerry said. "I know. She was all right. She climbed up on my back and tore some more threads out of my coat."

"Good," Pam said. "Lively, then."

Jerry agreed she was lively. He drank again. He turned to Pam.

"Look," he said, "I suppose she's all right? Mentally?"

Pam was indignant. Of course she was all right mentally.

"Well," Jerry said, "she behaves very oddly about her tail. She doesn't know it *is* her tail. She doesn't have any control over it, as far as I can see. Or even recognize it. The tip thrashes around and she looks at it and moves her head when it moves, as if she were watching a tennis game. Do you think that's bright?"

Pam wanted to know why not. Jerry raised his shoulders and dropped them. He said he didn't know. He said it didn't seem very bright, somehow. After all, it was her own tail. She washed it, when she thought of washing.

"So why," he asked, "does she always look so surprised when she sees it?"

"Because she has blue eyes," Pam told him.

"What?" Jerry said.

"Cats with blue eyes look surprised," Pam explained. "It's because you're surprised that they have blue eyes, I expect."

Jerry shook his head slightly to clear it. He looked at his cocktail glass. He emptied it.

"Listen, Pam," he said. "That's your surprise. I mean the cat's surprise."

Pam looked at him, puzzled. Then her face cleared.

"Oh," she said, "well, we attribute to animals what we feel ourselves. So it's really our surprise." She paused. "Of course," she said, "Martini does seem to think her tail is just something that follows her around. But she's not very old yet. She's very bright, for her age. Do you know any other cat who retrieves alternately for two people, no matter who throws?"

"No," Jerry said. "All right, she's bright. She—"

The waiter captain came and told them he had a table for five. They went to the table. Now they could talk about the murder. Pam and Bill Weigand, but mostly Bill, told, in summary, what they knew to date. Jerry drank and listened. Dorian Weigand, her greenish eyes fixed on her husband, her cocktail glass turning round and round in her pointed fingers, listened almost without other movement. Now and then, looking at her, Bill forgot precisely what it was he was talking about. When he did, Dorian smiled faintly.

"Personally," Pam North said, when the returns were in, "I vote for Mr. Smith. He's the one I want it to be."

"Why?" Jerry said.

"Because I like the others better, of course," Pam said. "I vote against the son—Dan."

"Because the girl's in love with him," Jerry told her.

"Well," Dorian said, "she sounds like a nice girl."

Mullins looked at his old-fashioned, shook it, and tilted it for a drop he thought he saw. He looked a little disappointed. Then he looked over the glass at Weigand, who was shaking his head.

It didn't work that way, Weigand told them. It was too bad, but it didn't. Nice girls had, before now, fallen in love with murderers. And would again.

"And he ran," Weigand pointed out. "It isn't conclusive. But it needs explanation. Why did he run?"

Pam shook her head at that. She wished he hadn't.

"As for your favorite," Weigand said, "I'm afraid not, this time, Pam. If his secretary confirms his story." He paused. "As she will," he said. "Smith doesn't seem to be a fool. If she got back not later than one fifteen, if he was there until three, he's out. Obviously."

The others nodded. Pam said, "Yes," with a little sigh.

"It's disappointing," she said. "You could work it out so—so neatly. He's lost Dan's money, not the doctor. The doctor had found out and was going to—oh, do something. So Nickerson Smith killed him. It's—convenient."

It would be convenient, Bill Weigand agreed. The chances were ten to one against. The—

The waiter captain came and got Weigand, who was wanted on the telephone. Weigand was gone only a few minutes. He came back, sat down, finished his drink.

"The chances are now a thousand to one against," he said. "Unless a Miss Conover, of Brooklyn, is lying. The boys dropped around. She came back at one thirteen—she noticed the time because she was due back at one and was late, and wondered how late. She checked herself by a wall clock in the office, which is electrically controlled. And Smith was there. He was at his desk. As soon as he heard her come in, he buzzed for her and began dictating. He was there until he was telephoned for by the nurse. A couple of men, whose names she has, came in to see him. One of them at about one thirty, and stayed perhaps fifteen minutes. One of them a little after two, and stayed almost half an hour."

"You'll ask them?" Pam said, not hopefully.

They would ask them, Weigand agreed. "We ask everybody," he told her. "Everything. As you know." But they would tell the same story.

"And the girl is telling the truth?" Dorian said.

The boys thought she was, Bill told her. The boys were good judges. So many people tried to lie to policemen.

"So," Bill said, "you'd better pick somebody else, Pam."

Pam North agreed. She brightened.

"Why not one of the patients?" she said. "One of the men he examined. Suppose—" She stopped, figuring. Bill waited, half smiling.

"Suppose one of them didn't really go out," she said. "The nurse didn't see four of them go. She just saw the rooms empty and decided they had gone. But suppose one of them—say the man in the first room, because that would be easiest—really went into the doctor's private office and—and waited. And when the doctor came back, killed him. And then—sneaked out somehow?"

"How?" Bill said. "The nurse was in the corridor. If we believe her."

Pam wanted to know if they had to. Bill shrugged. He said they didn't have to believe anybody. Also, he said, all they had to go on was what people told them, so in the end they had to act as if they believed somebody. He granted that Nurse Spencer's testimony was uncorroborated. Actually, her story of the doctor's leaving might have been pure invention. But in that case, it was also desirable to assume that she had killed him herself or, less probably, was shielding somebody who had.

"Which," he said, "is something to bear in mind. Not necessarily something to accept. Personally, I think she was telling the truth, as she saw the truth. I think she has a good mind and is probably, therefore, a good reporter. I can be wrong. But—we have to start with the belief that at least part of what we are told is true—that the innocent people concerned are coming as near the truth as they can. Otherwise—well, otherwise we can't start."

"Actually," Pam said, "I think Miss Spencer was telling the truth. But couldn't the man—this patient who's hiding in the doctor's office, and has just killed the doctor—couldn't he get out without her seeing him?"

Bill Weigand thought it over, and after a moment he nodded. But his nod was doubtful.

"Starting a couple of minutes after the doctor himself went out," he said, "for Miss Brooks was the only person in the office until Miss Spencer came back and Miss Brooks was at her desk—or, anyway, in that vicinity. Maybe at the files. I suppose somebody could have slipped out then, before the nurse came back. But that would mean Dr. Gordon went out, came back in less than half an hour and got killed. Which is possible, of course. After about two, and until she found the body, the nurse was in the examining-room area—or, anyway, wandering around the office. That would have made it harder. I suppose somebody could have got out then, but he would have been taking a chance. Playing his luck."

He paused, considering again.

"However," he said, "it is more possible than I thought at first."

"Then," Pam said, but Weigand's expression stopped her.

"But," Bill said, "the obvious first. We have a man who had opportunity, possible motive—and who ran away. Right? So we don't make it hard unless we have to."

"Yeah, Loot," Mullins said, suddenly. "Like the old boy says." He looked around at the others. "The inspector," he explained.

"Right," Bill said. "We—"

He was interrupted by the arrival of food. They had almost finished eating, with a minimum of conversation, when Bill was called again to the telephone. When he came back he was walking rapidly and his arms seemed to be full of hats and coats. Mullins was on his feet by the time Bill Weigand reached the table. Weigand nodded.

"We move," he said. "The girl's started. She's got her car and is headed uptown. You can—"

But the others were standing too, and Jerry was looking for the waiter. He came, as waiters come when customers, who have not got their checks, stand up. He supplied the check and Jerry put a bill on it.

Weigand was already moving toward the door, with Mullins after him. He turned and said, "No" over his shoulder, and the others continued after him. His car was parked just ahead of the Norths's, and Weigand looked at the two cars and then at Pamela North, and then he half smiled.

"Be seeing you," Bill said, and got behind the wheel of his car. Mullins got in after him.

"Oh, yes," Pam said. "Oh, yes, Bill."

The police car started, U-turned and went uptown.

"It's a lovely night for a drive," Pam said. "Come on, Dorian. Jerry."

She was moving, quickly, toward the Norths's Buick. Jerry hesitated only a moment. He looked at the trim, quick figure of his wife; he looked at Dorian. Dorian said, "Oh, well, Jerry." They were all in the front seat of the Norths's car when Jerry U-turned and started up Madison.

"I've kept track of it," Pam said. "It turned west in Fifty-ninth."

They turned west in Fifty-ninth. The police car should be somewhere ahead. They could not see it. Then, apparently at Fifth, they heard the harsh demand of its siren.

They were lucky. The red light which the siren had protested was green when they reached Fifth. The way was clear through Fifty-ninth. The siren sounded again at Sixth. They went through on the tail of a green light. "Avenue of the Americas indeed," Pam said, looking at it with disapproval. "Central Park South and the Avenue of the Americas!" Again, now obviously at Columbus Circle, the siren sounded.

Beside Pam North, between her and the window, Dorian laughed. It was a soft laugh, at once amused and gentle.

"My Bill," she said. "He doesn't want us to get lost. After he's told us officially not to follow."

They were going through Columbus Circle, not very fast, when the siren sounded again. It was downtown, now, and for a moment Jerry looked puzzled and hesitated. Then his face cleared and he turned down Eighth Avenue. Lights stopped him at Fifty-eighth.

"Oh," Pam said, annoyed. "Now what?"

"Listen," Dorian said. "He ought—"

They heard the siren, very distant; its location confused by the buildings. But Jerry took his right hand from the wheel and waved it toward Pam.

"Of course," Pam said. "Through Fifty-seventh to the West Side. Then—" She paused, thinking. "Do you know the way to North Salem, Jerry?" she wanted to know. Jerry, starting the car with the change of light, took time to turn and grin at her. He turned west in Fifty-seventh. He said he thought he did. Farther ahead, now, the siren sounded faintly. Bill could give them a hint; he wouldn't wait.

"Such a nice balance," Dorian said, thoughtfully. "So like Bill."

They turned up the West Side Highway. They rolled rapidly north—and listened. The siren was faint—hardly distinguishable—when it sounded again. But it was still ahead.

"You could keep up," Pam pointed out. "Only—"

"Only I'd get pinched," Jerry told her. "We'll have to guess at it from now."

"But you agree, North Salem?" Pam said.

Jerry swerved right to the center lane, swerved left after a dawdling taxicab was behind them, and went up to fifty-five. Then he said, "Yes, I agree" and sank lower in the seat. "Cigarette, baby?" he said. Pam lighted a cigarette, steadied her hand with fingers against his cheek, and put the cigarette between his lips.

"It *is* a nice night for a drive," she said, as if she were a little surprised. "I do hope Martini won't mind."

• 5 •

Monday, 10 p.m. to Tuesday, 12:20 a.m.

"This," Jerry said, grimly, "is what you call a nice night for a drive."

Pam peered ahead, said, "Watch out!" and then said, "No, it's all right, I thought I saw something." Then she said well, it had been a nice night for a drive. At first.

It had been all right to Hawthorne Circle where, after a very brief consultation, they had turned right toward White Plains. It had been all right until, beyond White Plains, they had turned up Route 22, which began in such deceptive magnificence. Then, just when they had finished climbing the first curving hill, the fog got them. It was wispy at first, and unpredictable as always. They encountered it at high spots of the road, but not at all high spots. They would drive for minutes with the lights bright and then they would plunge, while Jerry swore and braked, into dripping dimness. The headlights would then throw white dazzle back into their eyes and Jerry would dip them and they would crawl, fearful of the ditch on their right, fearful of other cars groping toward them on the left. Approaching lights were dim, baffled; two cars would creep toward each other hesitantly, worriedly sounding horns. Dark objects would loom out of the fog ahead and then vanish mysteriously. Then they would run out of the fog for a moment, think it was over and pick up speed, suddenly find themselves again immersed.

"The best way is to turn off on one twenty-one," Pam said. "If we can find it."

"If," Jerry said, "we can find anything."

Dorian was mostly silent. She looked out of the window on her side of the car.

"The funny thing," she said once, "is that it isn't really thick. You can see houses and lights, only a little dimmed. Only washed over."

Jerry crept to a stop behind a car which seemed to be blocking the road. He discovered it was almost off the road, parked. He pulled out and went cautiously around it and said it was a hell of a place for anyone to park. He answered Dorian.

"The lights," he said. "Without lights you can see, but not enough. With them—" He swerved toward the center of the road, avoiding a culvert wall.

"With them you can see too much fog and not anything else," Pam said. "Watch it, Jerry!"

Jerry swerved a little to the right, to avoid a car groping toward them in the center of the road. He yelled at the other car, with exasperation.

"One twenty-one ought to be along pretty soon," Pam said. "Maybe it will be better."

"Why should it?" Jerry had asked her. "Probably it will be worse. And probably we'll miss it."

They had not missed it, although they had driven past the intersection and had to back, perilously, to make the turn. It was no better—no worse—no different.

"Anyway," Dorian said, "it will be as bad for everybody. For the girl—what's her name?" Pam told her. "Debbie. For Bill."

Both the Norths shook their heads. Pam explained.

"It may be," she said. "But it needn't. Sometimes ten minutes one way or the other make all the difference. Perhaps they came a different way—there are a lot of ways. That might make a difference. It might be perfectly clear."

"Yes," Jerry said. "And it might be twice as bad. Air currents. Lakes. Differences of temperature. They may have sailed through."

"We aren't," Pam said. They weren't.

Two hours should have done it, even with cautious driving—an hour and three quarters would have done it as Jerry had been going before the fog. Now it had been at least that long since they had started and there was, actually, no telling where they were. They were on a twisting road which ambled through Westchester on its way to half a dozen places; a road which branched into other roads, intersected absent-mindedly and lost itself in intersection. It was easy enough in daylight, if you knew it; it was not difficult on a clear night. But it was full of traps in fog or rain.

It was difficult afterward to determine where they fell into a trap. Their lights picked up a road marker, held it momentarily through the fog. It was not NY 121. It was NY Something Else. They could not make out what. Jerry swore again. He said that did it.

"Are we lost?" Dorian said. She was not alarmed; she was interested. "Actually," she said, "the fog is beautiful. Out of the side window."

They were lost, Jerry said. As nearly as you could be lost, where they were. It would be temporary.

"All the roads around here go to pretty much the same places," Pam said. "Only in different directions."

It sounded odd, Jerry told Dorian, staring ahead through the windshield. It sounded odd, but it was about the truth. It was impossible really to get lost. You merely got delayed. This road, whatever it was, would come into another road which would, in the end, take them to most of the places Route 121 would have taken them. By different turnings, through other places. By this Bedford and that Bedford.

"Or," Pam said, "back to twenty-two. Most of them do that, given long enough."

That was true, Jerry said, and stopped the car because his lights had picked up a stop sign. Beyond it was a road sign.

"Speaking of twenty-two," Jerry said, and turned right. "Now we're not lost. We're merely wandering." They drove a mile through heavy fog. Then, with no warning, the lights shone brightly on the road and far up ahead little lights in houses became sharply clear. Jerry went up to fifty, and asked what time it was. Pam looked at the car clock, computed, and said it was about a quarter of eleven. Jerry went up to fifty-five and stayed at it.

It was clear in Brewster, where the traffic light stopped them. It was clear beyond where they turned right on US 6 and, after a few miles, right off it. Even as they skirted Peach Lake there was no fog.

"It's funny," Dorian said. "Water—and no fog."

"It's always funny," Pam told her.

It was ten minutes after eleven when they stopped at the crossroads in North Salem and asked directions at the tavern. It was ten minutes later when, following the directions, they turned in between stone pillars at what they hoped was the Gordon place. There was no house at once; there was a graveled drive between trees. It was quiet and clear and they rolled along the drive silently, so that they could hear the tires crunching on the gravel. They passed through what had been an old barway in a dry stone wall and came out in a more open field, with a big, white house ahead, among trees. The house was near the center of what had once been a great rectangular field, bounded all around by stone walls and rows of trees. There were no lights in the house. It was white and dead in moonlight.

Then a light flashed at them, went out, went on again, went out a second time. Jerry stopped. The car was just beyond the old barway, on the white gravel drive which led straight toward the house.

A State trooper came toward them. The lights picked him up. Jerry switched off the headlights and the little parking lights came up on the front fenders. The moon made it seem almost as bright, after a moment, as it had been with the headlights on. The trooper came to Jerry's side of the car, stood looking at Jerry and said, "Well?" Then he turned his flashlight on Jerry and shifted its beam to Pam and then to Dorian.

"Well?" he repeated. "Aren't you a little off the road, bub?"

"Is Weigand here?" Jerry said.

The trooper put one elbow on the car door and looked at Jerry.

"What do you know about Weigand?" he said. He looked at the other two. "Homicide?" he said, obviously doubting it.

"This is Mrs. Weigand," Jerry said, indicating. "We're—friends. He's probably expecting us to show up."

"Is he?" the trooper said. "Why would he be expecting you?"

"Because he sirened at us," Pam said. "So of course he knew we were coming. Only we got lost because of the fog."

"Well," the trooper said. "Well. Well. He sirened at you. What did he say?"

"What?" Pam said.

The trooper shook his head.

"All right, bub," he said. "Move her on up. Easy. About as fast as I can walk. Eh, bub?"

Jerry moved her up, very slowly, with only the parking lights. There were several cars standing in a widening of the drive near the house, in front of a three-car garage. One of them was the police car which had brought Weigand. It looked very long and formidable in the moonlight.

"Lots of people, apparently," Pam said, with interest. "Are they sitting in the dark?"

"I don't know what they're doing," the trooper said. "Do you want to see Lieutenant Weigand or don't you?"

Dorian and Jerry simultaneously opened the doors beside them. Pam followed Dorian out on the right side. Jerry went around the car and joined them in front of it.

"We—" Pam began. Then, as if it were a cue, lights seemed to go on everywhere. There were lights in most of the windows of the house and a light over the Colonial entrance; there was a bright light, under a shade, beating down on the cars in front of the garage.

"Found it," the trooper said. "Come on, bub." He looked at Pam and Dorian. "And ladies," he said. He led them to the front door, opened it and raised his voice. "The lieutenant in there?" he demanded.

"Who wants him?" a strange voice said.

"People," the trooper said. "Say they're friends of his. In fact, one of them says she's his wife."

"Well," the voice inside said. "Ain't that—"

The voice stopped as if somebody had stepped on it. Bill came to the door. He looked at the Norths and Dorian a moment. His face was grave.

"All right, Graham," he said. The trooper saluted. "Get back to it,"

Bill told him. The trooper turned and went back down the drive. It appeared he was guarding the driveway. "It took you quite a while," Bill said, to the three of them generally. "Get lost?"

"Fog," Jerry said.

"Funny," Bill said. "We didn't hit any fog." He smiled. "Not until we got here, anyway," he added. "Come on in."

They went in to the big central hall, with stairs leading up from it. Bill motioned to the right and they went into a long living room, with french doors along the opposite side.

"What a nice house," Pam said. "See, Jerry, that's what I was talking about. With a terrace outside."

"Yes, baby," Jerry said. "I knew what you were talking about. It's fine."

"Bill," Dorian said. "Are you all right?" She looked at him. "Something's happened!" she said.

Bill nodded.

"We got him," Bill said. "Now we haven't got him. Somebody was helpful." They looked at him and waited. "Somebody turned off the lights on us," he said. "At the fuse-box switch. Just as Mr. Gordon was about to explain things to us."

"And he got away again," Pam said. It was a statement.

"Since you don't sit around a lighted room with a pocket torch in your hand," Bill said, "he got away, Pam. For the moment. It's a little confused. Everybody seems to have got away. That's why Graham is watching the entrance." He smiled faintly. "Not that their cars would be much good to them," he added. "We fixed that."

"Look," Pam said, "we just came in. We seem to have missed a lot."

Up until about fifteen-twenty minutes earlier they had missed nothing of much importance, Bill told them. Except helping to count noses. There were quite a lot of noses. Bill counted them. Dan Gordon. Deborah Brooks. Mrs. Andrew Gordon. And a new one—Lawrence Westcott. A neighbor, by all accounts. Very good looking, in tweeds and a sweater, probably in his late thirties. A big man; a pipe smoker.

"No dog?" Pam said.

Lots of dogs, Bill assumed. But not with him. He had heard of Dr.

Gordon's murder. On the radio. ("Was it?" Pam said. "It was," Bill told her.) He had come over to see if he could do anything.

"Mrs. Westcott?" Pam said. "Or isn't there one?"

Westcott had not mentioned one, Bill said. It had not come up, however; not directly. He told them the rest of it.

The troopers—two of them—had been at the house since about nine, on Weigand's request. Merely to watch; to do nothing unless somebody tried to leave. Nobody had tried to leave. Bill and Mullins had picked up Debbie Brooks, guided to her by a radio car and trailed her, driving at a moderate speed, up the Saw Mill River Parkway and seen her turn right at Hawthorne Circle. They had lost her then, but had been undisturbed, because by then they were reasonably certain where she was going. They had been right; the troopers had timed her in, about fifteen minutes before Weigand arrived. He had reached the house, having to stop to ask the way in North Salem, at about a quarter of eleven.

Weigand and Mullins had driven up to the house, like casual guests, and had rung the front doorbell. Dan Gordon himself had come to the door. He had looked at them and said, "Well?"

"Like the trooper," Pam said.

Weigand said he supposed so. Weigand had politely, unnecessarily, introduced himself and Mullins. Dan Gordon had been surly. That was the word for it, Weigand thought. He seemed to be, generally, a surly young man. He had said, specifically, "what the hell?"

"We want to talk to you," Weigand said. "Didn't Miss Brooks tell you?"

"Suppose you leave her alone," Dan Gordon said. "Or do you like to scare little girls?"

He had said it nastily. Then, without waiting for them to answer, he had said they might as well come in. He had taken them to the living room. Deborah Brooks, Mrs. Gordon and Westcott were there—Deborah was standing in front of a chair as if she had leaped out of it. She looked very young, and frightened. Dan Gordon had gone to her at once, and put an arm around her, and she had put her face against his coat a moment and then lifted it.

"Well?" he had said, again.

Weigand had said the obvious things—it was murder, an investigation of murder; they had to see everyone and ask all the usual questions. "And," of course, Weigand had said, "we have to ask what made you run away, Mr. Gordon."

Gordon had glared at him. Weigand had noticed that the young man was perspiring; that his forehead was wet.

"He didn't run away," Debbie said. Her voice was frightened, but still eager. "You don't understand."

"No?" Weigand said.

"All right, Debbie," Dan Gordon said. His voice was gentle, suddenly. "It's all right, darling."

"Of course," the girl said, and looked up at him. Her eyes were wet. "Of course, Dan."

"Is it?" Bill said. "I'm afraid—"

He had been interrupted then by the ringing of the front doorbell. Dan had started toward the door; Bill had shaken his head; Mullins, finally, had opened it. Grace Spencer had come in. She seemed hurried. She spoke, it seemed, before she saw who was in the room. "I had—" she began. Then she caught herself. "I didn't know," she said. "I'm sorry."

She had come in, and everybody had sat down while Weigand sorted things out. He sorted Westcott out; he passed him over for the time. When he asked if there was anybody else in the house, Mrs. Gordon had said, "only Eileen—my little girl." And her nurse. And Mr. and Mrs. Gustaf. Mr. and Mrs. Gustaf were the "couple."

Weigand had thought things over and decided to start on Dan Gordon. Gordon, irritably, admitted there was some place they could talk. He had led Weigand out of the living room, across the central hall, into a study beyond. Weigand closed the door; found there were two other doors leading into the small room, and closed them. Gordon had sat down in a deep chair and watched him. Weigand had crossed and looked out through the french doors which were on the far side of this room, also, and then had gone back and sat in another deep chair opposite Gordon. There were only deep chairs in the room. Weigand offered

Dan Gordon a cigarette and noticed that the fingers which took it trembled. Weigand had lighted Gordon's cigarette and his own. They had smoked silently for a minute or two, each waiting for the other. Gordon waited longer.

"Now," Weigand began, finally. Then the lights went out.

Bill Weigand had lost time getting out of the deep chair. Not much, but enough. He heard movement, and was blind and lunged toward Gordon's chair. But Gordon's chair was empty. After a little Bill's eyes adjusted and then there was enough moonlight coming in through the french doors to make it apparent that the room was empty. If somebody had been giving Dan Gordon another chance to get out from under, he had taken it.

Bill went back, fast, toward the living room and almost ran into Mullins, who was coming fast out of it. There was a good deal of confusion, Bill admitted. Both of the troopers had come on the run and had been sent out again, to immobilize the cars which had brought Gordon, Deborah Brooks and Grace Spencer to the house. Westcott, it appeared, had come across country, afoot. Mrs. Gordon's big Cadillac was in the garage. Dan's convertible, also a Cadillac, was headed toward the garage door, but not inside. A Ford coupe—Debbie's by its position—was alongside. An older Plymouth—Grace Spencer's, that would be—was behind it. The troopers took care of those, and posted themselves so that they could watch the house, after a fashion. It was not too good a fashion; the house rambled, possessing wings and minor protuberances. There were no positions from which two men could watch it all.

Weigand and Mullins had had flashlights by that time. They did not need them to discover that the living room, moonlight flooded, was empty—unless, to be sure, people were hiding in the dark shadows cast by chairs and tables. They brushed those shadows away with the light from their torches. Nobody. Then they started searching.

"It's a damn big house," Weigand told Dorian and the Norths. "Bigger even than it looks from outside. It twists and turns."

They twisted and turned with it. Then, down a corridor, they saw the light from another flash, and yelled at it. Westcott, big and burly—

and calm—turned the light on himself for identification and said it was a hell of a note.

"Eve's with the kid," he said. "Kidnappers, she's afraid of."

It seemed to be stretching an irrelevant fear a good distance. But perhaps it wasn't. Reasonably, it would be in a mother's mind. As an explanation, it would stand up.

"Power failure," Westcott told them. "Happens all the time in the country, you know."

Bill didn't know. He said so curtly. It happened, chiefly, during thunderstorms. Where was the thunderstorm?

"What else?" Westcott said. He sounded interested.

If he couldn't guess, there was no point in explaining. Weigand assumed he could guess, if he wanted to.

"Where did you go?" Weigand asked.

"With Eve."

"And the others?"

Westcott shrugged, dim in the reflected light from the torches. Weigand let it go for the moment. It could be true. Very possibly it was true. In any event, it was secondary.

Westcott did not know where the fuse boxes were; he assumed in the basement. He looked at Weigand when he was asked and shook his head.

"Everybody was in the living room," he said. "Everybody was surprised."

"No, Loot," Mullins said. "The girl wasn't there. She—" He paused. "She had to be excused."

That had been a minute or two after Weigand had taken Dan Gordon out. Mullins, considerate—and probably, Bill thought, a little embarrassed—had approved her departure. She had been gone another minute or two when the lights went out.

"The little fool," Bill said. "Twice is too much."

They blundered in search of the main fuse boxes, which presumably would be in the basement. They opened wrong doors; they found stairs going down and went down them and came back up, because they led into a storeroom which led nowhere—and contained no fuse boxes.

They found the kitchen and opened a door beyond it and a blurred, accented voice wanted to know who was there. The voice belonged to Mr. Gustaf, who was short and heavy and in a nightshirt. His hair was a fringe, standing up around the circumference of his head like a bristling fence. It was apparent that Mr. Gustaf had been asleep.

With Weigand's torch light on him, he reached to the wall at the left of the door, and Weigand heard a wall switch click. Nothing happened. Gustaf looked surprised. Then he looked frightened. It took time to bring him out of it. Then he went back, rumbled an explanation to someone inside—someone who was, they would assume for the time, Mrs. Gustaf—and came back with trousers over the nightshirt and slippers on the broad feet. He led them to the fuse box, which was in the basement. It was a triple box, for three circuits. Each circuit had its own knife switch. All were down.

"Vell!" Mr. Gustaf said, with what appeared to be hurt surprise in his voice. He pushed them back up again. In the basement, nothing happened. Then Mr. Gustaf found a switch and pushed it. Light returned. Upstairs, when they got there, there was no lack of light. They called one of the troopers in, then, leaving the other at the road. They sent Mr. Gustaf back to his room, and told him to stay there. They took—were taken by—Westcott to the little girl's bedroom. Mrs. Gordon was there; the child's nurse, middle aged and comfortable, was there. The little girl, with hair like her mother's—but softer, flowing as it wished—was asleep. Bright hair spread over her pillow; her face was flushed. Near relaxed fingers lay an object which must have started life as a felt animal. A rabbit, perhaps. It had been around.

Evelyn Gordon looked frightened—and wondering. She spoke very quietly, not waking the child. She said, "What?" and waited. Bill Weigand shook his head; he indicated Westcott. He could answer that. "Stay here, all of you," Weigand said, and went out and closed the door—very gently, so as not to waken the child.

It was not a new house. There was a minimum of open space, particularly on the second floor. There were many rooms, with closed doors. And there were only three of them to look. They left Mullins to start upstairs. Weigand took the trooper and went down again.

"Then you came," Bill said.

"So somebody threw the main switches so Gordon could get away," Pam said. "And he got away."

"Why somebody?" Bill said. "Deborah Brooks. The sweet young thing."

"Well," Pam said, reasonably, "she is. Or isn't she?"

The sweetness was wearing thin, Bill told her. She kept getting in the way.

"Do we help?" Jerry said. "Help look?"

They did, Bill told them. Then he hesitated.

"You girls stay together," he directed. "Jerry and I, the trooper, Mullins—we split up. You don't." He looked at them. "Gordon is very—jumpy," he told them. "I should hate to have either of you—"

"We'll be careful," Dorian said. "Very careful."

Bill Weigand looked at the two of them as if he didn't believe what Dorian promised. But he went off with Jerry toward the center hall, talking as he went. Pam and Dorian were alone in the big living room.

"This is the kind of room I've been telling Jerry about," Pam said, waving at it generally. "Long, with french doors and everything. And a terrace outside."

She looked down the room toward the rear of the house.

"Only," she said, "I'd like it a little longer, if anything, and that end down there used as a dining room. Maybe with some way of shutting it off."

She walked down the room and stopped near the end.

"About here," she said. "Some sort of a partition. Movable. Or screens. Or one of those what-you-may-call-'ems that fold up. Here there must be—" They had reached the end of the room. There was a doorway arch at the left. "Here there is a dining room," Pam said. "Rather nice, too. Do you and Bill want a house?"

"Very much," Dorian said. "Doesn't everybody? But a policeman—"

Pam said she knew.

"Do you still mind his being one?" she said.

"Not any more," Dorian said. "I see it his way." She stopped and looked at a picture on the wall. "Nice," she said. "I wish I could paint."

"But—" Pam said.

Dorian said she meant paint. She didn't mean do fashion drawings. She meant paint.

There was no one in the dining room. They went through it to a swinging door beyond.

"Pantry," Pam said. "Then kitchen."

They looked at the kitchen.

"Actually," Pam said, "I suppose it's very sanitary, and everything. But it looks clinical."

They had turned on lights. The kitchen was very bright. And very empty.

"A *really* big refrigerator," Pam said, and went over to look at it. "Big enough to keep anything." She heard herself and stopped suddenly. She looked at it again. "Anything," she repeated, in a changed voice. She touched the handle, drew her hand back, pressed on it with resolution. The door of the refrigerator came open. Dorian from across the room and Pam, from closer, looked in.

"Food," Pam said. "Just food." She sounded relieved. "Look," she said. "It's got a special freeze compartment and—"

She explored. Dorian watched her. Then, because there was a door, half glassed, in the wall at her right, she turned to it and opened it and looked out. It opened on a sheltered terrace. The kitchen was a wing; it and the quarters of the Gustafs were a wing. The door was in a corner made by the wing and the french doors which formed a wall of the dining room. The terrace was paved and white in the moonlight. And Dorian, her hand still on the door, was suddenly motionless and she drew her breath in quickly. Pam heard that before she heard Dorian Weigand, her voice oddly hurried, call "Pam!"

They opened the door a little wider and looked out. Grace Spencer lay there, on the flagging, as if she were asleep, face down. But her head was not pillowed on an arm, as it would have been if she had been asleep. The moonlight was white on her. It made the blood around her head look black. It was a spreading blackness.

They went out together—close together. It was Pam who knelt beside the nurse. She knelt briefly and then stood up.

"Her whole head—" she said, in a voice which shook a little. "Her whole head, Dorian."

Dorian put an arm around Pam North, and Dorian did not look down at what lay by their feet. She drew Pam back into the bright kitchen, and Pam was shaking under her arm.

"I'm—" Pam North began, and then closed her mouth and did not finish. Her face was very white; lipstick was sharp against the pallor. She waited a moment, quiet; using all her strength, and not moving. "All right," she said. "I'm not going to be. You—didn't look?"

"Not—closely," Dorian said. She was white, too. "Not after—after I saw from the door."

"Somebody struck her with an iron something," Pam said. "A rod. More—more than once. The rod is there, in the—by her head."

"You're making a picture of it," Dorian said. "Don't."

"I know," Pam said. "I know now. It's a spit from a broiler. One of those charcoal broilers. It—Dorian, it *bent* a little!"

She put her hands up and covered her face. Dorian waited. Pam took her hands down.

"All right," she said. "But I had to get the picture over with. We've got to find Jerry."

They went, almost running and still close together, back through the pantry and the dining room. In the dining room Pam began to call. "Jerry!" she called. "Jerry!"

They were in the living room. Halfway up its length five people were standing—all facing them; one expression on their very different faces. Jerry and Bill, Mullins—Dan Gordon and Debbie. Then Jerry broke from the little group and came to meet Pam and Dorian. Pam ran into his arms and clung to him for a moment.

"Out there," she said, gesturing behind her. "Oh—Jerry!"

Dorian Weigand was beside her husband; she clung to his left arm with both her hands. She was very white, too. Bill looked down at her.

"The nurse," she said, trying to keep her voice steady. "Miss Spencer. She's out there. She's—somebody beat her skull in. Pam—Pam looked."

Bill and Mullins moved fast, out through the french doors of the dining room. They did not stay long. Their faces were hard when they came back. They looked like policemen. They walked back, looking at Gordon and the girl. Then Weigand stood in front of them, and looked at them without saying anything for what seemed like a very long time.

"You say you were together?" he said. "All the time? In the—in whatever you call that room?"

His voice was without expression.

"Yes," the girl said. "Oh—yes."

But almost at the same time, Dan Gordon spoke.

"Not all the time," he said. "No."

He looked back at Weigand, and his eyes were steady. But perspiration stood out on his forehead.

"Sit down," Weigand told them. "Both of you."

There was a deep chair near and Debbie Brooks sat in it. She did not sit back in it; she sat on the edge and she held Dan Gordon's left hand tight. With his free hand, Dan drew a lighter chair near enough and sat beside her. His free hand gripped the wooden arm of the chair.

Bill Weigand turned back toward a table behind the sofa which stood before the fireplace. He seemed to hesitate a moment. He picked up a book lying on the table and looked at it idly. Then, with no warning, quickly, he slapped the book down hard, flat, on the polished wood. It made a sharp crack, almost like an explosion. Everybody started, and then looked at Bill.

But you could not call Dan Gordon's movement a mere start of surprise. It was convulsive. But it was a convulsion which shook his whole body. His head went back against the back of the chair, the neck twisted. His left hand broke from Deborah's grasp, his right came away from the chair arm. Both hands went to his face and covered it. Both hands, his whole body, trembled.

They looked at him, then, in the instant before Deborah's young arms went around him, holding him; before she turned toward Weigand defiantly, her eyes hot with anger. They all looked at Dan Gordon, tall and, in a lean fashion, powerful—and cowering like a frightened child.

After a moment, Dan Gordon recovered himself. Gently, he pushed the girl away. He looked at Weigand and his eyes told nothing.

"I'm sorry, Gordon," Bill said, and for the first time he spoke to Gordon in a tone which was not his official tone. "I'm sorry. I wanted to know."

"Well," Gordon said, and his voice was controlled. "Now you know."

"Yes," Bill said. "Now I know."

Debbie Brooks put her face down in her hands, and her hair flowed down, covering face and hands. Dan Gordon reached out toward her bent shoulders and then, hesitantly, withdrew his hand. His face flushed, and then he turned back toward Bill Weigand. Anger grew on his face, twisting his mouth. Then, with a kind of confused violence, he was on his feet and he began to talk. He talked too loudly. His anger was ugly in ugly words. Weigand listened only a moment.

"Stop it!" he said. His voice was harsh, breaking through the other's words. "Stop it, Gordon!"

Gordon moved toward Weigand, hurling the ugly words. His face was contorted. He was taller than Weigand and his fists clenched. Bill stood, not moving, not seeming to tense his muscles, his arms hanging loosely at his sides and his hands open. Only his eyes seemed alert. Mullins moved in from a position near the fireplace, and he moved easily and without hurry.

"Stop it, Gordon," Bill said. His voice was not so loud. It was almost matter of fact. Gordon did not seem to hear him. "Watch yourself, Gordon," Weigand said. "Watch yourself." His tone was almost quiet, now.

Debbie Brooks was looking up. She pushed back her hair with both hands.

"Dan!" she said. "Danny!"

Gordon was within arm's length of Weigand and still coming toward him. And then he stopped. It was hard to say what had stopped him; hard to guess whether he had heard the girl's low, pleading voice. For a moment after he had stopped, and fallen silent, he stood unmoving, looking at Weigand. Hatred began to fade out of his eyes, and purpose left them. He seemed puzzled, suddenly—bewildered. You would have thought he was surprised to find himself standing there, so close to Weigand and so threatening. Then he looked embarrassed.

"Sorry," he said. "Don't know what—" He broke off. "Sorry," he said again. He went back to his chair and looked down at Debbie a moment and shook his head. Then he sat down beside her and took the hand she gave him. He held it tight.

"You mustn't," Debbie said, and looked at Weigand anxiously. "Please! Can't you understand?"

Weigand nodded.

"I understand, Miss Brooks," he said, and he spoke slowly. "Do you?"

She looked at him and shook her head. Her eyes were wide and, Bill thought, frightened.

"How long has it been, Gordon?" Weigand asked. His voice, again, was matter of fact. He looked at Dan Gordon, and saw perspiration standing out on his forehead. Gordon freed his hand from Debbie's and took a handkerchief out of his coat pocket and wiped both his hands, carefully. Then he took the girl's hand again.

"Several months," he said. "It started after things were over. Delayed reaction, they say."

He might have been talking about someone else.

"Better than it was?" Weigand said.

Gordon said he guessed so.

"Oh, yes," Debbie said. "Much better, Danny."

"All right," Dan said, and smiled down at her. "Much better, Debbie."

But he looked at Weigand almost immediately and his eyes held no confidence.

It was all there, Weigand thought. Extreme irritability, restlessness, excessive perspiration, convulsive reaction to sharp sounds—all of it you could see from outside was there. You didn't need to be a psychiatrist to put a name to it—the name they were using this time. Combat fatigue. But you needed to be more of a psychiatrist than Weigand was to know what it did inside, where you couldn't see. Maybe it needed more of a psychiatrist than anybody was.

"Why did you leave the office?" Weigand asked. "You knew we wanted to talk to you."

"What the hell," Gordon said. "You made me wait. I've done enough waiting in the last few years. I was tired of being there."

"Why did you think you could get away with it?" Weigand asked.

Gordon looked at Weigand, shook his head, and repeated "get away with it?"

There was, in theory, a patrolman who would have stopped him, Weigand said. Only in theory, but Gordon couldn't have known.

"I don't know," Gordon said. "I didn't think of it particularly. I just went."

"And got your car and drove out here?" Weigand asked him.

"Yes," Gordon said. "Sure." He hesitated a moment. "I wasn't hiding, or anything," he said. "I wouldn't have come here if I had been."

"Right," Bill said. "Not if you thought of it. But—was there something you had to do here, Gordon? Something that wanted doing before we came?"

"Such as?" Gordon said.

Bill declined to be drawn. He said he had no suggestions. "At the moment," he said.

"And in the library," he went on. "When the lights went out. Why did you run again?" He watched Gordon's face. "Hold onto yourself," he said. "It won't get you anything to blow up." He waited, interested to see what would happen. Gordon got hold of himself.

"I didn't run," Gordon said. "When the lights went out I—I went to find Debbie."

"You were afraid something would happen to her?" Weigand asked.

"I guess so," Gordon said.

Weigand turned to the girl.

"Miss Brooks, did you throw the light switches?" he asked, his words coming quick.

She looked at him. Then she looked at Gordon.

"Why would I?" she said. "Dan hasn't anything to hide."

She looked back at the tall young man beside her when she said that. Her eyes questioned him. Again, Weigand thought, there was fear in them.

"I think you did," Weigand said, and his voice was almost gentle. "I think you don't know whether he has anything to hide or not, Miss Brooks. I think you're afraid he has."

The girl looked quickly at Weigand and then back at Dan Gordon. She was looking at Dan as she spoke; she was speaking to him.

"No," she said. "Oh, no! I'm not afraid. I know he didn't—" She stopped. "I know," she repeated, but her voice wavered.

"And," Weigand said, "you will do anything to help him, won't you, Miss Brooks? The thing you think of first—even futile little things, like turning off the lights. Is that it?"

"He doesn't need help," Debbie said. She looked at the detective now. "Why should he?"

Weigand nodded. He said perhaps Dan Gordon didn't need help.

"I don't know," he said. "Do you need help, Gordon?"

Gordon said he didn't know what Weigand was talking about.

"Yes," Weigand said. "Oh, yes. You know. I'm talking about your stepfather's murder, Gordon. Did you know most of your money was lost?"

"Some of it," Gordon said. "So what?"

"You knew your stepfather had lost it?"

Gordon shook his head.

"I don't know what happened to it," he said. "I don't know anybody lost it."

"Really?" Weigand said. "Really, Mr. Gordon?"

Gordon did not say anything.

"Suppose I think you did," Weigand said. "Suppose I think that you heard something—perhaps your stepfather warned you that there wouldn't be as much money as you had expected. That a major part of it had been lost—somehow. Perhaps as a result of his bad judgment. Suppose I think you got to brooding about it, and wanted to know more—and arranged to meet him yesterday to find out more. Suppose I think you waited in the lobby downstairs until he came down and that you went up to him—and by that time you were very irritated. As you were here, a few minutes ago. Suppose I think he persuaded you to go back to the office, because he didn't want you making a show of it in the lobby, and that you went—and started in again when you were there, in his private office—which is more or less soundproof. So Miss Brooks wouldn't hear you."

He stopped and looked at the girl, consideringly.

"Or perhaps she did hear you," he said. "In spite of the soundproofing. And went in—and found that you'd grabbed up a paperweight and gone after him. The way you started to go at me a few minutes ago. And stood by you—and tried to help you. And making the kind of mistake—doing the kind of wrong, useless thing—she did tonight when she turned off the lights. Because she's young and—frightened—and will do anything to help you."

"No," the girl said. "No—nothing like that—"

"No?" Weigand said. "Suppose I still think it was, Miss Brooks? It wouldn't be murder, maybe—if you had called the police, and Gordon hadn't run from questioning—so he would have time to make up a good story, perhaps? Or work out an alibi?—it wouldn't have been murder. Manslaughter, at worst. An accident—one of those unhappy things we can blame on the war. You see, Miss Brooks?"

"It didn't happen," the girl said. "Tell him, Danny. Tell him."

"What's the use?" Gordon said. "Let him guess. That's what he's for."

"Oh," Weigand said, "perhaps you didn't hear anything, Miss Brooks. Perhaps you don't know anything. Perhaps you're just—afraid it was that way."

The girl shook her head, her hair swaying.

"Why don't you leave her alone?" Gordon said. "Why don't you stick to this—this story about me? The one you're making up."

"Am I?" Weigand said. "I don't know. You had motive. So far as I know you had the opportunity. You have the—temperament. If it happened the way I've described."

"And I suppose I had another—disturbed period—and killed the nurse," Gordon said. "Or had you forgotten about her?"

Bill Weigand said he hadn't forgotten.

"That wasn't the same thing," he said. "That was murder. That was murder of someone who knew too much—and had come out here to talk it over with somebody. I should think with you, Gordon. Did she see you, after you killed your stepfather? Was that what she was going to give you a chance to explain? When you killed her?"

"What's the use?" Gordon said. "I didn't kill anybody. And I'm not crazy."

Weigand agreed with that. He said he didn't think Dan Gordon was crazy.

There were lights and voices outside, then, and the sound of men moving. Mullins went to one of the french doors and looked out.

"Troopers," Mullins said. Weigand nodded. It hadn't taken them long—now that they had a murder of their own. The doorbell rang.

The man who came in first was a short powerful man in civilian clothes. There were two younger men in civilian clothes with him. They were cops, all right, Pamela North thought. Then she thought something else.

"Why—" Mrs. North said.

"Well," the short man said, in a strong, heavy voice. "Well. Old Home Week." He looked around. He nodded to Bill Weigand. "Hello, Weigand," he said. He made a joke. "Having another vacation, Lieutenant?" he said.

"Hello, Heimrich," Weigand said. "Not a vacation, this one. Our murders cross. I've got one. You've got one. Division of labor."

"O.K.," Heimrich said. "They tie in?"

"Right, Lieutenant," Weigand said. "They tie in." He looked at Gordon and the girl beside Gordon. "Tight," he said.

Lieutenant Heimrich, Bureau of Criminal Identification, New York State Police, looked at Gordon and the girl. He snapped his fingers.

"Sure," he said. He spoke to Gordon. "You kill your dad, son?" he asked, in an interested tone. He waited for Gordon to speak. Gordon merely looked at him.

"O.K.," Heimrich said. "Not my headache anyway. You kill anybody around here, son? That'd be my business, you know."

He looked at Weigand. Weigand shook his head. Heimrich joined him and they walked down the room, out of earshot. They conferred for a moment. They walked back.

"I'll talk to you two later," Heimrich said. "Meanwhile—I'm going to have you wait in your rooms." He looked at the girl. "You're Miss Brooks," he told her. "You got a room here?" The girl nodded. "O.K.," Heimrich said. He spoke to the two detectives who had come in with him. "Take them up," he said. "See that they stay put. Get a couple of the boys on their doors. Get it?"

The detectives got it. They took Gordon and Debbie Brooks out. She was holding to his hand. Lieutenant Heimrich looked at those who remained.

"There are a lot of us," he said. He looked at them. "You're Mrs. North," he told Mrs. North. "I remember you, from last time." He looked at Jerry North. "You I've seen somewhere," Heimrich said.

"With me," Mrs. North said. "My husband."

Lieutenant Heimrich thought this over a moment. He looked at Jerry North again.

"O.K.," Heimrich said. "If that's the way you want it. Who are you?"

This was to Dorian Weigand. Bill smiled at her. He told Heimrich he ought to remember her.

"Dorian Hunt," Bill said. "At the same time you met the Norths. And Mullins and me. Now she's Dorian Weigand."

"Well," Heimrich said. He looked at all of them. "That was quite a vacation you had," he told them.

"Oh yes," Pam North said. "It was one of our most interesting—"[*]

The doorbell interrupted her. Mullins went to the door.

"Get along in, you," a voice said, and the door closed. Mullins came back, but there was a heavy-set man of medium height in front of him.

"Why, hello, Mr. Smith," Pam said. She looked at him with a pleased smile. "I've been wondering about you," she said.

---

[*] The Norths first met Lieutenant Heimrich in *Murder Out of Turn,* J. B. Lippincott Co., 1941.

• 6 •

Tuesday, 12:20 a.m. to 3:55 a.m.

Nickerson Smith stood in the doorway and looked at them. He looked with the hopefully polite, and blank, expression of a man who has walked in too late on a story.

"Wondering about me?" he said, repeating Mrs. North's remark. "Why?"

"Where you were," Pam told him. "Everybody was here but you."

Smith shook his head and looked at Lieutenant Weigand. Weigand's expression told him nothing in particular.

"I'm afraid," he said, and waited for somebody to pick it up. Bill Weigand, after a moment, picked it up.

"Where have you been, Mr. Smith?" Bill asked. "And, for that matter, why are you here?"

"Driving out," Smith said. He looked puzzled. "To see my nephew, naturally. Want to have a talk with him."

"About the money," Bill said, with no inflection of enquiry.

"Yes," Smith said.

"How did you know he would be here?" Bill wanted to know.

Smith shrugged. He said it seemed the most likely place. He looked at Weigand shrewdly.

"What's going on?" he asked.

"Murder," Pam North said, for Bill.

All of them looked at Nickerson Smith. He looked sad.

"I know," he said. "Of course." Then he looked puzzled. "But all these State troopers," he said. "They're all over the place."

"A new murder," Pam said. "That is—" She stopped speaking and looked at Bill. She looked at Jerry, who shook his head at her. But Bill Weigand nodded.

"Right," he said. "A new murder. Grace Spencer." He said it flatly.

Nickerson Smith looked shocked.

"Grace—" he said. "Why, that's the nurse!"

"Right," Bill told him.

"But," Smith said, and paused. "I don't understand," he said.

"Try," Mrs. North advised him. "Grace Spencer. Somebody killed her. Because she remembered something—something odd. Something she couldn't be allowed to tell. Where were you, Mr. Smith?"

Smith looked puzzled again. He shook his head.

"I don't know," he said. "When was she killed? If it wasn't too long ago, I was driving here."

Pam looked at Bill Weigand, and he nodded.

"About an hour," she said. "Less, perhaps."

Jerry shook his head.

"More," he said. "A little more."

"On the road, then," Smith said. He looked without anger, almost with amusement, at Mrs. North. "Do I need an alibi?" he asked.

"Heavens," Mrs. North said. "You ought to know that, if anybody. People who kill people need alibis. You ought to know."

"I do," Smith said. "On that basis, I don't." He looked at Mrs. North. "I'm not sure I get the basis," he added.

"Look," Mrs. North said, "it's guilty people who need alibis, isn't it? So that they will be some place else when they weren't? If you killed Miss Spencer, of course you need an alibi. Like a gas station."

"Listen, Pam," Jerry said. He ran the fingers of his right hand through his hair. "Why a gas station?"

"To stop at, of course," Pam told him. "While the lights were off."

Nickerson Smith looked at Weigand; and Dorian suddenly, quite unexpectedly, laughed from the deep chair in which she was sitting. It was a subdued laugh, and brief.

"You all look so funny," Dorian said, when everybody looked at her. "Pam's perfectly clear."

"Of course," Pam said. "It's simple. You got ten gallons and he remembers you because you asked what time it was."

Jerry shook his head, looking again at Pam.

"What time was it?" he said.

"About twenty minutes after eleven," Pam said, without hesitating. She looked at her watch. "You were right," she said. "It's twelve thirty now. More than an hour."

"So you mean," Smith said, speaking very slowly and carefully, "where was I at about eleven twenty, and did I stop at a gas station so I can prove it?"

"Of course," Pam North said. "What would I mean?"

Smith shook his head.

"I was on the road somewhere," he said. "On my way here. About at Hawthorne Circle, probably."

"Why?" Pam said. "Did you look at your watch?"

Smith looked confused again, but only for a moment.

"Oh," he said, "at the Circle. No—it would just be about right."

He looked at Weigand then and his eyes challenged Weigand.

"Lieutenant," he said, "what is all this? This—lady—seems to suspect me. Am I supposed to take that as the official attitude?"

Weigand smiled a little, but it was not an informative smile.

"This lady suspects everyone," he said. "So do I. So does Lieutenant Heimrich here. This is Nickerson Smith, Heimrich. Dan Gordon's uncle. Brother of the doctor's first wife. And—one of the executors of his sister's will. Dr. Gordon was the other."

"And," Nickerson Smith said, "Gordon managed to throw away about three fourths of the money. Leaving me to hold the bag."

Heimrich made deprecating consonants with his tongue and teeth. They could mean anything.

"And," Smith said, "I was in my office when Andrew was killed."

Heimrich looked at Weigand, who nodded.

"That's right," Weigand said. "He was."

"Oh, so you talked to the girl," Smith said, enlightened.

"Right," Bill said. "We talked to your secretary. You were in your office."

"Then?" Smith said.

Then, Bill said, as far as he was concerned Smith could talk with his nephew. But it was up to Heimrich; they were in Heimrich territory.

"Why not, Mr. Smith?" Heimrich said, pleasantly. "He's in his room. Tell the man at the door I said you could talk to him. You know where his room is, of course."

Nickerson Smith shook his head. Oddly enough, he said, he had been at the house only once before, and then had stayed on the first floor. Heimrich looked surprised. He said he understood Smith was a relative; it was clear from his tone that relatives knew one another's houses. Smith smiled faintly.

"We didn't see much of one another," he said. "After my sister died, and particularly after Andrew remarried, I saw them only occasionally. In town. I'm afraid that, even with Dan, I wasn't a—a good relative." He thought a moment. "Apparently it would have been better if I had been," he said. "All around. I left too much to Andrew."

Nobody had anything to say to that. Smith looked at all of them, said morosely and to nobody in particular that it was water under the bridge, and went off with a guiding trooper. They looked after him for a moment. Pamela's gaze was oddly speculative. She continued to regard the place where Mr. Smith had been for some time after the others had turned away.

"You look," Jerry said, after they had contemplated her preoccupied face for a moment, "very speculative. Like Teeney when she sees a cigarette package, which maybe somebody will empty for her."

Pam started. She looked at Jerry and said, "Oh!"

"Well," she said, "I do want him."

"Hey!" Jerry said.

"Platonically," Pam said. "As a murderer. Is that platonic?"

Bill Weigand shrugged. Not platonic, he thought. "Hopeless" was the word.

"Don't set your heart on him, Pam," he said. "Because he couldn't have killed Gordon. And whoever killed Gordon, killed the nurse." He paused. "I hope," he added, with some fervor.

"Yeah," Lieutenant Heimrich said. "No doubt about it." He was relaxed, contented. "So you can work it out all nice and clean for both of us, Weigand. We'll make the motions and you do the work." He was almost purring. "Different from that other time," he said. "This time you shake the tree and we'll catch the apples. O.K.?"

"Right," Weigand said, "and I think we'll leave you to your motions, Lieutenant."

"O.K.," Heimrich said, still contented. "You'll hear from us." He smiled at Weigand, and his smile was a police smile. "Naturally," he said, "we'll do a little tree shaking, too." He regarded the ceiling momentarily. "Starting with Mrs. Gordon," he said. "And her boy friend. If he is."

"The neighbors might know," Pam North suggested.

Heimrich regarded her.

"Why, Mrs. North," he said. "You wouldn't want us to listen to gossip, would you?" He was heavily jocose; it was a joke.

"Personally," Pam North said, "I like gossip. As long as it isn't trivial."

The Norths were home, Bill Weigand thought—with that just perceptible twinge of uncertainty which was so often a concomitant to making up one's mind about Pam and Jerry North. Dorian was home, he knew, having just talked to her. He pushed that thought away; he pushed away the thought that it would be better to be with her. He whistled a bar or two of Sullivan's music and thought of Gilbert's lyrics. For a couple of laymen— He looked at his watch, and learned what he could have guessed. It was getting on toward three o'clock—three o'clock in the morning. Another song came back into his mind, which was an indication that his mind was tired. And it was less applicable; they hadn't danced the whole night through. They had driven through the night, guided by a radio car which was trailing another car, they had found a sick man and a dead woman; a man in tweeds and a wife unprostrated by grief, and a little girl asleep with bright hair strewing her pillow. And they had wallowed back through fog. Weigand's eyes were as tired as his mind. He ran a hand over them and held them closed a moment. Then he opened them and looked at his desk, and at the reports piled in front of him.

The report on Nickerson Smith was on top, and it told him nothing he had not already heard. From one fifteen certainly, from one ten probably, until he had taken the call from Nurse Spencer, he had been at his desk. That much of his story was true, and that was what was significant. So far as they had got, which was not far, the rest of his story was true, at least in its factual elements. He had been named co-executor with Andrew Gordon of the estate left by his sister, and Gordon's wife. The will did provide that the principal go to Dan Gordon on his twenty-fifth birthday. The rest of it was more obscure and would require further enquiry—laborious, careful enquiry by accountants. Presumably this enquiry would show that the estate had wasted badly; if Nickerson Smith had a motive for lying about that the motive was surpassingly obscure. The enquiry might show that Gordon had lost the money; whether by financial incompetence, bad luck or chicanery there might be a way of telling. It might show that the fault—if there had been fault—was Smith's. His motive for lying at that point need not be obscure.

Weigand conjured a picture of Smith into his mind. A solid, substantial man with a square face and a habit of looking at people he spoke to with an unwavering gaze. He had bristling gray hair—or did he have? The picture was not clear. Weigand passed the detail and sought the general effect. The general effect was a substantial businessman in his middle fifties, with no noticeable peculiarities. There was an additional factor to be considered—Mrs. Gerald North openly preferred him as the murderer. Weigand was impartial as he considered this; he weighed Pam's insight—if insight was what you called it, and Bill Weigand had given up being sure—against the facts. Pam had been right in the past. She had also been wrong. Her average was good. But the facts were against her.

Nickerson Smith was tempting, because you could give him a

motive. But he was, so far as Weigand could see, unobtainable. Weigand dismissed the mental image of Nickerson Smith, put the report on him in the file basket and regarded the report on Mrs. Andrew Gordon. It was, he decided as he read it, rather interesting.

A waiter captain at Longchamps had been found who believed, without certainty, that he remembered Mrs. Gordon lunching there, coming in at some time around one. The picture they had showed him had helped. If the woman he was thinking of was Mrs. Gordon, it was true that she had seemed, at first, to be waiting for somebody. But, still if he was thinking of the right woman, she had not, as she said, waited fruitlessly. About ten minutes after she arrived—this was always if the woman the waiter captain was thinking of, was the woman they wanted him to think of—she had been joined by a man. The waiter captain did not go beyond that. There was a man and that was the end of it. It could be presumed that the waiter would have noticed if he had been an Indian with feathers, or an Indian with a turban. Failing these peculiarities, he was merely a gentleman who had joined a lady for lunch.

But, even so vaguely established, it was interesting. Presuming the waiter captain was remembering Mrs. Gordon, and Weigand thought he was, she had had a companion at the luncheon she had pictured as solitary. Her husband, after all? Or the tweed-covered Westcott? Or someone else? If it had been Dr. Gordon, it would be very interesting indeed.

From the restaurant she had, as she had said, gone to a Madison Avenue shop. There was no question about it this time; she was known there—and she had bought dresses for a little girl and had them mailed to an address in North Salem. But—and again this evidence was more assured—she had not been alone. There had been a man with her. He had merely stood and waited, not taking part in her decisions among the dresses offered. But he had certainly been there. And, as certainly, he remained vague. Again he was merely a man. Apparently, he had been unassertive, whatever—and whoever—he might have been. Dr. Gordon? But would he not have been interested in helping to pick out clothes for his little girl? Westcott? Or, again, somebody new?

And, after the shop which sold the dresses, Mrs. Gordon had gone to another shop which had sold her a hat. There was no doubt of the identification here. And, this time, she had mailed back to North Salem the hat she had been wearing and put on the new hat. But—this time there had been no man. They were sure of that at the shop. If there had been a man, it appeared, they would have noticed him.

The rest of the report made the already known, official. Bill Weigand tossed the report into the file basket. There would be some new questions to ask Mrs. Gordon, when next she was asked questions.

Dan Gordon came next. The reports added little, as far as his actions went, to what they already knew—and did not either contradict or confirm what they had been told. Young Gordon had spent Sunday night at the Harvard Club and had left early. The elevator starter in the office building had said "oh yes, sure" when shown Gordon's picture, and had remembered seeing him come in some time between nine and ten—and remembered that he came down again a little later.

The same starter had remembered him coming into the lobby again, he thought a little before one, with a very pretty girl and thought they had stopped for a few moments to talk, letting one elevator go up without them. But this memory was vague; the starter supposed they had gone up together but, pressed, he admitted that this was only a supposition. "May just figure that people who come into the lobby always do go up," the precinct detective who had made the investigation noted. At any rate, it appeared that Dan Gordon had not loitered, obviously, in the lobby waiting for his father to come down. But the lobby was busy, with offices emptying and refilling at the lunch hour. He might easily have hung around, unnoticed. Queried as to whether he had seen Dr. Gordon come down, the elevator starter threw up his hands. If it had been a little after one, then he had come with a swarm. There were outgoing swarms at a few minutes after twelve, minor swarms half an hour later, returning and departing swarms just before and just after one. That Dan Gordon was noticed at all was because his arrival, with the pretty girl, was during a comparatively slack period in lobby traffic. Which checked, Bill Weigand reflected. And the rest—proved nothing.

The Army in Washington, reacting to an urgent plea, confirmed and amplified what had been partially a guess. Dan Gordon had served as an infantryman in the ETO for two years, and had been around. He had been around where it was thick and he had been good—good enough to be commissioned in the field just before the German collapse. And there had been nothing wrong with him; he had been wounded once and had recovered and been sent back, and thereafter there had been nothing wrong with him. Then, in midsummer, when they were merely sweating it out, he had, unexpectedly, cracked up.

This was unusual, but not unprecedented. Almost nothing was unprecedented among the things which could happen to combat soldiers in a war like that. Gordon had been hospitalized and, in the course of time, returned to the States. Combat fatigue, but the prognosis had always been good. He had responded normally; late in the previous autumn he had been released from the hospital and, at his own request, from the Army. It was to be expected, the Army psychiatrists indicated, that he would continue to improve and that, within a year, he would be entirely normal. No treatment was indicated; time and peace could be expected to take care of things.

Bill Weigand made a note, tossed the report on Dan Gordon into the file basket and looked at his watch. After three, now. He ran a hand again across his tired eyes. He sat for a moment looking at nothing, tapping the top of his desk. He went back to it.

There was a brief report on Deborah Brooks—a report consonant with the brevity of her life. It seemed to tell them nothing the girl had not told them; it told them less—"said to be engaged D. Gordon" was an almost absurd summary of what her eyes said—what her whole face said—when she looked at "D. Gordon"; of what her foolish, impulsive actions had told them that afternoon and night. The report on Grace Spencer was longer, but it, too, told less than they knew. There was no hint in it of what the girl—whose body was now lying somewhere under glaring lights; was now no longer sentient, but merely a fact in an investigation—had revealed when she dropped her head on her arms after she had answered their questions and sobbed with a kind of hopelessness.

There was nothing on Lawrence Westcott, the attentive neighbor.

Nothing had been known of Westcott when the Police Department—which meant unhurried, ingenious men in ordinary clothes, turning things over methodically—had started that community effort which would not end until, somewhere, at some time, a jury said: "We find the defendant guilty—" of whatever they found the defendant guilty of. In this instance, Weigand supposed, murder in the first degree would have to be the answer. Because of the nurse.

That would hang somebody—or send electricity through somebody. Not even Dan Gordon would beat a conviction on that. (The chair was another matter; in the end he would almost as certainly not go to the chair.) You could imagine circumstances which would make the first killing merely manslaughter. In connection with Dan Gordon, you could imagine those circumstances with little difficulty. But it would take stretching—very expert stretching, by a very expert defense—to make uncontrollable irritation, or whatever psychiatry chose to call it, cover the killing of Grace Spencer.

He was thinking a good deal of Dan Gordon, Weigand realized. It fitted very well; it was the way to play it. Which would, Bill Weigand realized, not suit Mrs. Gerald North. Bill smiled involuntarily when he thought of Mrs. Gerald North. It was too bad they weren't going to be able to work things out for her; work them out so Debbie Brooks and Dan Gordon had a chance to live happily ever after. But the chances were they weren't.

If there is much more of this, Weigand thought, blinking his eyes, it would have to go over until morning. He looked at his watch again. Morning was now; it would have to go over until he had slept a little. But there shouldn't be much more of it.

There were five reports clipped together. Those would be the reports on the afternoon compensation cases. There should be six. A note explained that. Two efforts had been made to talk to Robert Oakes, who lived on the East Side, not far from Stuyvesant Square. Oakes had not been at home. Another attempt would be made later.

The men who had been at home were Henry Flint, Fritz Weber, John Dunnigan, George Cooper and Jose Garcia. All agreed that they had been at the office the day before; all had employments and all argued that their work had led to eye ailments for which the insurance company should pay; all had been examined by Dr. Gordon for the first—and, as it turned out, the last—time that day. And even detectives, always suspicious in accordance with regulations, had found nothing about any of the five to connect them, in other than the most casual fashion, with Dr. Andrew Gordon. To them he had been a name and an address, and a time of day, handed them on a slip of paper; he had been an abstraction of science, wearing a white coat. On what he noted down on cards depended their immediate futures—perhaps more. But he, himself, was impersonal. Only what he wrote mattered.

Presumably these men varied—they were tall and short, they had beliefs which were all the more intense for being muddled, they had at some time loved, or hated, according to their capacities; some of them might be alive thirty years from now and some of them might die within a week. In their past lives, or in those they might live, there were, it was conceivable, the seeds of other murders. The police might meet them again, and would not entirely have forgotten them. Their names would be in files, somewhere, and might turn up. They might get themselves run over. Or they might drive through traffic lights. Then it might appear that, once, murder had brushed them.

But, so far as the reports Bill Weigand tossed into the file basket showed, it had this time only brushed them.

That, for now, was the size of it. Bill thought of Dorian. She would be asleep, now, relaxed and quiet. But there would be a dim light in the bedroom, because she always kept a dim light on when he was not at home. If he could go home she would awaken, without surprise—merely opening her greenish eyes slowly—and look at him and then, after a moment of gravity, she would smile and say something to him, using a language which was nobody's business but their own.

"Damn!" Bill Weigand said. He went out of his office, down a corridor and into a small room which could have stood another window. Mullins was asleep on one of the two cots; he was not as ornamental asleep—or in any other condition, come to think of it—as Dorian. Bill undressed, sufficiently, and lay down on the other cot.

Now what the hell did Grace Spencer know? Bill wondered. What had she seen when she returned from lunch and made her check on the empty examining rooms and waited to call the doctor to meet his patients at three? Had she seen something and decided not to tell it, and then, perhaps, changed her mind, too late? Or had the significance of something she had seen impressed itself on her, again, too late? There was the crux of it—there was the crux of both cases.

Sergeant Mullins snored once, resonantly. Bill Weigand said "Damn!" again and turned his back to Mullins and after a little while he went to sleep.

• 7 •

TUESDAY, 8:30 A.M. TO 12:07 P.M.

The story was prominent in the newspapers. It was prominent in the *Herald-Tribune,* which Mrs. North read. It was prominent in the *Times,* around which Mr. North reached groping for his cup of coffee. Martini tossed a wadded cigarette package into the air, jumped straight up after it and came down twisted, with her tail and back bristling. She made a lunge for it, paused suddenly to scratch her right ear, and then batted it to Pam North's feet. Martini sat and looked at Pam expectantly. Ignored, Martini spoke. She put out a paw and touched Pam's nearest leg.

"Last pair of stockings, Teeney," Pam said, in a reasonable tone. "Don't."

"What?" Jerry North said. "Say something?"

"Stockings," Pam said. "Last pair. The *Herald-Tribune* didn't get North Salem in."

"No?" Jerry said, pleased. "The *Times* did. New lead." He read it to her. "Police of Westchester County and New York today were investigating the apparently linked murders of Dr. Andrew Gordon, widely known oculist, slain yesterday in his office in the Medical Chambers, and of Grace Spencer, his nurse, beaten to death hours later at the Gordon home near North Salem, in Westchester County," Jerry read. He paused. "A mouthful," he added. "Ouch!"

"What?" Pam said.

"Teeney," Jerry said. "The *Herald-Trib* hasn't got the nurse?"

"It's an earlier edition," Pam said, defensively. "We usually get an earlier edition of it. Don't!"

Martini, deciding that Pam's leg offered the greater responsiveness, had returned to it. Martini made comment, deep in her throat, comprehensible only to herself.

"And don't talk Siamese," Pam said. "Talk cat."

"Yah," Martini said, drawing it out.

Nobody answered her. She kicked the wadded cigarette package aside, ran after it, jumped on it, smelled it, and wandered back, talking low in her throat. Still nobody paid attention. Seemingly without effort, almost absent-mindedly, she floated to the top of the breakfast table.

"No!" Pam North said. "No, Martini!"

Martini could ignore with anybody. She moved, delicately, to the cream pitcher, looked quickly at Pam, and hurriedly put her face in it.

"No!" said Pam, explosively.

Martini did everything at once. Her head came out of the pitcher, her fur bristled and she got under way. It was all one movement. It took the cream pitcher with it for an instant, and left the pitcher on its side, cream spreading. Martini landed in the cream she had spilled. Infuriated, she went up and over Jerry North, sailed to the windowsill and bounced to a chest. She stopped there, shook her feet one after another, looked at the Norths with an expression of hurt astonishment, said "Yah!" with anger and began to lick her feet. As she licked them, she began again to make the low, throaty noise.

"I do wish," Pam said, mopping up the cream, "that you wouldn't let her on the table."

"*I* wouldn't!" Jerry said, mopping cream tracks off his shoulder with a napkin. "*I—*" He ended, baffled. He tried again. "Listen," he said, "it was your leg she was at. Not mine."

"No discipline," Pam said. "That's the real trouble. No discipline at all. Poor Teeney."

She went over to Teeney, who stopped licking her left hind foot, but remained in position. "Poor Teeney," Pam said. "Nobody tells her anything."

She stroked Martini's head. Martini purred briefly and called attention to the fact that she still had a foot to lick. There would be time later, Martini indicated, for head rubbing.

"Which reminds me," Pam said, coming back and sitting down at the table again. "What was Grace Spencer going to tell?"

Jerry put his *Times* down, looked at the empty toast plate, said, "oh" mildly, and pointed out that they did not know that Grace Spencer had been going to tell anybody anything.

"As good as," Pam said. "Otherwise why?"

"Why go there?" Jerry said. "Or why killed?"

"They're both the same thing," Pam told him. "Part of the same thing. She remembered something and was going to tell Bill—no, she didn't know Bill was there, did she?"

"I shouldn't think so," Jerry said.

"Then Dan Gordon," Pam said. "Or the wife. So that they could take it up with the police. What?"

"She saw young Gordon come back with his father between two and three," Jerry said, promptly. "She saw Mrs. Gordon having lunch with a gangster and paying him money. She saw somebody—Smith—say, carrying the doctor out of the last examining room, and began to think, later, that there was something a little strange about it. She saw Debbie having lunch with Westcott and urging him to do something to—I can't finish that one."

"To kill Dr. Gordon, who was keeping her under hypnosis for his own evil ends," Pam said. "Anybody can finish any of them if you want to make it easy. What did she really have to tell?"

Jerry discovered cream that he had missed, and rubbed at it, dampening his napkin in his glass of water. He shook his head.

"Two times," Pam said. "When he was going out, before lunch. After she came back from lunch and before she found the body. One or the other."

Jerry shook his head again.

"Any time between the doctor's return from the hospital and the time she found the body," he corrected. "Something she saw or heard, either one. You can't shut out the time she was at lunch. It's quite possible she ran across something then."

Pam considered; she nodded. He was making it harder, she said. But you couldn't get away from it.

"Actually," she said, "you know what I think?"

"Good God, no," Jerry said.

Pam ignored this.

"I still think it was something she saw when he was leaving," she said.

"I know," Jerry told her. "Because people who are about to be murdered look different from people who aren't. It—shows in their faces."

"Well," Pam said, "I should think they'd be worried." She looked at Jerry and smiled quickly and shook her head before he could speak. "No," she said. "Really. Because murders are the end of something else, almost always. They don't just—just come out of a clear sky. They come out of circumstances—worrying circumstances. And the victim is worried too, just as much as the murderer." She paused. "Oh," she said, "differently, I suppose. But you don't just get up all bright and cheery in the morning, all's right with the world, and get murdered at eight A.M. with the orange juice."

Jerry said he saw what she meant, although he thought her example badly chosen.

"Everybody's worried in the morning," he said. "It's the natural state of man. Particularly at what would be about seven thirty. Unless he didn't take his shower."

"What?" Pam said. "Oh. That's frivolous."

All their guessing was frivolous, Jerry told her. Any guessing when you had nothing to go on was frivolous.

"And," he said, "I've got to see an author about a contract. You know what they want now? Control of reprints." He stood up and sighed. "Authors used to be milder in the old days."

"And, to be honest, broker," Pam said. "Did you ever hear of a publisher dying in a garret?"

"Thousands," Jerry assured her. Pam looked doubtful.

"Anyway," she said, "I think that Dr. Gordon probably looked worried, because he was going to be murdered. Or was in a hurry, as if he had an appointment. Or said something that didn't mean anything at the time, but did afterward."

"Like 'we who are about to die'—?" Jerry said.

Pam stood up, too.

"Go see about the contract," she said.

Jerry came around the table and kissed her. He said she tasted of jam. "Very nice," he said, consideringly. "Strawberry."

"Black raspberry," Pam told him. "Lunch?"

Jerry said he would call her up.

"You'll be here?" he said, getting his hat off the sofa.

Pam North looked vague, suddenly.

"Look," she said, "suppose I call you? About noon? And then we can go to Charles early, because otherwise they're full up and it's so embarrassing for Hugo. And we have to have two drinks while we're waiting and sometimes I wonder whether they're good for us."

Jerry looked at her, not without suspicion.

"Look," he said, "you're not going to be here. Right?"

Pam told him he sounded like Bill.

"Listen, Pam," Jerry said, "wouldn't it be fun just to let Bill do it? For—for a change? Instead of leading with that agreeable chin?"

"Jerry," Pam said. "You *can* say nice things."

She kissed him, and this time he did not think of jam. He was still not thinking of jam when he remembered, as he got out of the elevator, that Pam had not, even remotely, agreed not to lead with her chin.

It had been hardly any trouble at all to get the names and addresses she wanted from Sergeant Mullins, although he talked at some length, and anxiously, about the inspector. Pam had had a twinge of conscience at circumventing Bill Weigand, but she paid no attention to it and obediently went away. She had more trouble circumventing Martini, who, chagrined that Jerry had escaped while she was giving a final polish to the right rear leg, was determined to block the escape of the one who smelled different, but did supply food when sharply spoken to. Pam backed out again—and almost bumped into a very surprised young man she had never seen before—but she caught Martini in the air as the little cat sprang, put her back and closed the door firmly after pushing out of it one hopeful, enquiring paw. This time, however, there was no taxicab. She waited ten minutes on the curb of Sixth Avenue, under a sign which called it "Avenue of the Americas," and then was forced to take a bus.

Four of the addresses she had were in Manhattan, one was in Harlem and the sixth was—distantly, she feared—in Brooklyn. She would take the Manhattan ones first and then Harlem and then, if her strength and time lasted, the distant Brooklynite. The first, she decided, was the one in West Fiftieth, beyond Ninth Avenue.

It was a tenement and the one she wanted was on the fifth floor. It was a long way up; above the third floor the narrow wooden stairway sagged away from the wall, so that walking up it one instinctively hugged the wall and fought against a tendency to slip outward. "Some day," Pam thought, "fire will go up these stairs and—and spread out at the top." She shivered. The fifth floor was the top; that would be where the fire would mushroom. The air was staler there than it had been below, where a sometimes-opened door let dead air out. But there was a glimmer from a dirty skylight above the stairwell—a skylight ideally situated, Pam thought, to provide a draft for the fire. She picked out one of the doors and knocked, and the door opened almost immediately. At first there seemed no reason for this response, and then Pam looked down.

"Hello, dear," she said, looking into round brown eyes, "is your father Mr. Dunnigan?"

"I'm Mabel," the little girl said, each word formed carefully on small lips. "Mabel Dunnigan. Who are you?"

"I'm Pamela North," Mrs. North said.

"That's a funny name," Mabel told her. "Goodbye."

She started to shut the door.

"You mean 'hello,' dear," Mrs. North said. "Hello, Mabel."

"I mean goodbye," Mabel said. "They're different woids. Goodbye."

"Words," Pam said. "But I want to see your father, Mabel. I—"

A woman came out of a door into the inner corridor of the flat. She picked Mabel up and held her under an arm. The woman was taller than Pam by a good deal, and heavier by more. She looked down.

"Whatever it is," the woman said, "we don't want it. My husband's sick."

"I know," Pam said. "I want to see him. About yesterday. About Dr. Gordon."

"There was a cop here," the woman said. "You from a paper?"

"No," Pam said. "I—"

"You're sure not a cop," the woman said, looking at Pam.

"In a way," Pam said. "I help Lieutenant Weigand." She looked at the woman. "And Sergeant Mullins," she said, making it stronger.

A man's voice came out of the room the woman had left.

"Who is it?" the voice said. "Mabel! Who is it?"

"Some woman says she's from the police," the woman said, and raised her voice. "I said you'd seen the police."

"Well, bring her in," the man's voice said. The woman looked at Pam, made a gesture with her head, and stood out of the way, still holding little Mabel.

"She's pretty," Pam said, moving in. "Sweet. Hello, Mabel."

"Goodbye," Mabel said, still under her mother's arm. The woman said nothing, but she smiled. It was a worried smile, but it was there.

John Dunnigan was sitting in a morris chair by a window which opened on an airshaft. He half got up when Pam went in. The room was unlighted; gray light came in unwillingly from the window, but Dunnigan faced away from it. When her eyes were adjusted to the gloom, Pam saw that his eyes were red and swollen.

"If you're from the police," Dunnigan said, "I've told everything I know. Which is nothing. The doc was all right when he finished with me. I went out and came home."

He spoke as if he had planned it; had it ready.

"We know he was all right," Pam said. "That is, we know he was alive, Mr. Dunnigan. That isn't what I want."

"Well?" Dunnigan said. His eyes blinked when he looked at her. They were bloodshot.

"It's hard to say," Pam North said. "Had you ever been examined by him before?"

Dunnigan shook his head.

"Then maybe you wouldn't know," Pam said. "What I want is—something odd. Something out of the ordinary. Was he nervous? Excited? Anything like that. As if, say, he'd just got bad news? Or heard something—frightening? But you don't know how he usually was, do you?"

Dunnigan blinked at her. Then he shook his head again.

"To tell you the truth, lady, I didn't pay much attention," he said. "He was just the doc. You know?"

"Just somebody looking at your eyes," Pam said.

"Sure," Dunnigan said. "All I wanted to know was, when could I go back to work? Do I get the insurance money?"

That was natural, Pam told him.

"Sure," he said. "That's what any guy would be interested in. Outside of that, I didn't pay much attention."

"He wasn't nervous, that you noticed?" Pam said. "Or anything?"

"Nope," Dunnigan said.

Pam North said nothing. She waited.

"I told the detective all about it," Dunnigan said. "What there was. I heard him moving around in the next room. Then he came in and shut the door. I said 'hello, doc' and he said 'hello.' Then he sat down on the stool and told me to look at a place on the wall and turned on a light and looked at my eyes. He made me look this way and that way and then he wrote something down on my card and that was all."

"He didn't say anything?"

"Sure. He said, 'Don't worry, mister'—and, then he looked at the card and said, 'Dunnigan, I'll get in touch with your doctor. Leave the card here as you go.'"

"That was all?"

"Sure. He went on into the next room and I got up and got out of there. Went down a sort of hall and—"

"By the way," Pam said, "how did you know to go out that way?"

"Nurse told me, when she told me to go in the room," Dunnigan said. "She said something about when I went out, go down the corridor and turn right and I'd find a door. Sure enough."

Sure enough he had, Pam interpreted.

"And nothing—strange?" Pam said.

"Not as I noticed," Dunnigan said. "If there was, I wouldn't know, lady."

Mrs. North stood up.

"Oh, by the way," she said, "which room were you in?"

"Third from the end," Dunnigan said.

Pamela North turned to go. Small Mabel was standing in the door of the room and Pam smiled at her.

"Goodbye, Mabel," Pam said.

"Hello," Mabel said.

Really, Pam thought, as, outside the flat, she started down the canted stairs, it can't be me altogether. It must be the little girl, this time. There's simply no pleasing her.

Pam went on down. She was disappointed, and almost inclined to give the whole thing up. Whatever it was she had vaguely hoped for— and she had to admit to herself that her hopes could hardly have been vaguer—she had not got. Like Teeney the time she had jumped for Jerry's leg, intending to climb to his shoulder, and Jerry had moved at the same moment. Like Teeney when she went sailing through unoccupied air, with a blank look on her masked face.

"Well, what do you want?" Henry Flint, occupant of Room No. 5 the previous afternoon at Dr. Andrew Gordon's office, demanded. He was uncompromising. He stood at the door of his furnished room in the far West Eighties and bristled. He was hardly taller than Pam herself; he was square and broad shouldered and he looked as if something had recently disagreed with him. Me, Pam thought; I disagree with him. But probably lots of things do.

"Who're you?" Henry Flint demanded. "You don't look like a cop." He looked at her again. "Or a do-gooder," he said. "What do you want?"

He did not leave the door.

Pam North, speaking as briefly as she could, told him what she wanted. Not so concisely—a little confusedly, even—she told him who she was. It might have been understood that Mrs. North, while not exactly a cop, was not exactly not a cop either.

"Hell," Henry Flint said. "Nothing strange. Is it strange to get kicked around? Is it strange to have some big shot treat a workingman like he was a animal? Like he was trying to grab something off, when all he wanted was to get what was coming to him? What the big shots were trying to gyp him out of? What's strange about that, huh?"

"Well," Pam said.

"Like I was inanimate," Flint told her, still standing in the door and bristling at her. "Like I was too low to have any feelings, see? That's your Doctor Gordon or whatever his name is."

"Was," Pam said. "He's dead."

"All right," Flint said. "So he's dead. Teach him to push good Americans around, that will."

"Well," Pam said, involuntarily. "I doubt it."

"What?" Flint said. He seemed really to look at her for the first time.

"I doubt that being dead will teach him to stop pushing Americans around," Pam said. "I doubt that it will teach him anything, particularly."

"Now you said something," Flint told her. "Now you sure said something. You an atheist?"

"No," Pam said, "Not particularly. Why?"

"Sure you are," Flint told her. "When you're dead you're dead. Nobody can teach you nothing. There you said something. Come in, why don't you?"

He moved away from the door and let Pam in.

"Do you good to see the way a workingman lives," Flint said, with animus. "Ain't pretty, is it?"

It was neither pretty nor, arrestingly, unpretty. It was clean and bare; it was without character. But the window opened above the street, and spring air came into it.

"Actually," Pam said, "I think it's rather comfortable, Mr. Flint."

"'Comfortable,' she says," Flint repeated. "'Comfortable,' she calls it. Would you like to live here, lady? That's all—would you like to live here?"

"No," Pam said. "But it wouldn't kill me. Or make me so terribly sorry for myself."

"Who's sorry for whose self?" Flint said. "You ain't talking about me, lady. I'll get what's coming to me. They can't kick me around."

They seemed to go in circles, Pam thought. People so often did. They remained standing inside the room and Flint's eyes—black eyes, she thought—blazed at her. There seemed to be nothing wrong with them, outwardly.

"Listen, Mr. Flint," Pam North said, "I don't want to argue with you. All I came for was to find out if Dr. Gordon acted strange when you saw him yesterday. As if—as if something had gone wrong. As if he expected to be murdered."

Flint looked at her carefully.

"Scared?" he said. "People like that doc ain't scared. They don't know what's coming. He was broos-kue."

"What?" Pam said. "Oh. Broos-kue, of course. But not frightened?"

"Took about two minutes with me, he did," Flint said. "Like I was a animal. No proper examination. Didn't even have me take my coat off."

Pam North shook her head slightly and, for some reason, reminded herself of Jerry.

"Coat off?" she said. "To look at your eyes?"

"How did he know it was just eyes?" Flint demanded. "Didn't take the trouble to find out. Just looked at my eyes through a little metal thing and said, 'Don't worry, Mr. Flint. I'll contact your doctor,' and went on to the next sucker. You call that a proper examination?"

"Did he really say 'contact'?" Pam asked.

"Why not?" Flint said. "What's wrong with it?" He seemed sincerely puzzled.

"Nothing, I guess," Pam said. "You feel that he gave you an—an inadequate examination? Cursory?"

"Like I was a animal," Flint said. "Like I was a—" He caught himself just in time, but Pam could see the participle which had formed on his lips. "Animal," he ended, rather halfheartedly.

"Then," Pam said, "you thought he was hurried. Not bothering to give you a real examination. Just—going through the motions? That was what I wanted, really. Something strange?"

"What's strange about it?" Flint said, with renewed animus. "They're all together, ain't they? Push guys around. Gyp them out of what's coming to them. Treat them like they were animals. What'ud you expect?"

"Then," Pam said, carefully, "you don't think there was anything out of the ordinary about the way he acted?"

"Didn't you hear what I said?" Flint demanded. "He rushes in, gives me a quick once-over with my coat on, writes something down and kicks me out. Takes about thirty seconds. Is that any way to examine a man?"

"Really, I don't know, Mr. Flint," Pam said. "I'm not a doctor."

"Doctors!" Flint said, disposing of them. "What else you want to know?"

"Nothing," Pam said. "Thank you, Mr. Flint." She turned toward the door and stopped. "By the way," she said, "not that it makes any difference. Are you a Communist?"

Flint glared at her. There was rage in his eyes.

"Me?!" he said. He almost shouted it. "Me a Commie?" His face was red with anger. "Watch out who you call a Commie, lady. Just watch out. Dirty foreign—"

His voice pursued Pamela North down the first of the flights of stairs which led to the street.

"Well!" Pam said to herself. She did not know whether she was disappointed or not, this time. Mr. Flint was baffling.

Fritz Weber was small and quiet, he was almost apologetic. His eyes were invisible behind dark glasses; his voice was soft and resigned. His wife, who let Pam in, had been crying. She was a small, gray woman and her eyes were red from crying. Both of the Webers, Pam thought, were in their late fifties. Their little apartment near Stuyvesant Square—their very neat, clean little apartment—seemed to have been lived in for a good many years. Mrs. Weber met Pam North at the door, and it was so dim in the apartment, so quiet, that Pam suddenly felt embarrassingly vigorous—discordantly bright and alive. She told Mrs. Weber who she was and, as nearly as she could, why she had come.

"The police?" Mrs. Weber said. "I'm sure I don't know what my husband— A detective was here yesterday." She paused. "He said he was a detective," she said, doubtfully, almost as if she were apologizing.

Pam explained again. She was not a detective; she was a friend of a detective. The position did not seem entirely clear even to Pam as again she tried to explain. She was looking for an oddity, not even knowing that an oddity existed. But she was trying to find out—to help find out—who had killed Dr. Andrew Gordon. And Mrs. Weber asked her to come in.

"Doctor was a good man," she said. "I'm sorry about doctor."

Fritz Weber was sitting in a chair; he sat with odd, careful precision. His arms did not rest on the chair arms; they were tight against his sides. He was looking straight ahead of him and he seemed to be waiting. But when his wife and Pam North came in he turned his head toward them and there was, then, a personal quality in his waiting. He was polite, in his quiet; he even smiled a little.

"This lady, Fritzl," Mrs. Weber said, and Weber began to nod. He spoke and his voice was soft and patient.

"I heard, mama," he said. "I heard very well. She has come about doctor."

"Yes," Pam said. "About Dr. Gordon."

"He was a good man," Weber said. "He could do nothing. For me he could do nothing. But he was a good man. I will tell you. It was a piece of steel. I was a toolmaker and there was a piece of steel. In my right eye. A very small piece of steel and the other doctor took it out. But it did not go well. Even after he took it out, it did not go well."

"I'm sorry," Pam said. "I'm very sorry, Mr. Weber."

"Yes," Weber said. "Thank you. So he—the other doctor—sent me to Dr. Gordon. And it was not the small piece of steel. There had been the small piece of steel, but it was not that. It was a disease. It did not have anything to do with the piece of steel. And there was nothing doctor could do."

"Oh!" Pam said. "I'm—" It seemed futile to say, again, that she was sorry. But Mr. Weber waited politely. When she did not go on, he nodded and smiled a little.

"Yes," he said. "I can see—I can understand—that you are sorry. It is—unpleasant to hear such things. Naturally. Doctor also was sorry. He said he wished he could say it was the small piece of steel. So that I would receive the insurance, you know. But he said he could not say that. Doctor was an honest man, so he could not say that. It was a disease, not the small piece of steel."

Pam said, "Oh!" again, realizing what the quiet little man was telling her. There had been an injury, which would have meant compensation. But what was wrong was not the injury; Dr. Gordon had not been able to attribute it to the injury.

"It will be a long time?" she said. "Before—I mean—" She broke off again.

"It will be always," Mr. Weber said. "In a few weeks, I will not see anything. Now there is only a little light. And shadows. In a few weeks—shadows."

The little man had dignity. He stated a fact.

"Even the doctor I did not see clearly," he said. "That is what you wanted to know? He was a shadow. And, of course, I could hear his voice. He was sorry about what he had to tell me."

"His voice," Pam said. "It was—there wasn't anything odd about it? Anything you wouldn't have expected? As if he were—oh, nervous? Worried?"

"No," Mr. Weber said. "I do not think he was worried. He was sorry he had to give me bad news after he examined my eyes. He told me to come home and—wait. He gave me the name of some people to see afterward. People who—he said there were things—work—one could do afterward. He said I should come and see him again in a week or two, although he did not think there was anything he could do. Doctor was an honest man."

"I'm—" Pam said. "I wish there were something I could do."

"You are good," Mr. Weber said. "Isn't she good, mama? But there is nothing." He paused. After a time he said, "Things happen."

Pam went, then; she made small, half-phrased sounds to Mrs. Weber and it seemed to her, grotesquely, that Mrs. Weber was comforting her. She left the little apartment, and its faded neatness, and Mr. Weber, waiting in the dusk for darkness. This time, she thought, I got more than I asked for. And then, against her will, she realized how much more she had got than she had asked for. It didn't fit, all her emotions told her; it did not fit, all that she believed to be true about the aging, beaten people she had left. Humanly, it was unbelievable. But her mind stopped her there. About people little was really unbelievable; about people you had met but once you merely thought, without remotely knowing, that things were hard to believe.

Shut the people out of it. Make Mr. Weber merely a name. Turn him from a small, waiting man into a designation on a police file, and it was different. Then you had a man with a motive; with, she thought, the best motive they had found. Suppose his quiet was bitterness; suppose that repeated "honest" used to describe Dr. Gordon was bitter irony. Because what it amounted to was this—Dr. Gordon had ruled not only against Fritz Weber's eyesight. He had, at the same time, ruled against the money which might have palliated blindness. He had said that the shop accident, which would be covered by the workman's compensation law, was not the cause of what was wrong with Fritz Weber's eyes. He had not stretched a point, as perhaps he might have. However sorry he had been, he had told Weber that his blindness was to be without recompense, while having it in his power to say something else. Men had been bitterly, violently hated for less. It was likely that men had been killed for less. And you could not guess what flaming hatred, what violence, there might be in even the smallest and quietest of men.

Pam North wished that she had not visited the Webers. She did not want to put into Bill Weigand's mind what she would have to put there.

* * *

It was noon, and before very long she should call Jerry. Perhaps, Pam thought, she ought to give the whole thing up and call Jerry now. She didn't really want to see any more people. Not after the Webers. It would be simpler to let the rest of it go, and it would please Jerry, who would think—if he knew about it—that she should have let all of it go, from the start.

But on the other hand, Robert Oakes lived very near. She could walk to the address on Second Avenue which was Oakes's, and it was foolish to be so near and not finish things off, since she had gone this far. She hesitated outside the building on Stuyvesant Square and then, as if she had flipped a coin in her mind, turned and walked toward Second Avenue. Her heels clicked on the pavement. She walked as if she were under orders.

Robert Oakes, No. 2 examining room, lived in a five-story tenement which had been reconverted. It was now of yellow brick instead of red. It had an entrance two steps down instead of several steps up. Pam pressed a downstairs bell, waited, pressed it again and tried the door. The door was unlocked. She went up a rebuilt stairway; a fireproofed anachronism, surrounded by inflammable walls. Mr. Oakes lived on the third floor—third floor rear. And, as she climbed, Pam North realized that probably he wasn't at home. People who were at home answered their bells.

She reached the third floor and went back down the hallways toward a door at the end. She was about ten feet from the doorway when something happened which was surprising and which was afterward difficult to describe. There was nothing in the hallway, except much used air, and yet something picked her up in gigantic, amorphous hands and threw her backward.

There was a feeling of being struck, but of being struck everywhere at once, and at the same time there was a tremendous roar and things began to come apart around her. The door she was looking at disintegrated while she still saw it, and while she was still throwing her hands up to protect her face. Then there was movement and a sudden, jarring, interruption of movement and a sharp pain in her left shoulder, which cut through a general feeling of terror and lesser pain. And then blackness swirled in around her and poured over her, except that at the last moment there was a red glow to the darkness.

"My," Pam said, "that blew up in my face. My, that blew up in my face. My that—" And then, although she tried to stop she could hear herself giggling. "It isn't me because I don't giggle," Pam said, "but it certainly blew up in my face. My but it—"

• 8 •

TUESDAY, 1:20 P.M. TO 3 P.M.

Gerald North looked at his watch for the third time in ten minutes and said "Damn!" It was true Pam had not said definitely that she would call him. It was true she had not said, definitely, that she was going to be at home. It was true that nothing fatal had happened to her yet, and that past performance was still the best basis for a guess of present safety. It was true— The telephone rang. Jerry reached for it convulsively, knocking it from its cradle. He grabbed it, took a deep breath and said: "Yes?" Then he said, exhaling the deep breath rather suddenly, "Good. Put her on."

"Darling," Pam North said, before he could say anything. "I'm all right."

"Of course," Jerry began, and then heard her. "What do you mean you're all right?"

"But I am, really," Pam said. "Except—Jerry—you'll have to come and get me. Not that I'm not all right." The last was hurried, anxious.

"Listen," Jerry said. "Where are you? Where've you been?"

"Lots of places," Pam said. "The last one blew up. So I kept saying it blew up in my face and laughing. And so naturally, they thought I had concussion. But I haven't, really."

"Pam!" Jerry said, his voice demanding. "Where are you?"

"Now you mustn't get excited," Pam said. "Because I'm perfectly all right."

"Where are you?" Jerry said, his voice heavy.

"Well," Pam told him, "I guess you'd call it a—a sort of a hospital, Jerry. But I'm all right."

"*Pam!*" Jerry said. *"Are you all right?"*

"Look," Pam said, "I've just been telling you I'm all right. That's what I called up for. And to tell you to come and—"

"This sort of hospital," Jerry said. "What is it?"

"Well," Pam said, and she sounded reluctant. "Bellevue." She went on hastily. "Just because it was convenient, Jerry," she said. "After I got blown up." She paused, but not long enough for him to speak. "Before the building burned down," she said. "And really, it only partly burned down. The firemen were so quick."

"Pam!" Jerry said. "Are you hurt?"

If he would only listen, Pam said, she would explain it. Of course she wasn't hurt.

"Shaken," she said. "And maybe I was out for a few minutes. And there's sort of a bump. And my shoulder hurts a little, but it's just a bruise. And whatever they say, I know I haven't got concussion."

"What who says?" Jerry demanded. "For God's sake!"

"The doctor says I sound disturbed," Pam told him. "He says there isn't anything wrong, except the bump and shock, and much less shock than you'd expect. And they want the bed. But he says concussion is the only—"

"Pam," Jerry said. "Pam, darling. Start at the beginning."

"Listen, Jerry," Pam said, and she was severe with him. "That will have to wait. The beginning was Mr. Oakes, but he's dead now and so there's no hurry. And the doctor just thinks I've got concussion because I don't talk the way he expects, which is silly of him, because if I waited for him to catch up he never would. And now I've got to have some clothes, so I can leave."

Her voice sounded all right, Jerry thought—quick and clear and—yes, even now—oddly gay. So probably she was all right.

"Clothes?" he said. He paused and thought about it. "What happened to your clothes?"

"Well," Pam said, "it's a funny thing, but they sort of got—well, blown off, I guess. Anyway, when the firemen got there—" She interrupted herself and then went on, hurriedly. "Not all of them, Jerry," she said. "I still had quite a little on, really. And of course the man in the ambulance covered me up right away. But there isn't enough to go to lunch in."

"My God!" Jerry North said. "Lunch!"

"Well," Pam said, reasonably, "of course it was awful about poor Mr. Oakes. But I didn't see him, really." She considered. "Any part of him," she said. "So I'm still hungry, and the doctor says I can go if you'll bring me clothes and—wait a minute." She spoke to someone, apparently, at Bellevue Hospital. "My husband," she said. "He's bringing me some clothes." Then she came back to Jerry. "Look," she said, "they say we're tying up the line. So you go around and get me some clothes. The black dress with pockets, I think. And a slip and—no, there aren't any stockings. I'll just have to—" She lapsed, apparently, into thought. "Oh yes," she said, "and some pants, please, Jerry. Then we can go to lunch."

The odd thing was that Pam, dressed in the black dress with the pockets, looked to be in excellent health. The bump on her head did not show, under hair, but it was a good-sized bump as Jerry discovered when she guided his fingers to it. She was a little pale, perhaps; her eyes were a little larger than usual. And there was a quick lightness in her voice which showed that, under everything, she was excited and keyed up. That, the doctor told Jerry, was the aftermath of shock. She would, if she were his wife, spend a day or two in bed. ("Not if I were his wife," Pam said cryptically, when they were outside. Jerry examined that remark and, in the interest of finding out what had happened, decided not to pick it up.) And her left shoulder, she admitted, hurt when she moved her arm. But she was, she insisted, doing much better than was to be expected.

She had picked up the rest of the story at the hospital, it turned out. She gave it to Jerry firsthand up to the moment of the strange, impalpable force which hurled her from her feet, outside Robert Oakes's door. After that it was what she had pieced together.

She had arrived, by somewhat devastating coincidence, just as the pilot light on the gas stove in Oakes's tiny apartment had set off the gas which had been accumulating for, probably, some hours. It was the blast which had knocked her down—and the red tinge to the blackness had been the fire which started in the apartment. The blast had hurled her backward and sideways, so that she was brought up against the wall and banged her head. She apparently had lost consciousness then; it was when she came to in the ambulance that she kept saying, over and over, "my, it blew up in my face" and then had giggled because she thought it was funny to use that phrase about anything so literal. That together with her subsequent remarks had, Jerry concluded, led to the now-abandoned diagnosis of concussion.

Altogether, she had been extraordinarily lucky. Her clothes had been, apparently, very largely blown from her body; at least, there seemed to be nothing she thought worth salvaging, except her shoes. The firemen, who had come very quickly indeed, had found her lying in the hall, just beginning to return to consciousness, and had bundled her up and taken her to an ambulance. Then they had stopped the fire before it had much more than burned out Oakes's apartment.

Oakes's body had been broken by the explosion, and somewhat burned. But it was easily identifiable. He had been a man easy to identify—very tall, and very thin, with a small head on a long neck. (That, Pam had gathered from a precinct detective who had questioned her briefly.) But it was the theory of the police—a theory now being verified at the morgue—that neither explosion nor flame had killed Robert Oakes. He had been dead, they thought, some hours before the pilot light set off the collected gas. He had been dead of gas poisoning and there was every evidence that this was what he had planned.

"Those damn pilot lights," the detective had said. "Half the time somebody decides to bump himself off with gas he forgets the pilot light. And the whole place blows up. They never learn."

It was not entirely clear who never learned. As nearly as Pam could work it out, the detective seemed to mean that the people who committed suicide never learned. It seemed, Pam told Jerry, an odd thing to reproach them with.

The taxicab had got them to Charles by the time Pam finished her account. They decided that, in view of everything, they deserved cocktails, and they watched thirstily while Gus twirled gin, and a very little vermouth, with a great deal of ice. They beamed at Gus when he had finished and drank with thirst. Jerry, lifting the brim-filled glass, found that his hand was shaking a little.

"But why Oakes?" Jerry said then, putting the glass down on the bar. "What did he have against the doctor?"

Pam put her glass down, regarded it a moment and then turned her regard to Jerry.

"I suppose that's the simplest," she said. "Suicide before the police got him." She considered. "You'd think he'd have waited until they were—well, closer," she said. "He was in an awful hurry, if that was it."

"Panicked," Jerry suggested, and returned to his glass. "Why? Why did he kill the doctor?"

"Why," Pam said. "And how? Of course, he might have a motive like Mr. Weber's." Jerry opened his eyes and waited. She told him about Mr. Weber. "Except," she said, "it would be a rather remarkable coincidence. Two men in the same fix." She considered again; she finished her glass. "Of course," she said, "there's no denying there's another theory."

Jerry emptied his glass, looked at it, looked at Gus and raised his eyebrows and nodded toward the empty glasses, and then looked at Pam again.

"Yes," he said. "Naturally. Somebody knocked him out, turned on the gas and left him there. The same one as before. Because—well, I suppose because Oakes knew something, too." He considered that. "Our man—or woman—must have been mighty careless about who was looking," he said. Then, because Pam was looking beyond him and beginning to smile, he turned on his stool.

"Oh, hello, Bill," Jerry said. "Imagine meeting you here."

"Right," Bill said. "It's a small world." He looked beyond Jerry, and smiled. "You look very well, Pam—considering," he said. "All right. Let's have it."

Pam North let him have it. It took time; they left the bar, found a table, interrupted themselves to eat, sat with cigarettes and coffee afterward as the tempo of the restaurant slackened—as John went by from the bar to the waiters' dining room with a glass of beer in his hand, and came back from it with his hands empty; as Gus went by with his glass of beer.

"So," Pam said, "we can boil it down. Dunnigan—nothing. Flint—I don't know. He's a sorehead. Perhaps he got an offhand, hurried examination. But he'd think so anyway. Weber—he apparently got a careful, unhurried examination and learned that he was going blind. And Dr. Gordon refused—or didn't offer—to connect his blindness with an accident where he worked, so that Weber doesn't get insurance. And Oakes blew up."

Weigand nodded slowly and said, "Right."

"Actually," he said, "I don't know what you were after. Do you?"

She was, Pam told him, after something strange. Anything strange.

"Not, of course, as strange as being blown up with Mr. Oakes," she added. "That was stranger than I'd expected."

"Yes," Bill said. "Oakes. Oakes died of gas poisoning, not of the explosion. Not of the fire. And in a couple of months he would have died of cancer. Behind his right eye. So he had reason enough to turn on the gas."

Pam said "oh," and shivered.

"On the other hand," Bill said, "it is quite possible that someone got in, knocked him out and turned on the gas for him. Taking the chance, obviously, that he wouldn't recover consciousness before the gas got him. A considerable chance."

"Can't they tell?" Jerry wanted to know. Bill Weigand shook his head. He said it was doubtful, because of the damage done to the body by the explosion and, afterward, by the fire. He said they were trying to tell. He pressed a cigarette out in the ashtray and almost at once lighted another.

"The chances are he killed himself because he was sick," he said. "Not because he was guilty of murder and afraid of being caught. The chances are that Weber—you got more than we did from him, Pam—is merely the quiet, beaten little man you thought he was. But it is true we can make out a motive. The chances are that Flint is merely a sorehead, and would have complained no matter what kind of treatment he got." He paused. "The chances are that young Gordon killed his stepfather," he said. "In a fit of—'uncontrollable irritation,' call it. And has tried to cover up since."

"But," Pam said, "you aren't satisfied."

Bill Weigand smiled at her and shook his head.

"Chiefly because I can't see him killing the girl," he said. "And a guy I talked to can't. He's not very much taken with the idea that Gordon would have killed his stepfather. He's less taken with the idea he would have killed again. And he's supposed to know about that sort of thing. Combat-fatigue cases are easily irritated—sure. But he can't remember one who's been irritated enough to kill anybody. Particularly one as far along toward recovery as Gordon seems to be. But—give a motive and lack of control—well, maybe. He would hesitate to predict."

"Sounds like a doctor," Jerry said.

"Right," Bill said. "He is a doctor."

None of them said anything for a moment.

"I still wish it could be Mr. Smith," Pam said. "I think he's—ideal."

Bill smiled and shook his head. Then he said one word. "How?"

"All right," Pam said, "erase him. How about Mrs. Gordon? How about this—friend of hers?"

"Westcott," Bill said. "Lawrence Westcott."

"How about both of them?" Jerry said. "In the tradition. Wife and lover do in husband."

Bill Weigand nodded.

"That one Heimrich will buy," he said. "He'd like to buy it. And—he's beginning to think he can pay for it. Westcott and the lady went around together a good deal. Quite a good deal. Neighbors noticed. She's a lot younger than Gordon was. Westcott's nearer her age. He has more time, and apparently likes to spend it with her. And—I think he had lunch with her yesterday and went along with her on, anyway, part of her shopping trip."

"Look," Pam said, "no woman's going to buy a new hat just before she and her lover kill her husband."

Jerry shook his head at that. He didn't, he said, see why not. Women would, as far as he could see, buy hats any time.

"A pickup," he said. "Like a pill. Benzedrine. Probably very stimulating to murder."

"Jerry!" Pam said, with reproach.

Bill Weigand smiled at both of them.

"Possibly," he said, "they figured that a little shopping expedition would look very innocent, just then. That we'd figure the way Pam does."

Pamela North was not content and murmured slightly. Then she made a small motion, indicating tentative acceptance, with her shoulders.

"All right," she said. "How, then?"

That, Bill told them, was no problem—at least at the moment. There was nothing to indicate that Westcott had not been free during the crucial time. Since he was, they thought, with Mrs. Gordon, he could not obviously have any alibi except one she would give him. Which they needn't buy. Since she would presumably have a key to the back door of the offices, he presumably could get it—with her knowledge or without it. He could go in, taking a chance on being seen—ready to call the whole thing off if he was seen. He could kill Dr. Gordon in the doctor's private office, go through the examining rooms or along the corridor—probably the former, since the rooms gave cover—and go out the back door again. Taking the chance of being seen when, now, it would matter a great deal. But taking no greater chance than many murderers took. He could then meet Mrs. Gordon at some place prearranged, tell her the job was finished, send her to the office to play the shocked and grieved wife; himself go home to North Salem. Or, if she were not in it, not see her after the killing and let her shock and grief be real. Always, either way, planning to marry her and, through her, Dr. Gordon's money.

"Was there a lot of money?" Pam said. "And does he need it?"

"Plenty," Bill said. "Not particularly, as far as Heimrich's got. But that sort of checkup takes time. Just as it's taking time to find out about the trust fund—Dan Gordon's money. All we've got so far is that it's shrunk all right—just as Smith said. Smith's cooperating fully, incidentally. Shaking his head and looking shocked and saying 'tut, tut' at appropriate intervals."

"What I want to know," Pam said, "is why I don't like Mr. Smith unless it's because he's the murderer?"

They both looked at her. Jerry ran his right hand through his hair.

"*Pam!*" he said. He considered. "You don't like the way he wears his hair," he suggested. "You don't like his voice. You think he's too fat."

Pam shook her head. She said he wasn't fat. She said he wore his hair short and straight up, to which she didn't object. "Although," she said, "it makes him look a little like a brush." She guessed she just didn't like him.

"I never thought of his looking like a brush," Bill said. "However— I guess you can't have him, Pam. Alibis are a nuisance."

Bill smiled at her.

"By the way," he said, "if you want to worry about something profitable, I'll give you something. Where did Dr. Gordon's glasses go? And why did they go there?"

"Go?" Pam repeated. "Didn't they just get broken—the way glasses do?"

Bill Weigand shook his head. Not, at any rate, in Dr. Gordon's office. Because, no matter how carefully the pieces had been picked up, there would have been traces. Tiny fragments, invisible to the eye—but recoverable when the floor was cleaned properly by the police, and the dust and lint examined under microscope. And no glass had been recovered.

They thought about that for a moment.

"You know," Pam said, then. "I think somebody's going out of his way to make it hard for us."

Bill and Jerry agreed that somebody was. They pushed the table back and stood up. Then Hugo came to them to tell them that Lieutenant Weigand was wanted on the telephone. Weigand went rapidly, and the Norths less rapidly, toward the front of the restaurant. Jerry paid the check and they waited. Bill was gone only briefly.

"Mullins," he told them. "Checking on Westcott. He was with Mrs. Gordon—a girl in one of the shops identified his photograph. And—he didn't go back to his office yesterday afternoon. He left a little before one and didn't return. So—you can have him, Pam."

They went out. They picked up a newspaper at the corner of Tenth Street. The murder was below the first page fold. Near it, also below the fold, was the story of Robert Oakes's suicide. There was nothing in it about Pam North; there was reference to an as-yet-unidentified woman who had been taken to Bellevue, suffering from superficial injuries and shock. And there was a picture of Oakes and a description in some detail—a description dropped in for color. He had been very tall—well over six feet—and disproportionately thin. Everybody in the neighborhood knew him by sight. "As Chesterton once said of himself," the rewrite man had tossed in, "if they didn't know, they asked."

"Did he?" Pam said to this. "Why?"

"He was noticeable, too," Jerry said. "For other reasons. He may have said something like that. Look, it's raining."

Because it was raining, Bill Weigand took the Norths home in the police car. They, Jerry told him with determination, were going to stay at home. The office could struggle on without him. He was not certain that Pam could.

Bill grinned and waved at them and drove off. He decided to look in on the accountants who were checking on the Gordon trust.

The accountants were deep in it. They were checking figures; they were comparing lists with stock certificates and bonds from safe deposit boxes which Nickerson Smith, cooperative to the last detail, had opened for them. And the overall picture was clear—much of the money which the first Mrs. Gordon had left to her son, invested in securities as stable as human ingenuity could provide, had been reinvested in other securities—stocks, chiefly—which had lacked stability. The depression had emphasized that lack.

"Good intentions. Bad judgment," one of the accountants told Weigand. "As far as we've gone. Of course, we have to guess at the intentions. They don't have to have been good. If somebody wanted to, he could have made a nice thing out of substituting here and there—buying outright on the market—lower grade stuff. Selling the good stuff and keeping the change."

"Which could have got somebody in the clink," Weigand pointed out.

The accountant shrugged. If you could prove it, it would. Things like that were hard to prove. They might later, or might not, find something more concrete. They went back to it.

Bill Weigand left the accounts and went to Nickerson Smith's inner office. Smith was dictating to a young woman with red hair. Wiegand started to apologize, but Smith would have none of it. He stood up, and the red-haired girl stood up with him. He had a desk lighter flaring as Bill reached for a cigarette from an offered case. The case was discreet leather; the lighter a silvered mechanism set in a curve of dark green stone. The chair to which Smith gestured Weigand was deep and comfortable. Smith was very substantial, very affable. And it was true that his hair did make him look a little like a brush, as Pam had said. Weigand had not remembered that Smith was so brushlike.

"By the way," Smith said, "I don't think you've met Miss Conover." Miss Conover was the red-haired secretary. Weigand was glad to meet her; she was glad to meet Lieutenant Weigand. "I owe a good deal to Miss Conover, I imagine," Smith said, and smiled.

"Perhaps," Bill agreed. "Miss Conover is the one who—?"

"Yes," Smith said. "Alibi Conover, I think of her now." He sobered a moment. "In the end, of course, you would have found the right man," he said. "I don't doubt that. But I suspect her memory saved me—inconvenience. Am I right?"

Weigand admitted, by implication, that he might be right.

"It's always useful to know the impossibles," he said. "Along with the possibles. Narrows the field."

"I was so glad," Miss Conover said. "And to think if I hadn't been a little late getting back from lunch, I wouldn't have noticed the time." She smiled at her employer; it was a joke. The two might have several jokes between them, Bill decided. Possibly more than jokes. Fleetingly, he wondered whether anything might be made of that, if it were needed. Anything which might raise a doubt in the minds of, say, twelve men and women. But almost at once he dismissed the idea. Smith and his secretary were too casual; too sure. Concocted stories were told with emphasis, with steady eyes and an air of deep candor. Only the truth could be told lightly, thrown away as a joke. Even Pam North, for all her prejudice, would accept the truth of Smith's alibi, whatever she might suspect about Smith and his secretary. Her doubts, however she tried to hold them, would slip through her fingers. As, he noticed, his had. It was worth the trouble to see, yourself, the people who made statements.

He had, Bill Weigand told Nickerson Smith, dropped around to see how the accountants were making out. He had dropped in to tell Smith that, so far, they had found no proof of anything but—well, call it ineptitude. Smith looked shocked.

"Really," he said, as if the affirmation had led to his first doubt, "Andrew was honest. Completely honest. I never thought anything else. He—meant well."

"But lacked experience," Weigand said. "And judgment. Yes. It looks that way."

He got out of the deep chair, wondering a little why he had got into it; why he had dropped in on Nickerson Smith. It could be, he reflected wryly, that he was beginning to let Pam North do his thinking for him; letting her raise doubts where there was no room for doubts. Clearly, there was no room for doubt here. His eyes, professionally observant, flicked over Smith's desk as he stood up. A fresh blotter, bound in leather. A desk set, with pens leaning stiffly toward the hand. A glass ashtray. A desk lighter. Boxes, to match the desk, for incoming and outgoing letters. All dignity and restraint. The physicians' supply business apparently did Mr. Smith very well. He smiled at Miss Conover and nodded; Smith told him to drop in again. Weigand nodded and said casually that he might and went out of the office and the building, and by car to his own office.

Mullins was there. He had just talked to Lieutenant Heimrich on the telephone. Everything was quiet at North Salem. Lawrence Westcott had come around about one and taken Mrs. Gordon somewhere for lunch, amid hearty explanations that she had to get out and not sit around brooding. She had gone, with no protestations at all. The little girl had played outdoors until a light drizzle began; now she was playing, under the eyes of her nurse, in the living room.

Daniel Gordon had had breakfast with Deborah Brooks and after it they had walked outside together, apparently talking. Then the girl had come into the house and wandered restlessly for a while and then gone to her own room. Gordon had stood on the lawn looking after her, had seemed about to follow, and then had struck off suddenly toward a secondary road which led away from the Gordon estate. He had been observed long enough to make it clear that he was setting out for a walk, drizzle or no drizzle.

There had been no attempt to follow him. The State Police had enough to do, Heimrich indicated. They had taken pictures, made measurements, looked for fingerprints. They had located the outdoor grill from which the spit rod had been taken, they had—

"Actually," Mullins said, "they're just sitting on it, Loot. Waiting for us to do the heavy." Mullins sounded aggrieved.

"Right," Weigand said. "As we would, in their place. Why break your neck over somebody else's headache?" He listened to that and regretted it. Mullins remained doubtful, but he said, "O.K."

"All the same," he said, "they've got a killing too, Loot."

"Which," Weigand told him, "they naturally expect us to solve for them. So they merely sit on it, and wait."

Mullins considered, and nodded.

"Listen, Loot," he said. "How's about it being this guy Smith. Like Mrs. North thinks."

Weigand sighed. Prejudice seemed to rule his roost. Slowly, with care, as if to a child, he explained why it could not have been Mr. Smith.

"Take it yourself," he said, when he had gone over it. "You know a phony alibi the first time you hear it, don't you? Even if you can't prove it's phony?" He waited and Mullins, after thought, nodded. "Right," Bill said. "So do I. We'll never break Smith's in a hundred years. Because it's the truth. He was in his office from, at the latest, three or four minutes after the doctor left his own office until the doctor's body was found. Three or four minutes wasn't—any way you can play it—long enough. For a good part of the time it isn't only the girl—and don't think a jury wouldn't believe the girl. It was a couple of customers. You want us to take that to the D.A. and say you and Pam North have got yourselves a couple of hunches?"

"O.K., Loot," Mullins said. "I guess it ain't Smith."

"Right," Weigand said. "So for God's sake—don't *you* get intuitional on me."

"O.K., Loot," Mullins said, temperately. "I won't get institutional."

• 9 •

TUESDAY, 5:30 P.M. TO 7:15 P.M.

Debbie Brooks had lain for a long time staring at the ceiling, her eyes seeing nothing. Too many things had happened, too suddenly. Andy was dead and that was hard to grasp. He was not dead the way people died; the way her father had died. Then there had been merely sadness, and a kind of emptiness where he had been. She had been unhappy, when he died and for a long time afterward, but it had been quiet. It was at once an emptiness and a weight, and slowly—very slowly at first—the emptiness filled and the weight lightened. But it had always been quiet in her mind. This was not quiet. Her mind was filled with it—with all of it—and all of it was moving in her mind, going over and over.

Andy was dead, but he had been killed. And Grace Spencer, who had seemed to know so much—to know so many of the things she had still to learn—and to be so sure—she had been killed, too. And she had been young; not young as Debbie herself was young, but still young. Young as the rest of them were not, except Dan, and not always Dan. Young differently from the way Eve was young and the way Lawrence Westcott—Mr. Westcott—was young. Although the three of them were, probably, almost of an age. But about Eve there was something different; something hard to reach. You could never really talk to Eve and be sure that she was talking about the same things you were talking about.

She was not certain about Eve and Mr. Westcott—not completely certain. They were both so far away. She thought—not yet. But she was not even certain of that. Eve had been fond of Andy. She was sure that Eve had been fond of Andy. Once Lawrence Westcott had made a joke about Andy and had laughed, and Eve had not laughed and had said, "Larry! You mustn't." But she had said it as if she had wanted to laugh, and had made herself not laugh. It was as if she and Lawrence Westcott, in spite of what she said, were sharing the laughter she would not permit herself to show.

Debbie thought of Eve and Westcott, and stared at the ceiling, her eyes blank. She tried to imagine murder; she tried to think how it would be to do something to someone, who was living—who might just have spoken—so that they would not be living. She tried to feel the way it would feel. How would Lawrence Westcott feel if he struck somebody, as someone had struck Andy, and felt the bones give under the blow—and knew that now nothing, nothing in the world, could change what had happened? But she could not decide how Westcott would feel. Eve would be sorry. She would think it was too bad. But, beyond that, Debbie could not decide how Eve would feel, either.

How much did the police know, she wondered. Did they know how often Lawrence Westcott came; how often he and Eve went away in his car, and how many hours, sometimes, they spent away? Did they know how they talked on the telephone—and how, sometimes, when Eve answered the telephone in the living room and heard the voice at the other end, she would look up at Debbie and smile and form, with her lips, still smiling, the words "Do you mind?" so that Debbie would go somewhere else? And did they know how, after such a call, Eve would so often dress quickly and go out in her car, driving very fast on the white gravel which led to the main road?

She did not want it to be Eve, or even Lawrence Westcott. Unless it had to be somebody she knew; unless it had to be somebody else.

It was raining. She could hear the rain against the window. And Dan was walking somewhere in the rain, as he so often walked nowadays. He had said, "Go in, Debbie. I've got the fidgets," and then he had smiled at her, but as if she were someone else, and had watched her walk toward the house. She had looked back as she opened the door and had seen him start off, walking very fast; walking almost as if he were angry. She had seen him walk that way so often since he had come back.

She knew about it. Andy had explained it to her, slowly, gently. It was nothing that would last. It had a name. Combat fatigue. It was not anything tangible, although it had evidences which were tangible. You could call it anything—it was nervousness, uneasiness in the world, a shadow of old anxieties lying across the mind. It was the memory of old fears. And it would pass. She had understood that; she understood it now. And the corollary which Andy urged—that she and Dan wait to marry until they could start on surer ground—she understood that, too. It was better for Dan; better to make only familiar adjustments, first. It was better for her, because Dan could not yet be different, and she would not always understand. She would think she could, but she could not. There would be quick angers and quick words; there would be that unconquerable restlessness. And, however she tried to remember that these things were not really Dan, there would be times, if they were married, when she would not be able really to remember that they were not Dan. Even now that was true. Today, for example. She had been hurt when Dan sent her away, so he could be alone. Walk alone. She had understood, but she had been hurt all the same. And when people were married, Andy had told her—still gently—there would be a new kind of intensity between them; a new kind of sensitiveness. If people were married at all. It was hard to explain, but words meant more then; gestures meant more. You saw things that you would, before, have overlooked. "If it takes at all," Andy had said, and smiled—and, it seemed to her, smiled at something he remembered from a long time back.

She had believed Andy; believed that what he said was said candidly, for their good. But Dan had not agreed; he had been violent in disagreement, as he was now so often violent about so many things. He had wanted her to ignore what Andy said, and when she would not, when she was unhappy at his insistence, and showed it, and still would not—he had demanded that Andrew Gordon withdraw his advice. He had demanded this, she knew, several times. And each time he had been unsuccessful, and each time he had been angry. The anger lasted only briefly; it was a violent irritation more than anger. Dan was often irritated; that was part of it.

He had been angry each time, but only within very recent weeks had he been more. Then it was intangible; it was guessing to say what other emotion there was, or could be. But she had thought he was suspicious. Of some thing, of some one. Presumably of Andy. She had said, only a few days ago, "But, Danny, he's only thinking of us" and Dan had said, "Of *us?* You're sure it's of us?" and had looked at her as if he were trying to read something in her eyes. Apparently he had not, because in a moment he had smiled and said, "Forget it, Debbie. You're a baby. Of course he's fond of you." He had not explained any further, although she had tried to get him to. Perhaps there was nothing more to explain.

But if Dan was angry at his stepfather—if he had been angry at him the day before, if he had met him when he was angry—it was because of Andy's advice to her about their marriage. Not because of anything else; not because of money. The police wouldn't understand that; it was too intangible even to explain to the police. And—

Lying, staring at the ceiling, her fingers had tightened suddenly on the spread.

It wouldn't help to explain it to the police. Even if it were something to make clear. Because it would give them two things—two motives. It would make them believe more than ever that it was Dan. They were wrong; they had to be wrong. Oh, please, somebody—*make them wrong.*

Because it can't be Danny, she thought. I won't *let* it be Danny.

Then she had tried to make her mind blank and, failing that, she had thought only about Dan walking in the rain. She had tried to think what he was seeing, in the gray spring, with the light growing dimmer long before it should. She thought of the rain, falling gently, and of Dan Gordon walking through it, down a road. And then, quite suddenly, she must have fallen asleep, because reality and dream intermingled, and she was walking down a lane with Danny and they were holding hands, and nobody had been killed and nobody was unhappy.

Then she woke. The light coming in the windows was pale and gray. She looked at her watch. But it was only half-past five, and not time for a day to end in April. She swung from the bed, her litheness unconscious, and went to the window. It was very dark; no, it was very lightless. There was a difference. This was an unreal darkness. Oh, yes, it was going to storm. And Dan was still out. Or was he?

Hurriedly, she dressed; she ran downstairs and into the living room. Eve and Lawrence Westcott were there, sitting on a sofa, not close together, drinking cocktails. She forced herself to speak quietly.

"Oh, hello," she said. "Dan around?"

Eve smiled and said she hadn't seen him.

"We just came in, dear," she said. She waved toward a cocktail shaker. "Daiquiris," she said. "Help yourself."

Debbie poured a drink into a small, flaring glass. She carried it with her and went to a window and looked out.

"It's dark," she said.

"Wind shift," Westcott told her. "A hard one and then it will clear."

"Yes," Debbie said, not thinking about it. She was restless. She went to another window.

"Sit down, Debbie," Eve said. "Dan can take care of himself. Walking?"

"I suppose so," Debbie said. "I know he can take care of himself."

She stayed by the window, looking out.

"She's upset, Eve," she heard Lawrence Westcott say, behind her.

"Of course," Eve said. "Of course, Larry. Who isn't?"

Debbie went out of the room and across the hall and into the study. She sat by a window, looking out, and sipped her drink. The trees were bending in the wind. She did not turn on the lights, but, after sitting for a time, she reached out toward a table radio and clicked it on. "Fifteen minutes of the latest news," the radio said, in cultivated tones, interrupted a little by distant static. "But first, a word from our sponsor." The sponsor had a good many words. "And now Frederick Erkhart, with the latest news," the announcer said. Frederick Erkhart said "good evening."

Things were happening in Washington. And in London and in the Balkans. And even, it seemed, in New York.

"Now," Mr. Erkhart said, "for the human interest story of the day. A tall ungainly figure, familiar to almost everyone living in certain blocks of New York's East Side—a figure so tall and emaciated, so almost grotesque—that no one could pass without a second glance—a figure of fun, perhaps, to the street-playing children—today played an inappropriate part in tragedy. Robert Oakes, six feet six inches tall, weighing under a hundred and thirty, killed himself some time this morning by inhaling gas in the small flat in which he lived alone. Several hours later the collected gas exploded, almost wrecking the building, seriously injuring an unidentified young woman who, it is thought, may have been on her way to interview Oakes. Why? Because Oakes, almost grotesque figure of fun, is now revealed as an important witness in the murder of Dr. Andrew Gordon, famous eye surgeon. Oakes, a patient of Gordon's, is believed to have been in the physician's office when Gordon was killed. Police are still seeking the person who, early yesterday afternoon, beat the doctor to death in his office. Now, the official forecast from the United States Weather Bureau. Tonight, showers or thundershowers and much cooler. Tomorrow—"

But Debbie Brooks did not hear the forecast. She was looking at nothing, and there was a puzzled line between her eyes.

"But that couldn't be," she said, speaking aloud. "That couldn't be. It wasn't in the afternoon. I *know* it wasn't."

She sat for a moment and then stood, suddenly. She went to the desk and took the telephone from its cradle. Then she hesitated, replaced it and stood for a moment thinking. Then she took up the telephone again. She dialed information. "I would like the number of Mr. Gerald North at—" she said.

Deputy Chief Inspector Artemus O'Malley was very enthusiastic about Robert Oakes. Oakes was God's gift to policemen; O'Malley was clearly annoyed that Weigand did not, freely, accept him as such.

"Why not?" Inspector O'Malley said, and leaned across his desk and brought a plump fist down on it. "Tell me that, huh?"

"Nothing to go on," Bill Weigand said. "Could be. Needn't be."

"You young cops," Inspector O'Malley said. He leaned back and sighed, pantomiming hopeless resignation. "Doing everything the hard way." He thought of something, and leaned forward again. "How did this Mrs. North get into it?" He was accusing, now. "I thought I told you—"

"Right," Bill said. "You told me." He felt he should say something else. But he could think of nothing else to say. Inspector O'Malley looked at him accusingly. Then, unexpectedly, he dismissed Mrs. North with a wave of his hand.

"This guy Oakes," he said. "He killed Gordon. He saw the police were about to get him. He suicided. What's wrong with that?"

"Well," Weigand said, "we weren't about to get him. That's one thing wrong with it." He spoke mildly.

O'Malley dismissed that with a wave of his other hand.

"Sure we were," he said. "The boys had been trying to find him."

"Merely to make a routine check," Weigand said. He would have gone on, but O'Malley interrupted.

"O.K.," O'Malley said, heavily. "So he knew it was just a routine check, I suppose? Here he is, jittering on account he's bumped a guy off. And here's a cop, wanting to see him. How's he going to figure it's a routine check?"

Weigand would give the inspector that. He did.

"Also," he said, "Oakes was going to die of cancer before very long—very painfully. Maybe he merely figured gas would be easier."

O'Malley leaned back across the desk. He was very earnest.

"Let me tell you something, Bill," he said. "You'll never get anywhere if you make things hard for yourself. Not in this business. You're wandering all over the lot. Sure—maybe that's the reason he did it. Maybe a girl turned him down. Maybe he lost a fortune. My God—maybe anything. Why don't you take what's in front of you?"

"Because—" Bill Weigand said, before he was interrupted again.

"Let me tell you something, Bill," O'Malley said. "You've got a setup. Here's a guy wanted in a kill. He bumps himself off. So what? So he did the kill. So we've got a nice clean job, all wrapped up and put away. So we forget it. What's wrong with that?"

"Only," Bill said, speaking rapidly, "that we've no real evidence that he did the kill."

O'Malley leaned back in his chair, regarded the ceiling, mutely abandoned Bill Weigand as moronically perverse. He sighed deeply and closed his eyes. He opened his eyes.

"Sometimes you're a great trial to me, Bill," he said. "With this we could make the A.M.'s. I suppose you hadn't figured that." He looked at Bill. "Damn near everything I have to think of myself," he said. "Damn near everything."

"Give me time," Bill said. "Don't spring it yet, Inspector."

"The last decent kill we gave the afternoons a break," he said. "O.K. So this time we give it to the mornings. You ought to see that, Bill."

"Right," Bill said. "I see that. But make it the mornings, day after tomorrow—or whenever we get it. Friday. Next week." He leaned forward in turn. "Look," he said. "We can't make this one stick."

O'Malley looked at him pityingly. He pointed out that they would not need to make it stick. Oakes was dead.

Bill Weigand stood up. When he spoke his voice was detached, without emphasis.

"Obviously," he said, "the decision is yours, sir."

O'Malley looked at him—and then he grinned suddenly.

"The hell with that," he said. "The hell with that, Bill. We'll hold it. Until day after tomorrow, anyhow." He continued to grin. "Only just don't make it too fancy, Bill," he said.

Bill Weigand said he'd try not to. He went back to his own office. Mullins got hastily out of Weigand's chair. Weigand sat in it. Mullins looked at him.

"Been seeing the inspector, Loot?" he said. He examined Weigand. "You look like it," he said. "Wants to pin it on this guy who bumped himself off, I suppose. This long stringy guy."

"Right," Bill said.

Mullins nodded.

"O.K., Loot," he said. "Why not?"

Weigand sighed, reminded himself of O'Malley, broke the sigh off.

"Why?" he said.

Mullins gave it thought.

"Well," he said, "it fits. Sort of."

Sort of wasn't good enough, Bill told him.

"Look," he said, "I want to find out what happened. As long as you're working with me, you want to find out what happened. Right?"

"O.K., Loot," Mullins said. He was equable.

"Look at it," Weigand directed him. "Maybe Oakes killed himself. But maybe somebody killed him. Maybe he killed himself because he'd found out what was the matter with him. Maybe he killed himself because he killed Gordon and thought we were after him. Maybe he was killed because he saw something—or didn't see something he was expected to see. Maybe when he was there he saw somebody do something suspicious. Maybe he heard something. Maybe—" He broke off. "Actually," he said, "we don't know anything at all, Mullins."

Mullins shook his head. He said they knew something.

"We know he was there," Mullins said.

"Yes," Weigand agreed. He spoke abstractedly. Then he stiffened suddenly and looked at Mullins. "What?" he said.

"We know he was there," Mullins repeated. "On account of the card. We—" Mullins looked at Weigand and stopped speaking for a moment. "Listen, Loot," he said then, anxiously, "we *do* know he was there, don't we?"

Slowly, his eyebrows drawn together so that a line was sharp between them, Weigand shook his head.

"Come to think of it," he said, and he spoke softly. "We just know a name was there. Just a name, Mullins."

"But—" Mullins said.

"Just a name," Weigand repeated again. "A name on a referral card. Remember what he looked like, Mullins. So tall—so thin—everybody noticed him. Not just average size—average weight—average face. A freak, pretty near."

"Sure," Mullins said. "But—"

"Did anybody—it would be the receptionist or the nurse—did either of them say anything about Oakes? Except as a name? Did either of them say—oh—'one of the patients was a funny-looking man, about seven feet tall.' Did they?"

Mullins went back into his memory. He shook his head.

"Not that I remember," he said. "But—"

"And this guy Oakes was a—a sensation," Weigand said. "Everybody who ever saw him remembered him. All around where he lived, people remembered him—'that funny-looking guy.' And neither Miss Brooks nor the nurse mentioned him."

Mullins shook his head.

"Why would they?" he said. "Why would they figure it had anything to do with—anything?"

Weigand shook his head while Mullins was still speaking.

"I don't know why," he said. "I know people do. Suppose—suppose one of the patients had been a dwarf. A guy about two feet tall. You mean to say that Miss Brooks, say, wouldn't have told us there were six compensation cases yesterday afternoon and then added—whether she thought it meant anything or not—'one of them was a dwarf a couple of feet high'? You mean to say anybody—you—me—O'Malley—anybody—would see a freak where he didn't expect to see one and never say anything about it?"

Mullins thought. His face showed thought. Then he began slowly, reluctantly, to nod.

"O.K., Loot," he said. "You make it sound—I guess I'd mention it. I guess anybody would."

"And," Bill told him, "nobody did. Nobody did, Mullins."

"Well," Mullins said, "where does it get us?"

For that, Weigand had no answer. He seemed to have forgotten Mullins, and he sat staring at the opposite wall, tapping his fingers on his desk. He sat so, for what seemed, to Mullins, like a long time and Mullins could tell that Weigand was working something out. This was always very interesting to Mullins, and very obscure. When Weigand reached for the telephone, Mullins was interested, because whatever Weigand did from now on would, he realized, be a surprise.

Weigand put in a call for the home of Dr. Andrew Gordon, in North Salem, New York—a person to person call, to Miss Deborah Brooks.

He replaced the telephone and went back to looking at the wall, and tapping out a kind of tune with his fingers on his desk. Then the telephone rang. Weigand picked it up, said, "yes," listened and put it back. Now the line was between his brows again.

"Temporarily out of order," he said. "There's a storm up there, apparently. I suppose—" He broke off and sat for a moment more, looking at the wall. Then, abruptly, he stood up.

"Get the car, Sergeant," he said. "We're going places."

When you live with a cat, certain conventions are adhered to by all parties. Certain places belong to the cat; other, and less desirable places, may be contended for on a basis of relative equality. Thus Martini had proscriptive rights to a position on Gerald North's shoulders when he was shaving with an electric razor, because Martini was interested in electric razors and found the sound they made soothing. Mr. North had the right to argue about the chair he and Martini both liked and, as a last resort, to pretend that he did not know she was there and to prepare to sit on her. Martini owned all emptied cigarette packages, and either of the Norths had a right to throw them for her, in which case she would bring them back if that were her mood. The question whether Mr. North's cigarette case was to be considered an emptied cigarette package was moot, Martini being in the affirmative. Martini also owned Mr. North's right hand, which she chose to regard as an animal—distinct from the larger animal which was Mr. North—and subject to periodic destruction. But it was understood on both sides that Martini did not use claws or, at any rate, did not use them fully extended. Whether Martini also owned the cream which was left in the pitcher after breakfast was not yet decided. The subject was opened afresh each morning, on Martini's part with an air of innocence; each morning, Martini found the cream pitcher anew, with a pretty pretense of surprise and pleasure.

One of Martini's inalienable rights was to help Mr. North make cocktails. Here the routine was established. Martha, the maid, brought in ice, glasses, mixer, and gin and vermouth. She put them down on the living-room chest which served as a bar. Martini arrived next, leaping from any convenient position, not quite landing on the glasses. She then awaited Mr. North, meanwhile experimenting to see whether her head still fitted into the mixing pitcher. On such occasions, Mr. North was always commendably prompt.

With his arrival, Martini sat back and watched. She watched with disconcerting intentness and, Mr. North sometimes thought, a rather censorious expression. It occurred to Mr. North, at intervals, that Martini was a conservative; that she thought three-to-one quite dry enough. She had been known to touch Mr. North's hand lightly, remindingly, when he was for the fourth time filling the measuring glass with gin. Once she had succeeded in upsetting the mixing glass and spilling its contents, but this was not unalloyed triumph. Some of the gin wet her right front foot and she departed angrily. She later licked the foot, without pleasure but also, so far as the Norths could determine, without ill effect.

When the drinks were mixed and the glasses filled—very full because the Norths tried to limit themselves to two each, and there was no sense in not making the most of them—it was understood that Martini would leap from the chest top to Mr. North's shoulder. This was always an interesting moment, since if Martini timed it perfectly, so that Mr. North had a brimming glass in each hand, there was almost certain to be spillage. The cause of temperance was thus served. Martini was then privileged to ride—moving now and then as it occurred to her—until Mr. North had given Mrs. North her cocktail and had sat down with his own. The game ended then; Martini was supposed to think of something else.

This evening went as usual. Martha entered at a few minutes after six, according to ritual. Martini entered two seconds later, having taken off from the mantelpiece. She put her head in the mixing pitcher and took it out as Mr. North arrived. Mr. North mixed and poured, took a deep breath for steadiness and reached to pick the glasses up. Then the telephone rang.

Bells excited Martini. The doorbell was best, because there was always a chance that it would lead to an opportunity to catapult herself into the outer hall. But telephone bells were all right too, and demanded attention. A cat could race to the box in the hall which held the bells and sit down and watch it. This telephone bell excited Martini and she took off—unhesitatingly, with grace, with no feeling of responsibility. She knocked over both filled glasses, scratched one of Mr. North's extended hands in her passage, and landed running. Mr. North started convulsively and his right hand hit the vermouth bottle. It tottered and he lunged for it, caught his sleeve on the handle of the mixing spoon and tilted the pitcher against the gin bottle with a sharp crack. Mr. North said, "Damn!" with intense feeling; Mrs. North said, "Teeney!" and then, into the telephone, "Hello."

"One moment, please," an operator said. "Here's your party." Then, on the heels of that, a girl's voice said, "Hello, hello. Is this Mrs. North? Mrs. Gerald North?"

"Yes," Pam said. "Ouch." Martini had returned, landing on Mrs. North's shoulder. "That was just the cat," Pam North said. "Who is this?"

"Deborah Brooks," the voice said. "In North Salem. Did you hear the radio?"

Her voice was quick and seemed excited.

"What radio?" Mrs. North said. "No, I don't think so."

"About the man who killed himself," Deborah said. "The man named Oakes. I just heard it. And I know him and he wasn't—"

And then the voice stopped. It was not as if Deborah Brooks had stopped speaking. There was a crackling noise, and then silence, except for a faint humming. Then, very far away there was a voice, which might still be Deborah's, saying something that sounded like "—had to tell—" Then there was silence again, and this time it was unbroken.

"Hello," Mrs. North said. "Hello. Hello."

Nobody answered her. She put the telephone back and looked at it. She looked at Jerry, who was examining the mixing pitcher.

"Not broken," he said. "But I'll have to start all over. And one glass is. Who was it?"

"Deborah Brooks," Pam said. "But something happened. And—it sounded important. About Mr. Oakes."

"What about Mr. Oakes?" Jerry wanted to know.

"I don't know," Pam said. "She said, 'he wasn't' and then something happened. I don't know what he wasn't."

Jerry went on mixing new drinks for a moment. He poured them carefully. Then he turned around.

"She seemed excited," Pam said. "Do you think we ought to do something?"

Jerry thought and nodded. He said they ought to call her back. Pam started it. It was slow—information, the operator, another operator, a sound as of a telephone ringing far away. But then—nothing. Jerry delivered drinks; Pam sipped and waited. She thought she heard a voice and said, "Hello?" quickly, but nobody answered her. She waited again and then the operator came on and asked what number she was calling. Pam told her. There was another pause.

"I'm sorry," the operator said, "that line seems to be temporarily out of order. Shall I try again later?"

"I don't know," Pam said. "Yes, all right."

She put the telephone back.

"Something happened," she said.

"Country telephones," Jerry said, swallowing. "Too much vermouth?"

Pam swallowed.

"Not for me," she said. "It's not strong at all."

Jerry smiled. He started to say something and decided against it. The more vermouth, the stronger. That was Pam's belief, amounting in intensity to a faith.

"I wonder what she wanted," Pam said. "It must have been important. But what was it? What is it that Mr. Oakes wasn't?"

"I don't know," Jerry said. "I've no idea. Wasn't really Mr. Oakes?"

Pam shook her head.

"Everybody says he was Mr. Oakes," she said. "They couldn't all be wrong. Maybe—" She paused. Then she spoke in a different tone. *"Jerry!"* she said. "Maybe—'wasn't the man who was there yesterday.' Do you think?"

Jerry considered it. He lifted his shoulders and let them fall again.

"Nothing to think on," he said. "Possibly. Maybe 'wasn't the man who killed Dr. Gordon.' Maybe 'wasn't the kind of man to kill himself.' Maybe—" He ended it and finished his drink.

"Jerry," Pam said, "I'm—I'm worried."

Gerald North put his glass down firmly.

"Listen, Pam," he said. "We're not going out there to find out. Not tonight. We've just started our drinks and dinner's—"

Pam did not seem to be listening. She looked at the telephone. She reached for it, and dialed. She said, "Lieutenant William Weigand, please," and waited. Then she said, again, "Lieutenant William Weigand, please," and, after a moment, "Oh" in a disappointed voice. She listened again. She said, "Well, who is there?" and then, "Can I speak to him, please?"

"Mr. Stein," she said, then. "This is Pamela North. I want to talk to the lieutenant. Do you know where he is? Or Sergeant Mullins?"

She listened, said, "Both?" and after that, "No, I guess not." Then she hung up.

"They've gone to North Salem," she said, and in a moment she was standing. "Jerry! Something's happening!"

"But—" Jerry said, and looked over his shoulder at the cocktail chest. "We've just—"

Martha, the maid, was resigned. She spoke to Martini and said, "Those folks of yours, cat" and Martini looked at her, enquiringly, with round blue eyes. Martha unmade the table; she took the roast out of the oven and put it on a kitchen shelf. Then she looked at Martini. "Even if it is too hot, cat," she said, and put the roast in the refrigerator. Martini made a low sound in her throat, but it was impossible to tell what she meant. It was probable, of course, that she was protesting the confinement of the roast in a place which she could not—as yet—open single-pawed.

The wind tore at the top of the convertible; clouds hurried across the moon. Far away, to the north and east, there was the flicker of lightning.

"We do pick the damnedest nights for little trips to the country," Jerry said. "The damnedest nights."

But there was no mist; the wind took care of that. So they went fast. They did not drive into rain until they turned off the Hutchinson River Parkway and started north.

· 10 ·

Tuesday, 6:20 p.m. to 8:45 p.m.

The trees Debbie could see from the study window were bending low before the wind; their small leaves, so newly out, must be hanging on for dear life. But it was too dark to see the leaves, except as a softness on branches which had been, only a few weeks earlier, bare and hard. The window rattled and cool air came in around it. Then there was a flash of light and, some seconds after it, the heavy roll of thunder. Summer was coming back; this was a foretaste of summer. It was like a summer storm.

The rain increased with sudden fury. Big drops splashed against the glass of the window, spotting a thin film of dust. Then it was as if someone, maliciously, had hurled a pail of water against the window. Debbie moved across the room to the window on the side. It was only splattered; she could see out of it across the lawn on the east. Rain was slanting through the air; the air was almost solid with water. Then lightning flashed again, and, for a second after, it seemed to rain harder than ever. Then the rain slackened a little, so that she could see the bending trees along the far'wall. One of them, a poplar, was sending out a rain of its own—a fleecy rain of cotton-supported seeds. But the real rain beat down the cottony particles remorselessly.

The storm was exciting; the world was suddenly tumultuous and unrestrained. Nature had abandoned all the conventions of good behavior and was having a fling. The wind was blowing everything away. There was a kind of savage gayety in the storm; it made Debbie feel excited and almost frightened, and at the same time almost gay. It was like other storms—like the storm she and Dan had been caught in, once, on a golf course, and had run through, wet and uncomfortable, with the rain molding their clothing to them. She had been wearing a thin blouse and slacks, and the soft, wet material of her blouse molded itself to her body and she had been embarrassed and at the same time glad—and had known how she looked, after they found shelter finally, and had not cared. Dan had looked at her and smiled and then, because they were alone—and wet and young and happy—had held her close to him a moment and kissed her, very hard. He had let her go and stood for a moment looking at her and then she had looked down at herself in the wet blouse and said, "oh," as if she were surprised, and had pulled the clinging material away from her body. She smiled, now, remembering. Always, she thought, I will remember that when there's a storm.

But now Dan was not with her; he was in the storm alone. Perhaps he was under shelter somewhere; surely he was under shelter. But he might merely be walking through it, head down, and if that was it she wished she could be with him. Always, until recently, he had wanted her to be with him; even when he first came home, although from the first he had been strange and nervous. It was only recently, since he had grown so angry because Andy wanted them to wait, that he had taken to going off by himself.

She turned from the window. Nothing would happen to him. A girl could walk through the storm, and nothing would happen except that she would be wet and cold and blown about. She had lived too much in the country to be afraid of the weather—at any rate of spring and summer weather. And Dan was strong and tough, and had been through a lot worse than this; had been through things which made all this fury of nature almost gentle. He would walk through it. Or he would find shelter. He would be all right.

She told herself this, knowing it was reasonable and true. But even while she reassured herself, the gay feeling which the storm, and memories of other storms, had brought, left her. It did not leave slowly, reminiscently. It went quite suddenly and, looking out at the driving rain and the driven trees, she shivered. The storm, instead of seeming an adventure, seemed all at once but another part of the turmoil which was in her mind—the turmoil which had filled the day. Uneasily, unexplainably, she was afraid—afraid for Dan, afraid for herself.

She turned quickly back to the telephone, dialed and listened for the sound which would mean that a light was flashing in front of the local operator. There was no sound. She replaced the telephone, put it to her ear again and listened. The hum which should have been in her ear—the "dial tone" they called it—was not there. There was an odd, subdued scratching sound, and nothing else. The telephone was still dead. But she had told Mr. North and Mrs. North—

Then she stopped, with her hand still on the telephone. Had she told Mrs. North? Or—had Mrs. North heard her? She had talked for a moment, as soon as she had explained herself to Mrs. North, and had told her about the mistake, and then something—the cessation, perhaps, of some sound so familiar that you knew of it only when it stopped—had made her feel that she was alone. Then she had said "Mrs. North? Do you hear me? Mrs. North?" and there had been no answer. While she had been talking, something had happened to the telephone. But how much had Pamela North heard before the telephone went dead?

Debbie realized then that she had merely assumed that her message had been heard, and that this assumption had given her some sort of reassurance. It was not that the message was important, because she was not sure that it was important. It might be. But the thought that she had shared this information—the only information she had which might help—had somehow freed her mind, given her a sense of release. Perhaps it was the beginning of her present doubt, as much as her uneasiness about Dan, which had erased the gayety from her mind.

It was dark in the room and she was suddenly lonely, "bereft," she thought; this was what "bereft" meant—loneliness in a dim room at evening. She switched on the lamp on the desk, but that merely deepened the shadows around her. She shook her head, as if she had been arguing with herself, and, abstractedly, picked up her cocktail glass. It was empty. She looked toward the hall and, beyond it, could see the light in the living room. Now that she listened, she could hear voices. Perhaps Dan—

She went quickly across the hall and into the living room. Evelyn Gordon and Lawrence Westcott were sitting close together on a sofa and they had started a fire. Westcott's arm lay along the back of the sofa behind Eve; and Debbie felt, without knowing, that he had just at that moment lifted it from her shoulders. With the other hand, as she stood there, he reached out to the coffee table in front of them and filled their glasses from a shaker. There was nobody else in the room and now they were not talking. But she felt as if they had just been talking, as she felt that Lawrence Westcott had just moved his left arm from around Eve.

Westcott filled the glasses and then, unhurriedly, looked back over his shoulder at Debbie. So they had heard her. He smiled at her.

"Come in by the fire," he said. He looked at her and seemed to be studying her face. Then he smiled. "Dan's all right," he said. "Come in and have a drink."

"Of course," she said. "I was just—watching the storm. From the study window. It's—quite a storm."

She walked across the room and stood for a moment in front of the fire. Then she sat on one of the chairs across from the sofa and stretched out her legs. She looked at her glass and tried to be careless, casual.

"Empty," she said, in a carefully plaintive voice. "Entirely empty."

They took care of that.

"That stepson of mine will be getting pretty wet," Eve said. Something in her tone, in the way she described Dan, underlined the absurdity of Dan's being her stepson. It made her sound, if anything, younger than Dan.

"You can say that again," Debbie said. And as she said it, she thought how strange familiar talk—the clichés of familiar talk—could sound when you thought of it, how far away, sometimes, the words you used were from the things you were saying.

"He'll get under something," she said. "He always does."

"Well," Lawrence Westcott said, "he's had practice." He said it in a dry, meaningless voice; too dry and meaningless. Eve suddenly patted his hand.

He smiled at her.

"All right," he said. "All the same, a man felt funny going around in—" He paused. "As if you didn't belong to anything," he said.

He means about the war, Debbie thought. He wasn't in it, for some reason, and he's—hurt about it. Inadequate. Even now. And it's made him, for some reason, not like Dan. She was embarrassed, and did not know what to say.

"He'll find some place," she said. "Definitely."

There was strain in the room; it had come into the room with her, Debbie thought. It had not been there before, when the two of them were sitting in front of the fire.

Eve looked at her watch.

"Almost seven," she said. "You'll stay to dinner, Larry."

Lawrence Westcott turned his head so that he could look out of a window at the rain.

"I'll have to, I guess," he said. He smiled. "Which is very convenient, since I'd like to. Only—"

He looked at Eve Gordon. She shook her head. What that meant, Debbie did not understand. Perhaps Lawrence Westcott thought he ought to go, even in the rain; that he had called long enough on a woman so recently, and publicly, widowed. Perhaps he was thinking about the neighbors. He had cause, Debbie reflected.

She sipped her drink and looked into the fire and remembered Andy. Her sadness about Andy came and went; her sense of loss came and went. He had been very good to her; he had been very kind and gentle, like a very good kind of uncle. But it was hard, precisely because his death had been so unreally dramatic, to think of him as Andy, dead. He was a—a "murder victim." It was sometimes hard to remember that he was also Andy, who had been like such a good kind of uncle. Sitting now, drinking slowly, she thought of him. The other two talked about nothing, leaving her out.

A maid came to the door of the dining room and stood as if about to speak. But just as she was beginning, the doorbell rang and, at a nod from Evelyn Gordon, she went across the room and out into the hall. Eve and Lawrence Westcott went on talking, but as if they were listening. Debbie stood up, thinking it was Dan, and then, although almost at once she realized that Dan would not need to ring, she continued to stand, looking at the door to the hall.

There was the sound of the outer door closing and then the maid's voice saying something which ended "—don't believe so, sir, but Mrs. Gordon is in" and then a man's voice which she did not at once recognize, except that it was not Dan's. "Wet night," the man's voice said, and there was the sound of a hat being slapped against something. Then the maid came to the door and said, "Mr. Smith, ma'am," and went on across the living room and out into the kitchen. Nickerson Smith came to the door, looked at them and then looked down at his trouser legs, which were wet.

"Quite a storm," he said, mildly. "Young Dan around?"

Lawrence Westcott stood up and Eve turned to look across the back of the sofa.

"Hello, Nickerson," Eve said. "No, he doesn't seem to be." She looked at Smith. "You're wet," she said. "Come over and dry out."

Nickerson Smith, deliberate, at ease, came across the room and stood in front of the fire.

"Turns out Dan's got to sign something else," he said. "Decided to bring it out myself."

"He went for a walk," Eve said. "He ought to be in eventually. Larry, give Nickerson a drink."

Nickerson Smith took the drink, raised it slightly toward Eve, raised it to his lips. He stood with his back to the fire, teetering gently from heel to toe to heel.

"Lovely night for a walk," he said. "Fit of sulks, I suppose?"

"Of course not," Debbie said. "It was nice when he started. He—he's not built just to sit around."

"My dear," Smith said. "My dear Miss Brooks. I didn't mean to imply—" He let the sentence finish itself.

"Anybody'd think there was something funny about Dan," the girl said. "Something—peculiar."

"I didn't mean—" Smith began, but Eve Gordon cut in.

"There is, Debbie," she said. "Why don't you face it? It's only just now, of course. He'll be all right. But there is something—well, funny, about him now. Naturally."

"Dan's all right!" Debbie said. She was defiant. Her cheeks flushed.

"Debbie," Eve Gordon began. Then she saw the maid standing in the door to the dining room. "All right, Susan," she said. She turned to the others. "Dinner," she said. "You'll stay, Nickerson? I'm sure Dan will be along."

Nickerson Smith hesitated. He had, he said, planned to drive back at once, getting a sandwich on the way. Later he was meeting— He looked out at the rain.

"However," he said, "it's rather important to get this signed. I suppose I can give him a ring and—"

"Of course," Eve said. But, at almost the same time, Debbie said, "No." They looked at her. "Because I'm afraid there's something the matter with the telephone," Debbie said. "I tried to call and I was—I couldn't get through." She did not know why she changed the sentence.

"Really," Eve said. "Telephones in the country! When was this, Debbie?"

"A little after six," Debbie said. "I'd just heard the news and I—I wanted to make a call."

It was lame. It sounded lame. It said too much—and too little. But nobody picked it up.

Perhaps the trouble was corrected, Nickerson Smith said, and he went across the hall to the study. But he came back in a moment, shaking his head, and said, "Nope. Still dead." He went back to the fire, stood in front of it for a moment and then shrugged. "In any case," he said, "I'd better wait for Dan. I'll just have to explain tomorrow."

They went in to dinner a few minutes later. The storm, which had seemed to lull, increased again. They were eating grapefruit when there was a sudden, very close, flash of lightning, with thunder almost on the flash. The lights went very low, came up for a second, went out.

It was a routine thing, an ordinary thing. There was no reason why anyone, knowing the way of electric storms with country power, should sit holding herself tight, trembling uncontrollably, while the maid brought candles, flickering in the semidarkness, throwing moving shadows which grew quiet as the candles began to burn steadily on the table. It was an ordinary thing.

But Debbie did sit trembling. I'm afraid of the dark, she thought; after last night, I'm afraid of the dark.

But this was an ordinary accident. Nobody had turned the lights off, as somebody had—as she better than anyone knew somebody had—the night before. This was merely something that happened, off and on, in the country when there were thunderstorms.

That would be Nickerson Smith, the man in the black slicker decided, from his glimpse of license numbers. Anyway, that would be Smith's car. So Smith would be snug inside, where Westcott was staying snug. The man in the slicker swore at the weather. He went back to the car, parked off the road not quite opposite the entrance to the Gordon drive. Snug indoors—that was swell. That was simply swell. He got into the car and turned on the radio, and static crackled and snarled at him. He got out and stood against the car, sheltering himself as much as he could. It wasn't much.

It was a hell of a night for this kind of thing. On a nice, moonlit night, with the peepers sounding, it wouldn't be so bad. It didn't help to think of the others snug inside. Maybe, the man thought, one of them won't be so snug after a while. Maybe the time would be coming when one of them would be glad to change places—if he could. There might come a time when being out in the rain would seem a mighty fine thing—and a mighty unobtainable thing—to one of those snug people.

He looked at the house, its windows softly luminous through the rain. Then lightning struck somewhere close and he ducked involuntarily. It was a fool thing to do; ducking lightning. A man did fool things, alone in the rain. He looked out from under the brim of his rubber hat and for a moment thought he must be looking in the wrong direction.

Then, as his eyes recovered from the flash, he saw the outlines of the big house through the rain. He wasn't looking in the wrong direction. All the lights in the house had gone out.

"Well," the man in the slicker said, aloud. "Well, well."

He left his shelter and began to cross the road.

The wind and the rain hit the police car near Elmsford, and the heavy sedan seemed to shudder. The windshield wipers fluttered, caught, swished across reluctantly and the glass streamed again as they passed. Bill swore and reduced speed; the road was suddenly bright in a glare of lightning, and as suddenly dark again. The speedometer arrow fell to forty and hung there. Then it crept up again.

Mullins looked at it with disfavor and wondered what the hurry was. When you couldn't see your way—

"If we've missed this one," Bill said savagely, "we can hand 'em in, Sergeant. Both of us. If we miss it again."

The speedometer needle went to fifty, although still the headlights caught little more than a torrent of rain.

"Watch it, Loot!" Mullins said. "Jeez!" Weigand watched it, leaning forward over the wheel, trying to force his eyes. But he did not slow.

"Ten minutes one way or the other, Loot," Mullins said, his voice mildly wistful. "Jeez."

"A day," Weigand said. "A day one way or another. And the nurse gets it." He wrenched the car around a curve. "Because we let routine become—just that. Because we figured we've got plenty of time."

"How could we figure it, Loot?" Mullins asked. "I don't see how we could figure it. Watch it!"

Bill swerved the car around a station wagon which groped, reasonably, through the rain.

"It hit us in the face," Bill said. "My God, Mullins—it hit us in the face. All the time."

"O.K., Loot," Mullins said, equably. "O.K., it hit us in the face."

He did not sound as if anything had hit him in the face. He sounded as if he were agreeing for the sake of calm. Weigand did not answer.

"O.K.," Mullins said. "Suppose it wasn't Oakes. Even so, how do you know?"

"My God," Weigand said. "Use your head. Who fits? Now we know the trick."

"Yeah," Mullins said. He sounded puzzled. "Do we?" he said.

"What other way is there?" Bill said, after a moment. The car slowed at a crossroads; suddenly swung right toward Mount Kisco. It went across railroad tracks, not hesitating. Mullins looked anxiously down the tracks on his side. They went through Mount Kisco, deserted in the storm. They went on beyond, cutting across country on secondary roads. In a dip of the road they plunged through water which slapped against the underside of the car. For a moment it was like being in a boat. Water fanned out on either side in great wings.

Mullins' silence was brooding. Bill broke it.

"There were six of them," Weigand said. "One of them wasn't Oakes. What more do you want?"

Mullins thought about it.

"O.K.," he said. "O.K., Loot." He thought a moment longer. "A name would be nice," he said.

"Oh," Bill said. "That! I'll give you a name. Where's your mind, Sergeant?"

Bill gave him a name. Mullins was silent again. Then he said "Yeah." Then he said, "It would be nice to have some evidence, Loot. It'd be real nice."

Bill Weigand was savage. He said it wouldn't be so nice to get the kind of evidence they were likely to. He said it wouldn't be so damned nice.

Mullins hung on to the door handle as the car sloshed fast, inside, around a curve. For several miles he said nothing. Then he said, mildly, that he didn't, after all, see how they could have known.

"My God, Mullins," Weigand said. "How else would you explain the glasses? The thing we didn't bother to explain?"

Mullins thought it over again.

"O.K., Loot," he said, finally. He was affirmative, this time.

The Norths's convertible shook in the wind; the top rattled. The car, wading away from the Sound, fought the storm.

"It oughtn't to do this in April," Pam said. "Ought it?"

"It can," Jerry told her. "God knows it can."

That, Pam said, was obvious. She still thought it oughtn't to. She said it was very extreme for April.

"Showers," she said. "May flowers. But not this. Can't we go faster?"

Not, Jerry told her, if they wanted to get there.

"Oh," Pam said. "We have to get there. Now we know it wasn't Mr. Oakes. But somebody who looked like him."

Jerry did not answer for a moment. The road seemed suddenly to have disappeared. He found it again just in time and was surprised to discover that he could see along it for what might be several hundred feet.

"Seems to be slackening," he said. Then he spoke in a different voice, as if he had just heard something which startled him. "What did you say?"

"We know it wasn't Mr. Oakes," Pam said. "What did you think I said?"

"I thought you said, somebody who looked like him," Jerry told her. "Which is absurd. If this—if this means anything—it was somebody who *didn't* look like him."

"But—" Pam began and then broke off. When she spoke again her voice was that of a person who has been enlightened. "Oh," she said, "you mean Mr. Oakes." She considered. "Of course," she said, "I can see how you would. A misleading relative."

"A what?" Jerry said.

"They're so difficult, sometimes," Pam said. "But it's so awkward to put a name after them in brackets. Don't you think?"

Jerry's hands were engaged; he could not run one of them through his hair. But his voice, when he spoke again to Pam, sounded as if he had just run a hand through his hair.

"Listen, darling," he said. "I don't think I quite—" Then he stopped suddenly. "Oh," he said. "*Him*."

"Naturally," Pam said. "What else would it be?"

Jerry had no answer to that. But as he thought it over—and as the rain did actually, for the moment, slacken—he drove the sloshing Buick faster toward North Salem.

"Only," Pam said, after several miles, "if it was that way, what did he use?"

The storm, having extinguished the lights, having contemptuously ended man's small attempt at emulation, seemed for the moment satisfied. They finished their dinner by candlelight, with their shadows flickering behind them on the wall. The wind was not so loud; the drumming of rain, which had seemed to fill the air even inside the solid old house, lessened. Eve Gordon and Lawrence Westcott talked; they drew Nickerson Smith into their talk and offered it to Debbie. She smiled, as if she had come back from a long way off, she said something, she went away again, the smile still on her lips—still meaningless. Westcott—or Smith?—was sitting where Dan ought to be. Nickerson Smith—he was opposite her. Where she wanted Dan to be.

She ate very little; she watched the shadows on the wall, hardly seeing them, but unconscious of them. They were part of the night which had come suddenly, come so furiously. The shadows—the beating rain—the odd new planes the soft light of the candles marked on familiar faces. On her own, she supposed; certainly on that of Nickerson Smith, sitting across from her. And Westcott's face. When Westcott turned momentarily toward her, so that the light of the center candles touched his face obliquely, the side of his face nearest her was shadowed. It was as if he had suddenly put on the mask of another man—an older man, a very different man. His face was no longer the open, uneventful—and undisturbing—face of Lawrence Westcott, man of the country, given to long, tweedy walks with dogs; given to philandering comfortably with an older neighbor's pretty wife. It was the face of a man with unknown purposes of his own, unrevealed determination and force. Debbie was startled, suddenly, seeing this new face where there had been, before, merely unconsidered familiarity. It was an odd trick for the light to play, she thought. If it was a trick.

Where was Dan? Why didn't he come? And why was Nickerson

Smith looking across the table at her with such complete attention? He seemed to be waiting for something from her, demanding something from her.

"Debbie, darling," Eve said. "Quit worrying. Come back. We're waiting for you."

"Waiting?" Debbie said. Then she looked at the others' dessert plates; at her own. She had eaten some of it, apparently. "Oh," she said. "I'm sorry. I've—I've finished."

"Good," Eve said. "Coffee, then."

Eve Gordon led the way into the long living room. It was very dim, now—very shadowed. There were candles near the door from the dining room; on tables by the fireplace there were other candles. Between there were deep shadows, chairs which looked as if they were crouched. Eve led them through the shadows, talking back to them, her voice unconcerned. On a low table by the fire the coffee things were waiting on a silver tray. Eve poured coffee into small white cups.

Nickerson Smith picked up his cup and walked toward a window. He stood looking out for a moment. Then he spoke without turning.

"I think it's really letting up a bit," he said. "I think—" Then he stopped speaking, as if somebody had put a hand over his mouth. They looked at him, and he was peering out through the window. He leaned close to it, put his left hand up and cupped it beside his eyes, shutting out the faint light in the room. His whole posture showed intense concentration on something outside.

Westcott stood up.

"What is it?" he said. "See something?"

Smith did not turn. He put down his cup absently and continued to peer out through the still rain-swept glass.

"Thought—" he said, and stopped again. He did not turn. "Somebody out there," he said. "Can't be sure. Somebody—wait a minute." He leaned closer still to the window and seemed to be listening.

Westcott moved toward him; Debbie and Eve Gordon stood up.

"Thought I heard somebody yelling," Smith said. "I don't know. A figure—seemed to be going back there—toward the back. A man, I think. And then I thought—" He ended with a shrug and turned toward them. "Seeing things, probably," he said. "It's too dark. But I thought I heard somebody calling."

"Dan!" Debbie said. "It was Dan!"

"I couldn't tell," Smith said. "A man—I thought it was a man. He was—running. Trying to run. As if—" He looked at Debbie and smiled. It was a forced smile. "Couldn't have been Dan," he said. "He'd come in. Wouldn't he?"

His tone sought confirmation.

"Trying to run!" Debbie said. "You said—*trying* to run. What did you mean?"

"The grass is wet," Smith said. "He—he slipped. Staggered. Naturally."

"No," Debbie said. "He was hurt. Wasn't he? It was Dan—he—"

Eve came to her quickly and put an arm around her shoulders.

"Don't!" Eve said, her voice challenging. "Don't! It wasn't Dan."

"You don't know!" Debbie said. She shook off the arm. "You don't know. How can you? It was Dan!" She turned to Nickerson Smith. "Wasn't it?" she said.

Smith looked at her. When he spoke his voice was slow, gentle—as if he were drawing a veil of reassurance over his own fears.

"I don't think so," he said. "Really I don't. It could have been—" he paused. "Anybody," he said. "Any tall man. If it was anybody at all. If I didn't—confuse a shadow."

"Look," Westcott said. "You saw somebody?"

Smith looked at him. He shrugged.

"All right," he said. "I think so. It needn't have been Gordon. I couldn't tell—couldn't come anywhere near telling."

The two men looked at each other. Then Smith nodded.

"I think so," he said. "Do no harm to look."

"You girls stay here," Westcott said. "Smith and I'll have a look around. Find whatever it was."

Smith started toward the hall.

"No," Westcott said. "Out the back—down here. You said he was going that way?"

Smith did not answer. He turned and started down the living room toward the french doors at the far end—the french doors which opened, like those of the dining room, like the door from the kitchen, on the terrace. The terrace the rain had washed of whatever might have clung to it; whatever might have seeped between the flagstones which paved it. The two men moved fast. Smith opened a door, and as it blew in toward him, caught it and held it for Westcott. They both went out and the darkness took them.

Debbie and Evelyn Gordon stood for a moment without moving, looking down the shadowed room. The door swung a little farther open as the wind, eddying in the protected terrace area, took it. The firelight flickered on the two women; it made lights in Debbie's soft hair. She stood with her feet together, her body tense, looking after the men—waiting. She still stood so after Eve, with a little sound—a tiny, worried sound in her throat—turned back to the fire. The older woman stood looking at the fire. But her body, too, was tense with listening.

A minute passed, slowly. And then, without warning, the rain began again, beating down on the house. It was a heavy sound, almost a roar; from the terrace, rain hurled itself against the windows. And the wind came up, raging in the trees. Through the open door, there was a sudden flurry of rain. Almost without thinking, Debbie moved down the room toward the door.

She had gone about halfway when there was a sound. It was a voice, indistinguishable—faint in the sound of the wind and rain. The words, if there were words, were lost in the rushing sound of the storm. And then, just as the voice died out, there was the sound of a shot.

Debbie ran, then, toward the door. Eve called behind her. "No, Debbie. No!" But the girl did not seem to hear. In a moment she was through the door. Eve had started after her; she stopped, now, and stood for a moment looking after her. Then, moving slowly, she went back to the fire and again stood looking into it.

It was like stepping into a wall of water. There was no moment of transition; no moment of preparation. Instantly, it seemed, Debbie's clothing was soaking on her. She was wearing a light suit, with a white blouse under the coat. The coat was heavy, pulpy, on her shoulders.

Her hair was beaten against her head and neck. She stood, ignoring the rain, trying to see into the darkness.

There was a flash of lightning and the lawn all about was clear for that instant. The trees, black in the rain, were clear—black and bending to the wind. She could see the rain itself, whipping across from the northwest. And, out at the far edge of the lawn—near the stone wall which bounded it—she saw the figure of a man. She could not, in the instant she had, see more than that it was a man, with his back toward her. He seemed to be standing there; she had an impression that he was looking down at something on the ground. But it was too momentary a glimpse for her to be sure of anything.

But her fears were as instant as the light which had come and gone. The man—he must be Larry Westcott or Smith. And what he was looking at—on the ground the thing he was looking at—! She heard herself speaking. But it was more a soft cry than speech. "No!" she said. "No! Dan—Danny!"

She started running, then. As she left the sheltered terrace the wind caught her. It pushed at her; for a moment she reeled, almost losing her feet. Then a stream of light lay momentarily across the lawn. It picked her up and lost her, as a car coming up the drive swung to the right in the circle and then, reversing itself, turned left toward the garage. The girl stopped for a moment and faced toward the car, which was fifty yards or more away. As she faced the car, she also faced the wind. It snatched at her breath. She stood there a moment, the rain tearing at her wet clothing.

Then she heard a voice. It was a man's voice. Again it was blurred in the sound of the storm. She could not identify it. But it called her name.

"Debbie!" the voice called. "Debbie!"

It did not seem to come from the direction in which she had seen the man looking down at the ground. It was behind her and, as she still faced toward the car circle—and the front of the house—it was off to her right. Behind the house, she thought.

She heard other voices, evidently from the people who had come in the car. She could not make out whose they were. She tried to call against the wind to them, but the wind seemed to force the words back into her throat. She stood for a moment longer, hesitating; then she turned and ran back, the wind pushing her, toward the voice which had called her name. As she ran, she heard someone shouting—perhaps at her—from where the car was. And as she ran, new lights swept the lawn as a second car turned in. But these lights did not pick her up.

"The girl," Mullins said. "Back there! Running."

He was opening the door of the police car as he spoke. Outside, he shouted down the wind. He shouted like a policeman—"Hey! Hey!"

Weigand ran around the car to him.

"Down there," Mullins said, and used his arm—seemed to use his whole body—to point the way. Then he shouted again. "Hey!"

"She won't hear you in all this," Bill told him, leaning close, his voice, raised, near Mullins' ear. "Go get her."

Mullins ran across the wet grass. His foot caught in a low hedge and he went forward in a heavy dive. But he landed with hands and knees ready, rolled in the slippery wetness, rolled to his feet. He ran on, yelling.

Bill Weigand ran to the house. A man came out of the protection of the garage and joined him. Bill turned a flashlight on the face, recognized it. "Well?" he said.

"The lights went out," the man said. "I came up. I thought I heard someone yelling."

"Mullins," Weigand told him.

"No," the man said. "Before you came. And something might have been a shot. You can't hear anything with all this damned wind."

"In the—" Weigand began, but the other was ahead of him. "Out back somewhere," he said. "I'm supposed to watch the front. But I was on my way when I heard you coming."

"Right," Bill said. "Help Mullins."

The man, his black slicker shining as the light from Bill's torch flicked it, ran the way Mullins had gone.

Bill pushed hard against the door, pounding on it. He twisted at the knob, and the door opened. He was halfway in when the lights of a car turned into the drive from the State road and came up it. He did not stop.

Evelyn Gordon stood in the doorway from the hall to the living room. She held a candle. Her face was pale in its small light.

"Weigand," Bill said. "Where are they?"

"Outside," she said.

"Who?" Bill said.

She told him, Debbie, Larry Westcott, Nick Smith.

"And somebody else," she said. "I don't know who. Dan. I don't know. Nick saw him. Then he and Larry went out and then there was a shot and Debbie went."

"And you didn't," Bill told her.

She looked at him.

"No," she said. "I didn't." Her voice was flat.

Bill turned, leaving her standing there, and ran out the door again. He was running hard, turning toward the rear of the house. His head was low, and the rain almost blinded him. Two running strides outside the door he cannoned into someone—someone light, who said something that sounded like "umph!" and disappeared. Then Weigand himself was grabbed, swung around.

"Where the hell do you think—" a voice which sounded very angry said and then, "For God's sake! Bill!"

Jerry North pushed Bill away from him suddenly and, with the push and the wind, Bill staggered. He caught himself and turned. Already Jerry was down on his knees by the side of the path which led to the door.

Bill was beside him in an instant and bending down. Pam North was already getting to her feet; she was pawing rain and earth from her face. Her hat was gone, her hair clung in a tangle about her face. She looked at Bill through the hair and mud, while her hand held onto Jerry's.

"My!" Pam said. "You ought to look where you're going. You're as bad as an explosion."

Debbie ran toward the voice which was calling her. She ran with the wind behind her. It came in gusts; sometimes it was so strong that she felt as if she were being thrown along; sometimes it slackened suddenly. As she ran she was conscious of voices behind her, near the garage at first and then coming nearer. The heavy voice of a man triumphed over the noise of the storm. He yelled "Hey! Hey you!" She thought that he must be shouting to her. But she did not stop.

Because the other voice, softer and nearer, called her name again. There was an urgency in the voice now, and a kind of caution, as if there were cause for alarm, for secrecy, in the growing confusion of voices and movement behind her. And now, although she realized that it was not the voice she wanted to hear, she realized, too, that it was a voice she knew. She was frightened and confused, and the voice—against the storm, against the shouting behind her—somehow offered reassurance.

Running, she reached the corner of the house. Beyond, in the shelter of the terrace, there was momentary protection from the wind. And then a hand took her arm, pressing it hard, decisively. There was a flash of lightning and, instantly, a crash of thunder. The hand tightened, convulsively.

"Quick," the voice said. "No! Not there!"

The last was in answer to the involuntary movement she made toward the french door which would let them into quiet and safety. "Not there, Deborah."

The voice sounded as if the man, too, had been running—running against the wind, from fears.

The hand—the strength behind the hand—took her across the terrace. In a moment they were beyond it and, as they drew away from the house, the wind caught them again. The pressure on her arm forced her into a run again, now away from the house, which was between them and the others—the pursuers.

"Dan," the man said, as they ran. He spoke pantingly. "After Dan. He wants you."

They ran across the lawn beyond the house, between fruit trees bending with the wind. The ground sloped down, here, to the stone wall which bounded the old field in which the house stood. They ran down the slope, the wind now more on their left than behind them. As they ran there was another flash of lightning; momentarily they could see the whole of the slope, down to the wall.

Their first speed diminished; they were walking now—a walk which was still so hurried as to be almost a run. And still the compelling hand was on her arm.

With the flash of lightning, Debbie slowed her movement, involuntarily. The grasp on her arm tightened.

"Hurry!" the man said. "They're after him."

"Dan?" the girl said. "After Dan?"

"Of course," the man said. "What did you think?"

"But—" Debbie said. The hand tightened, roughly.

"Keep your voice down," he said. "Do you want to take them to him? Kill his chance?"

"But Dan," the girl said. "Why Dan?"

"Later," he said. "He'll tell you. Just beyond the wall."

He turned back as he hurried her on, looking over his shoulder. There were flashlights now, dim in the rain. They seemed to be veering off toward the other side of the field.

The two ran on. The wall was close, now. The lawn on this side was mowed up to it, but beyond there was a tangle of bushes. They came to the wall. It was breast high.

"Over," the man said. "Keep low, for God's sake."

She reached out for the top of the wall, felt with a foot for a crevice, found one and lifted herself.

"Keep down as much as you can," he said.

She hesitated a moment.

"Go on," he said. His voice was harsh, commanding. "Dan's just beyond. He has to see you."

She went up, then, with a quick swing of her body; lay for a moment on top of the wall, twisted herself over. As she went down, something caught her suit coat and for a moment held her. She tore at it, and it held. She turned in the darkness, brush pulling at her skirt, and freed herself from the coat. It made no difference—she had been as cold and wet with the coat on as she was now. But the driving rain stung a little through the thin blouse.

The man was beside her in a moment. They stood for a second close together. Then, as she started to move, he reached out with both hands and took her shoulders.

"Wait!" he said. "He's here." He was silent for a moment. Then he called, very softly: "Dan?"

It seemed to the girl that his voice was too low—that nobody could hear it through the noise.

"Dan!" she called, her own voice higher and clearer. "D—" She did not finish. One of the hands left her shoulder and clamped hard on her mouth.

"Shut up, you little fool!" the man said, and his voice was harsh. "Want to lead them here?"

There was a lightning flash. It was not so sharp, so hard as the one before. But for a moment it lighted the thicket in which they were standing—and the field beyond, with tall grass bending in the wind, beaten by the rain. And there was nobody anywhere!

She turned on him then—on the darker shadow which was her companion in a world of darkness and shadows.

"He's not here!" she said. "Dan's not here!"

And the man laughed.

The lightning wasn't bad. The lightning didn't matter. It was the thunder with it; the sharp, explosive thunder. He fought against an almost uncontrollable impulse to throw himself on the ground, to burrow into the ground, convulsively, desperately. But he couldn't! He couldn't let himself! Not again. By God, he couldn't.

It had been too much, that once. Coming across the lawn toward the house, nearing it on his cross-field return from the side road, he had heard that voice and heard Debbie answer. Then, when he was tense with the implication of that, concentrating anxiously, the sudden explosion of thunder had beaten him. He had, then, thrown himself on the wet grass, clutching at it—trying to dig himself in with his fingers. Only for a moment—only for the time it took for consciousness to triumph over reflex. But it had been long enough—too long. Because when he was on his feet they were gone. And he could not tell where they had gone. He ran the few feet to the french doors of the living room; they would still be crossing the room. But there was no one moving inside; there was a woman at the far end, standing in the firelight, listening. But it was Eve, not Debbie.

He whirled around, trying to force his eyes to see through the darkness. Then there was another flash of lightning and he saw them. And with the thunder this time he started—for an instant he was shaking—but he did not drop to the ground.

They were halfway across the field, running away from the house toward the wall beyond. The man was holding the girl, forcing her along.

There were people running behind him. He was conscious of flashlight beams bouncing on the ground; of some man yelling through the storm. He did not know who these people were. Something was happening, but he did not know what it was. But he knew that Debbie was being forced across the lawn, among the fruit trees, away from the others.

And he ran after Debbie. He ran carefully, cautiously. He was still some distance from the wall when another flash of lightning showed him the man going over. He thought Debbie was beyond. He could not be sure.

But they had taken a bad place to cross. The old wall was uneven in height. Here and there the stones, piled artfully many years before to hold their place by weight and contour, had weathered loose and fallen. Above the high wall they had crossed there was a gap where the wall had fallen; fallen down to the lowest tier of stones. He remembered it; the picture of it was sharp in his mind. And beyond the gap there was a path through the brush. He saw that, too.

He veered from direct pursuit, heading toward the gap.

"How do I know where Dan is?" the man said, when he was no longer laughing. "Hiding from the thunder some place, I suppose. Getting under something and pulling it down on top of him."

"But you said—" Debbie began, and there was, in that first moment, only surprise and bewilderment in her voice. Then she stopped speaking, because the man laughed again.

They were sheltered behind the wall, in the brush. She could hear his laughter plainly. She could hear him when he spoke, although he did not raise his voice.

"Tough luck," the man said. "Mine. As a result—yours. How did I know he was a freak?"

It was clear, then. It was utterly clear—hopelessly clear. Because the man had a gun.

"Damned tough luck," he said, reasonably—somewhat regretfully. "Just because a man was seven feet tall. And, of course, because I'm not."

"Oakes," she said. She looked at the man. "Morning not afternoon. I remember him."

"Naturally," the man said. "Who wouldn't? As soon as I read about it, I knew you would. It was worse than the nurse. She just guessed something was wrong. You knew it. Or would know it."

"The radio," the girl said. "When they described him I knew he wasn't—wasn't the right man. It was you?"

"With dark glasses," the man said. "With stuff to flatten my hair. Naturally. I could have been anybody." He paused and then spoke bitterly. "Anybody except that bloody freak," he said. He looked at her. She could not see his face clearly, but she could feel the hatred in it—the anger.

She tried to move, then. She wrenched herself to free the hands on her shoulders; the wet fabric of her blouse gave under the hands. But they bit into her shoulders. The hands did not slip. And then one of them moved—to her throat. She tried to scream and the other hand bruised her mouth. She had never thought hands could be so powerful. Or so cruel.

The area to his right, as he looked down the side lawn toward the rear of the house, was covered. Mullins was there, and the State trooper—and, apparently, someone else, who seemed to be helping them. Weigand, running with a flashlight in his hand, veered toward the left, around the rear of the house. He ran across the flags of the terrace, and, as he went out onto the grass again, heard feet running behind him. One pair of feet clocked on the flagstones. That would be Pam North—wet and muddy and, Bill imagined, mad. Very mad. That, however, would be Jerry's problem.

Weigand's flashlight beam, swinging in arcs as he ran, at first picked up nothing. Then it picked up a shadow—a moving shadow—at the wall. The shadow seemed to go through the wall.

And then, distant, faint in the rushing of the wind through the trees, he heard a woman's scream. It was broken off almost as it began.

"Bill!" Pam called, her voice gasping. "Hear her! He's—got her!"

The hands closed on her throat. Pain shot through her throat where they touched. She writhed in the hands, but they only tightened. She tried to breathe, and breath was stopped by the hands. She fought; she tore at the hands with her own. Desperately—futilely—she tried to kick at the man who was holding her. But the brush caught her legs; the brush was helping him. Blackness began to circle in from the sides—she was looking down a narrowing channel, which was suddenly lurid with red light. And then she was falling. But even as she fell, she knew that something happened. There were two men, now. They were holding on to each other, swaying. And one of them was shouting.

Dan Gordon knew a good many tricks. But it was hard to play tricks when you were fighting a man knee deep—shoulder deep, almost—in bushes which grabbed at you, hampered you. He tried to bring his knee up, and missed. He swung with his right fist and it stopped, bruisingly, against the other man's jaw—and slid off. It was difficult, futile fighting. And the man was trying to get one hand into a pocket. Dan grabbed the hand, got the wrist, felt it slipping in his wet fingers. He struck again for the face—and missed, and floundered in the bushes momentarily from the swinging blow.

It gave the man time enough to reach the pocket. But the gun stuck in it. The man wrenched at the gun, got it free. He started to lift it and Dan jumped in on him and the gun went off. Dan got his hand on the wrist again, twisted sharply, raised his other hand and tried for the back of the neck with a knife blow. The man he was fighting twisted and Dan's hand slipped again. For an instant the man was free—and in that instant he turned toward the wall.

Dan jumped for him. Underbrush caught his feet and he half fell after the man, who reached the wall and kicked backward. One heel grazed Dan's chin and Dan put his hands up, quickly, to shield his face—and to clutch for the swinging feet. But the man, who was quicker and stronger than Dan had thought, went up the wall, flattening himself on the top of it. Dan jumped after him, his head came above the top of the wall and the beam of a flashlight caught him full in the eyes, blindingly.

During the moment in which he could not see, Dan grabbed instinctively for the top of the wall. His hands found cloth; found a leg.

"Let him go," Bill Weigand said, from the other side of the wall. "I've got him. And get your head out of the way, for God's sake!"

Dan moved abruptly, dropping out of the line of fire. He moved sideways and came up again.

Bill Weigand laughed suddenly.

"He won't go anywhere," he said. Bill laughed without humor. "He's stuck on a branch. In his coat. Aren't you, Mr. Smith?"

And then Pam North laughed, too. She sounded a little hysterical.

"How silly," Pam said. "How completely silly. For such a smart murderer."

And Nickerson Smith began to swear. There was a kind of ineffectual embarrassment in his profanity.

They got him off, with some wrestling, after they had got his gun. He did not make any effort to fight them; he seemed quite anxious to get the tree branch out of his coat and his feet under him. He was even helpful. When Mullins put handcuffs on him, Nickerson Smith looked at them with surprised resentment. Then he looked up at Weigand.

"That freak," he said. His voice was suddenly very bitter. "That god-damned freak. Who'd figure anybody to be seven feet tall?"

He seemed, somehow, to regard the whole thing as a personal, uncalled-for stupidity on the part of Lieutenant William Weigand.

Then Dan Gordon and Debbie came through the gap in the wall farther up and walked down toward them. Weigand threw the light from his flash on them, and then discreetly lowered it. A good many things had happened to the girl's clothes. But nothing of importance seemed to have happened to the girl. Dan was holding her so close that he seemed almost to be carrying her. They were both, the others could see in the instant before Weigand lowered his flashlight, very scratched, very muddy and, above all, very wet. You would have thought the girl, at least, would be very cold.

But neither of them looked as if they minded being wet and cold. They looked as if they were very warm and contented. From the expression on their faces, they might have been sitting in front of a fire. Actually, Pam North thought, they are. In the only sense that makes much difference.

· 11 ·

TUESDAY, 9:30 P.M. TO 10:45 P.M.

They came down to the fire one by one. Dan Gordon came first, and put logs on it and stirred it, so it leaped up brightly. Then Debbie came, in a pale blue slack suit, and walked into his arms. After a moment they sat down very close together on one of the sofas. He kept one arm around her. With the other hand he turned her face to him and gravely examined it. He told her she looked as if she had been playing with a cat. His voice was light, confident, and she smiled at him without answering.

Jerry North came next, in tweeds made for Dan Gordon and perceptibly long in the leg. He went over to the fire and stood in front of it and held out his hands. Then he turned and held out his back. Then, when Dan Gordon waved without comment, Jerry went to a portable bar and mixed himself a drink. He looked at the two on the sofa and they nodded, so he made more drinks. Then Pam came in, in a borrowed hostess coat—white with gold embroidery—and said, "me, too." So Jerry mixed a fourth drink. He took the drinks to Debbie and Dan; he took his own drink and Pam's—and Pam herself—and moved all firmly to the other sofa. He sat down and sighed. He looked at Pam, whose hair was wet and improbably curly. She nodded and said, "All right. Except for the shoulder. I landed on it." She paused, considering. "Again," she said.

Larry Westcott came next, and he had not changed; his tweeds looked wet; he brought an odor of wet wool with him. He stopped at a little distance and looked at them and said, "They've taken him along?"

"The State cops," Dan Gordon said. "Yes—they've taken him along. Not talking any more, they say."

Westcott said "Oh," vaguely. "I'll be getting along home, then," he said. He started toward the hall door. "By the way," he said, "Eve won't be down again. The kid's scared—the storm and everything. Eve said to tell you, Debbie."

"All right," Debbie said, without moving in Dan's arms.

Westcott went into the hall. There he spoke to someone. Then they heard a door close, and then Bill Weigand came in, with Mullins after him. They came across to the fire.

"Storm's over," Bill said. "Moon's out." He looked at them. "We ought to be getting along," he said. But he showed no immediate intention of getting along.

"A drink first," Debbie said, still without moving. "You and the sergeant?"

"O.K.," Mullins said. "O.K., Miss Brooks."

He went to the bar. He looked at Weigand, who nodded. He made drinks. He brought them back. Bill Weigand—in slacks and a sweater he had borrowed somewhere—stood in front of the fire. He drank and put his glass on the mantelpiece. He looked at Pam.

"All right, Pam," he said. "Say it."

"I told you so," Pam said, sweetly. "All along I told you so." She paused. "Only," she said, "I couldn't fit it together, which was what counted." She regarded Bill. "No help, I wasn't," she said.

Bill Weigand drank again. He put the glass back. He said he hadn't been any too bright himself. His face was shadowed.

"Not bright enough to save the nurse," he said. "Barely bright enough to help save you, Miss Brooks. I did all the things he expected me to do, right up to the end. Until the tall man died. Which he couldn't have counted on, since the card didn't show. Just a name—

and a pair of eyes—the card was." He paused, considering. He seemed disinclined to go on.

"We all did what he wanted us to do," Pam said. "Including Debbie. Running out in the rain, that way."

Bill nodded. He said, "Right.

"Including Debbie," he said. "Whom he had to get when his luck started to run out."

"Did he really see somebody out there?" Debbie said. "Before he went out? Or did he just pretend to?"

Nickerson Smith wasn't saying, Bill told her. He wasn't saying anything. So they had, still, to guess about a good deal of it. But, as a guess—"no, Smith didn't see anybody when he looked through the living-room window, out into the rain.

"He wanted you to think he saw Dan," Bill said. "He wanted you to think Dan was running somewhere, out there in the rain—and that he was hurt. You said he talked about the man's staggering."

"He said he seemed to be staggering," Debbie said.

Bill nodded.

"Right," he said. "Creating anxiety. Then he ran out, taking Westcott with him. Hoping we could blame Westcott for what was going to happen. Then he lost Westcott in the rain—and yelled and fired a shot. At nothing—at the air. To bring you."

Debbie nodded. "It brought me," she said. She looked up at Dan. "I didn't stop to think," she said. "I just—I was just—afraid."

"I know," Dan said. "You were just afraid."

His voice was very tender.

"So," Bill said. "He got you out—where it could be anyone. Where, after we found you, we'd think it could be anyone. Westcott. Dan, even. Or—anybody. It might have worked." He drank again. "The whole damn thing might have worked," he said, a little angrily. "And it was all there in front of us—spread out. And we didn't put it together."

"Finally you did," Pam said. "In time."

Not in time for Grace Spencer, Bill told her, and again his voice was bitter.

"How did he kill her?" Jerry said. "Why, for that matter?"

It was one of the things they would have to guess, Bill told him. He managed, in the darkness—after Debbie had turned out the lights to give Dan a chance to run. "And that was a damn fool thing to do," Bill interpolated. Smith managed to, somehow, entice her out onto the terrace. Presumably she had come out to talk to him; presumably she had remembered something and was giving him a chance to explain. But what she remembered—

"We won't know," Bill said. "Unless he decides to tell us. She remembered something that didn't fit. Presumably, when he was impersonating the doctor. Some gesture—some movement. Perhaps merely enough to make her doubt that it was really the doctor coming out. Perhaps not enough to make her realize that the man in the white coat was Smith. But—if we once suspected, he was in for it. He knew that. It had to be—perfect. Accepted as perfect. Otherwise—well, we'd all have thought what Pam thought."

"Step by step," Pam said, after a pause. "What did he do? What can you prove?"

Bill said he thought they could prove enough. As much as they needed to. Because, once they got around the alibi, he was always the likely one.

"As he no doubt realized," Bill said. "He had motive. The only good motive. He was around. Only—he *couldn't* do it. He thought we wouldn't break that down. He didn't care how much we suspected him as long as we couldn't break that down. But—step by step—"

First, he had—they were just breaking it down to details—stolen a large part of the fund for which he and Dr. Gordon were trustees. "We say he stole it," Bill said. "Perhaps he merely wasted it." But he was the one who had diverted the money from Dan, not Dr. Gordon. Gordon was the one who had left things to his cotrustee, not Smith. But—as the time came to pay the money over to Dan, Gordon asked for an accounting. Purely routine, probably. But Smith couldn't stand even a routine accounting. Possibly he had underestimated Gordon; possibly he had thought he would never have to explain. Perhaps he had always been ready to kill Gordon if it became necessary.

Then—he decided it had become necessary. Killing Gordon would serve two purposes. It would stop the investigation into the fund. It would give Smith a dead man to blame the loss on. But his motives were as obvious as they were compelling. He would have to move carefully. He did.

"Somehow, he got hold of one of the referral cards in Gordon's office," Bill said. "Oakes's card, by what turned out, for him, to be bad luck. I suppose Oakes had been in before and the card hadn't been returned. Probably it was on Miss Spencer's desk."

Bill looked at Debbie, who nodded.

"Yesterday morning," Debbie said. "It was the morning group he was in, not the afternoon. I remember him, of course. Anybody would."

Weigand nodded.

"Because he was so tall," Weigand said. "So odd. If he had been, as the chances were he would be, just an ordinary man you wouldn't have remembered, I imagine. As Smith, of course, assumed you wouldn't. Neither you nor Miss Spencer. He would have been just a name— hardly that."

"A number," Debbie said. "More a number than a name. A man in one of the rooms. No. 2, in his case."

"Right," Weigand said. "That's what Smith counted on. He slipped in after the doctor went to the hospital, while you were at your desk and Miss Spencer was—where was she?"

"In the storeroom, most of the time," Debbie said.

"Skipped in and got one of the morning cards," Bill said. "They were done with and filed; they wouldn't be checked for days; with the doctor dead they would probably never be checked."

Pam North thought of something.

"Why one of the morning cards?" she said. "Why not—oh, a card from last week. Because then there wouldn't be even a slight chance of somebody remembering."

Bill Weigand shook his head.

"Because he knew we would talk to the men," he said. "He could assume we would be rather careless about it, because they didn't have anything to do with the murder; couldn't have, as long as we thought

Dr. Gordon was alive after he had finished with them and gone out. But—he could be pretty sure somebody would be going around, just as a matter of routine, to ask Oakes and the rest if they had been at the office yesterday and if they had noticed anything out of the way. So it had to be somebody who *was* there yesterday."

"He took the chance," Jerry pointed out, "that your man would be specific—would say 'Were you at the doctor's office yesterday afternoon.'"

Bill nodded. He said that all murderers had to take some chances. He smiled suddenly and turned to Pam.

"What did you say to them?" he asked suddenly. "Yesterday? Yesterday afternoon?"

"Yesterday," Pam said. "I—I knew it was in the afternoon. We all did." She paused. "Thought we did," she added.

Bill said, "Right." He said Smith could count on that; had counted on it; would have been, a hundred times to one, safe in counting on it. So—Smith stole the card. He put on dark glasses, slicked his hair down.

"Why?" Pam said.

"Because Dr. Gordon did," Bill told her. "Because—Smith usually looked like a brush, Pam. Remember? And, of course, also to look less like himself. It worked both ways."

Pam nodded.

With dark glasses, with hair slicked down, in an unnoticeable dark suit, Smith had shown up at the office with the other compensation cases. The nurse and Debbie barely knew him by sight; there was hardly a chance they would recognize him behind the dark glasses, and they had not. He had come early, no doubt hoping to be the first. That would have made it a little easier. Actually, he was the second; Fritz Weber was even more prompt.

"That poor little man," Pam said. "That poor little man."

So Smith, posing as Oakes, had got in the second room, not the first. But that wasn't too bad. He got in the second room and waited—with the heavy, spherical base of a table cigarette lighter in his pocket. And, when Dr. Gordon finished examining Weber, when he came into the second room, Smith killed him. Probably he had stood inside the door and had struck Gordon just as the door closed behind him—while the oculist was still looking around an apparently empty room.

He made sure that Weber had left the first room; he could hear him as he left. Then he dragged Gordon's body back through the first room, into the private office and into the desk chair.

"Gordon's body was heavy," Bill said. "But Smith is strong."

"He sure as hell is," Dan Gordon said, reflectively.

Smith took a chance of being seen as he took the body through the first examining room, as Weber had left the door open.

"You might have seen him," Bill said to Debbie, but she shook her head.

"Not unless I leaned over the desk and tried to," she said. "Not from a normal position."

At any rate, there had been a chance. Grace Spencer might have happened by. But a murderer has to take some chances, and Smith took one. With the body in the private office, Smith did three things. He took off the white coat Dr. Gordon had worn and put it on; he took Gordon's glasses—which hadn't been broken, fortunately for him—and put them on. Probably he had trouble seeing through them, but he wasn't going to wear them long. And he took up the half sphere of the paper weight and pushed it against the wound he had made in Gordon's head.

"Why?" Pam said.

"To reinforce the assumption that Gordon was killed in the office, at his desk," Bill said. "If the question ever came up. Because, using the method he did actually use, Smith couldn't have used the paper weight. How would he have got it?"

They thought a moment.

"All right," Pam said. "Why not buy some glasses he could see through, instead of using Dr. Gordon's?"

Probably, Bill said, because there seemed less risk in using the doctor's own than in buying a pair which would have had to look like the doctor's. Somebody might have remembered his purchase, particularly as he would have had to be particular as to style. And, although he was in the business of supplying equipment to physicians, that did not include supplying glasses, so he would have had no special ease of access to what he wanted.

"Anyway," Bill said, "that's apparently what he did do. Which is why we couldn't find the glasses. He disposed of them later, of course."

Then with everything arranged in the private office, and both doors closed, Smith—in his white coat—went on through the remaining examining rooms and pretended to examine the patients. He knew the equipment, of course; he knew how it was used. Probably he had no real trouble in convincing the four men he examined that he was a doctor, proceeding normally.

"He didn't convince Flint," Pam pointed out.

Bill smiled. Nobody, probably, would have convinced Flint. Flint was not open to conviction. But even Flint had merely objected that the examination was cursory; not even he had suspected that it was no examination at all.

So—Smith had finished Dr. Gordon's chore, wearing Dr. Gordon's white coat, Dr. Gordon's glasses and what he was able to assume of Dr. Gordon's manner. He had finished and, then, taken his only serious chance. He had opened the door leading from Room 6 to the back-door corridor and, leaving the door open as a shield, stepped across the hall to the closet. For that moment, he would be in full sight of Grace Spencer, if she were at her desk. And she was. It was then, presumably, that she noticed whatever incongruity it was that had come back to plague her later—and led her to her death. But, at the moment, what Smith banked on had happened—she had seen what she was expecting to see: Dr. Gordon completing his examinations, hanging up his white coat, taking his hat, going out to lunch at a time which, later, would be easy to determine with reasonable accuracy. It had, in fact, been determined within a minute.

Outside, Smith had gone fast, to his own office. Probably, unless the indicators showed an up-elevator very near, he had gone up the fire stairs. In either case, it would have taken him two or three minutes to get from the back door to the desk in his own office. He had counted on Miss Conover to provide his alibi. She was due back at one. He knew her habits. She might be a little late, but she would, unless something very strange happened, be back by one fifteen. If she got there at one, he walked in on her—much too soon to have killed Dr. Gordon. If she came by one fifteen, she found him already at his desk, and the alibi was as good. Even if she had come at one twenty, Smith would probably have been safe.

Pam looked uncertain. Bill nodded at her.

"Think about it," he said. "Here is what he would have had to do: Meet Dr. Gordon somewhere—say in the corridor—after the doctor had left his office. Wait two or three minutes, engaging the doctor in conversation, until the nurse came out and got into an elevator. Then persuade the doctor to go back into his office, walk down the corridor to the private office, get the doctor seated at his desk and not only kill him but make sure he was dead. Then, after he had checked to see that he hadn't left any evidence, after he had taken whatever precautions he could take not to be seen, Smith would have had to go out again and get back to his office. I'd hate to have to prove that, working as fast as he could, he could have done all that in a quarter of an hour. And—if Miss Conover got back even as late as one twenty, he would have had only twelve minutes at the outside. So, unless something happened to the girl during her lunch hour, he was pretty safe."

Actually, of course, Miss Conover had got back at one thirteen and had looked at the clock and mentioned it. If she hadn't—well, Smith could have mentioned it himself, jokingly or chidingly. Anyway, to fix it in her mind. And so he was safe, sitting in comfortable assurance, with an alibi they couldn't break because, for the time it covered, it was true. It took the death of a tall man to trap him.

"And," Bill said, "so far as I know—so far as, I imagine, we'll ever know—that death was fortuitous. It was, as far as timing went, mere chance. Because there is every reason to think that Oakes killed himself solely because he was incurably ill. He planned it. But as far as Smith was concerned, it was pure accident."

They sat silent for a long minute, warm by the fire.

"Killing Grace Spencer was a mistake," Pam said. "His own mistake. Wasn't it?"

Bill shrugged. They couldn't know without knowing how much Grace Spencer had guessed. That they wouldn't know. But she was one of the calculated risks.

"And," he said, "I don't know quite how we would have tied him up with that. It was pretty open. He parked his car down the road, came across lots, got her out somehow and killed her. He took advantage of the lights being out. But if they hadn't been he probably would have rigged up another opportunity. Then he went back, got his car and drove around for an hour or so. Then he drove to the house and made an entrance. It was always obvious he could have done that, but there was no reason to think he had—as long as we couldn't think he had killed Gordon. Even now, I don't suppose we can prove that one."

"How did he know she was here? In North Salem?" Pam said.

Bill shrugged.

"Deduction?" he said. "Or, he went around to her apartment to see her, after she had indicated, in his presence at the doctor's office, that there was something which disturbed her, and saw her starting out in her car and followed her? Or, guessing where Dan was, guessing that we'd show up here, he came around, too, with no plan except to keep an eye on things—and took advantage of an opportunity? We won't know, Pam, until he tells us—unless he tells us. Fortunately, it's nothing we have to know."

There was another, longer pause. Again it was Pam North who ended it.

"So many things come up," she said, looking at her empty glass. "I should think it would be simpler not to kill anybody."

They digested this remark. Debbie and Dan looked at Mrs. North with some puzzlement. Jerry put a hand out and let it rest on her shoulder.

"Much simpler," he said, his voice slow. "Much simpler. For everybody." He looked up at Bill, standing by the fire. "Will you convict him?" Jerry said.

Bill thought about it a moment. Then he nodded. It was the old story, he said. Now they knew who, and how, they would get evidence to explain it to a jury. It worked that way, almost always. People had seen things, and remembered them. Somebody might remember seeing Smith come out of the doctor's office; might remember seeing him take off the doctor's glasses. Someone might have seen him going into his own office. A dozen little things which must have happened might now be remembered—now that they knew what to look for, knew what must have happened.

Pam was hardly listening. She was looking at Deborah and Dan, sitting very close together; looking at the fire they did not, after all, really need. She thought they would be sitting so, often now, and for a long time. She hoped so. And then a new thought entered her mind, fluttering its wings. She sat up suddenly.

"Jerry!" she said. "We've got to go home."

Jerry said he knew. He said it rather sleepily, and did not stir.

"Now," Pam said, and stood up. "Martini hasn't anybody to talk to. It will make her furious."

"Martini can—" Jerry began, and looked at Pam. Her eyes were gathering Bill Weigand in, too. Sometimes, Jerry thought, it was almost easier to understand Pamela North when she said nothing. Now she was saying, using no words, that they should leave the two alone by their fire. It was very easy to understand her. Jerry got up. But he thought, practically, of a problem.

"Our clothes," he said. "They're still wet."

"They'll lend us these," Pam said. "Everybody can send everything back later."

"Of course," Debbie said.

"But—" Jerry said, and looked at the hostess coat Pam was wearing. "Won't the drive be—"

Pam lifted her slim shoulders under the white coat. She said probably. She said it was too bad. She said it couldn't be helped.

"After all," she said, "murder is very hard on clothes." She thought a moment. "Especially on mine," Pam North said.